ANGEL WARS

Travis Minix
Angel Wars

All rights reserved
Copyright © 2025 by Travis Minix

No part of this publication may be reproduced, distributed, or transmitted in any form or by any means, including photocopying, recording, or other electronic or mechanical methods, without the prior written permission of the publisher, except in the case of brief quotations embodied in critical reviews and certain other noncommercial uses permitted by copyright law.

Published by Spines Publishing Platform
ISBN: 979-8-89950-541-6

ANGEL WARS
THE PROPHECY

TRAVIS MINIX

CONTENTS

Prologue	7
1. The Invitation	11
2. The Bum	23
3. The Ride	45
4. The Dojo	65
5. The Rescue	82
6. The Training	99
7. The Secret	131
8. The Deployment	145
9. The Sphinx	160
10. The Guest	191
11. The Island	216
12. The Sword	255
13. The Red Planet	281
14. The Nexus	326
15. The Homecoming	358
Epilogue	374

PROLOGUE

In the unforgiving silence of a vast, arid wasteland, where the sun's merciless glare has sculpted shadows upon the cracked earth, a primitive tribe of men gazes skyward, a congregation of trembling souls in awe and dread. Above them, the night sky shimmers with ancient secrets, stars whispering the legends of the cosmos. Then, piercing the darkness like a celestial omen, a blazing fireball streaks across the heavens—a divine herald of chaos and wonder. It tears through the atmosphere with fury, shattering into three fragments—harbingers of fate—racing toward the mortal realm.

One of these fiery messengers crashes into the sands not far from the tribe, shaking the earth with a deafening tremor. The tribesmen, hearts pounding with a mixture of fear and reverence, rush toward the impact site, eyes wide with the possibility that this might be a gift bestowed from the heavens themselves. As they approach, the flames die down, revealing a towering, gleaming sphere of metal—an alien monolith that defies understanding. Its surface flickers with multicolored lights, blinking and flashing in a chaotic symphony, pulsing with a rhythm that throbs like a heartbeat—faster, faster—until the very pulse seems to threaten to rip apart the fabric of reality.

Terrified, the tribe's scouts retreat in chaos, fleeing from the unearthly spectacle that defies comprehension. Yet among them, one lone figure is drawn irresistibly closer, driven by an unspoken call from the unknown. Against the protests of his kin, he steps into the crevasse—an act of defiance and curiosity. As his bare feet touch the sand, the glowing surface of the sphere grows brighter. A shriek erupts from the metal construct—a scream of alien anguish—followed by a blinding explosion. Deafening, it shatters the silence, unleashing a wave of destructive light that sears flesh from bone, reducing the others to remnants of their former selves.

When the dust finally settles, only one remains alive—an outsider amidst the wreckage, gazing around the crater with haunted eyes. Bleeding, battered, yet somehow alive, he begins to crawl back from the abyss, his mind haunted by the silence that follows the storm. As he turns to face the devastation, he sees the shattered remnants of the alien vessel, a symbol of divine wrath or inscrutable purpose. Alone in a world forever altered, he is left to wonder: was this a curse from the gods, or their greatest, most terrible gift? The answer lies hidden in the shadows of the cosmos, waiting to be revealed.

Chapter 1
THE INVITATION

2001:

The morning broke with a deceptive kind of beauty. It was one of those crisp, golden September days that made New York City feel immortal, like the skyline had been etched into the sky itself. The sun rose in a flawless cobalt sky, brushing the buildings with light so sharp it seemed to cut the air. A light breeze teased the flags above the Manhattan Convention Center, where four young boys—Jason, Adam, Henry, and Steven— bounded up the steps in their crisp white Taekwondo uniforms, their tiny feet barely touching the ground.

They were five years old. Just old enough to compete. Just old enough to believe today would be the biggest day of their lives.

Inside, the massive hall buzzed with nervous energy—children sparring on mats, proud parents with camcorders, senseis calling roll. Their own instructor, Master Kim Dae-jung, was pointing them toward their prep area when it happened. A deep, concussive boom cracked through the sky like the earth itself had ruptured. The building trembled. The lights flickered. Silence fell—then the stampede began.

Jason was the first to reach the convention center doors. The others followed, breathless and wide-eyed. What they saw froze them in place: a column of smoke—thick, black, even oily—pouring from the upper floors of the North Tower. Sirens were already wailing in the distance, but they seemed far away, like sounds from another world.

And then they saw it. Not everyone, not the adults, not the news cameras. Only the four boys.

Something moved in the sky. Not a plane. It flew fast and low, banking toward the South Tower in a blur of motion and shadow. A creature, twice the size of a large man, encased in gleaming, purplish-black skin that shimmered like oil in sunlight. It had wings—bat's wings—vast and sinewed, trailing tendrils of smoke. Its head was a nightmare of bone and rage: long, curling horns arched back like a ram's, and its eyes burned with a violent red spark.

Jason gasped as it raised something—a weapon, a massive cannon fused to its arm like an extension of its body. With a screech that sounded like metal screaming, it fired. The South Tower erupted. Flame burst from the impact point, windows shattering outward in a howl of heat and glass. The sky, moments ago so blue, was choked in fire and ash. The towers bled smoke.

People screamed that a plane had hit. Reporters would say the same. But Jason and his friends knew what they had seen. They stood there, paralyzed. Four children, fists clenched and bodies trembling, watching as something impossible vanished into the choking blackness.

That night, they made a pact to never speak of it again. And they kept their promise—three of them, at least.

Beep! Beep! Beep! Beep!

2012:

The alarm on Jason Fitzgerald's old iPhone 3 goes off, and he immediately rises from his bed, covered in dirty clothes and comics, knowing he has to be on time for his first-hour class.

"Jason! Jason, are you up?" his younger brother Luke yells.

"Yes," he grumbles. "And keep it down. You don't want to wake up Dad. He really tied one on last night, and I for one don't want to have it taken out on me. You know how he gets with his hangovers."

"Yeah. I do. His old Golden Glove days come back to him, and we're the punching bags," Luke whispers while picking up his older brother's soiled clothes off the floor, putting them on top of the already full hamper neatly.

"Exactly," Jason responds as he pushes himself up out of bed, running a hand through his messy cinnamon-light brown hair, rubbing the sleep from his hazel eyes, and says, "Now get ready, 'cause I can't be late."

"I am ready!" Luke exclaims with a huff, causing a frown to form around his bright blue eyes as he smooths down his already well-groomed light blonde hair. Jason realizes how insulted his brother must feel, because he's always a timely kid. He decides to apologize after showering and slipping out of their apartment in Hell's Kitchen. Plus, Jason needs to hurry if he's going to meet up with his friends and teammates Henry and Adam down at the Taekwondo dojo they're all members of.

After dropping Luke off at the bus stop, Jason hurries to meet up with the guys at the dojo. He rounds the corner, where they are being let in by Sensei Kim Dae-jung—a stern-looking Asian man in his mid-thirties whose kind eyes have never revealed the horrors of being a defector from North Korea. The three friends only slightly remember overhearing stories about it from other adults.

They aren't sure how Sensei keeps his modest little Taekwondo business running. For students who can't really afford lessons—which is most—their Sensei lets them work off fees by cleaning the dojo in the mornings or evenings after practice. Some of his more advanced students, like Jason, even help teach classes.

Outside the dojo, Henry sees Jason coming up as they open the glass door trimmed in weathered wood.

"Well, here's the Gold!" he shouts—his nickname for Jason, because he's never lost a tournament.

"What's up, fellas?" Jason says, exchanging fist bumps.

Right at that moment, Sensei Kim Dae-jung steps out. Jason puts his arms to his sides and bows. Henry and Adam fall in line as well, slightly embarrassed they still forget etiquette.

As the three enter the dojo, Sensei, with shoes off, bows in front of his family's sword, lighting and planting a stick of incense into a small pot of sand while offering a quick prayer.

Henry speaks up in the middle of munching on small donuts out of a white paper bag. "Now why do you worship that samurai sword again?"

Kim Dae-jung sighs. "It's not a katana. It's a Hwando, the Korean warrior's sword. I've explained the difference already, so no history lesson this morning. But as far as worship—it is not for the sword. I only pay respect to the ancestors. Now hurry along and post the training schedule on social media, then please take care of the dojo's website updates. And don't forget—you still owe me twenty push-ups."

"Yes, Sensei. I was hoping you'd forgotten that," Henry says, wobbling off to the office where their teacher's old, outdated computer sits.

Jason always thought it strange Sensei never says *his* ancestors, but it never surprises him that he always has Henry manage the website and social media accounts. The old Sensei isn't fond of technology much. He reminds Jason of the classic Kung Fu masters in all those old movies—minus the bald head and long, wispy goatee.

Funnily enough, Jason and his friends always think of Sensei as being super old, but he looks younger than their parents. They chalk it up to the Korean diet he talks so much about—well, mostly to Henry, because of his poor food choices and weight problem from excessive snacking.

Henry Ngo is a first-generation American. His mother came to the U.S. from Vietnam, pregnant and widowed, after losing her husband to an unsolved murder. She now works two jobs, so Henry's mostly raised himself—which is probably why he's become a wizard with computers.

To keep him connected to his heritage—and because being an Asian kid in Hell's Kitchen isn't exactly safe—she signed him up for Taekwondo. Henry's not much for martial arts, but their Sensei teaches more than just how to fight.

Adam grabs Jason and says in a hushed tone that he's been invited to an underground cage fight.

"I think we should join. The prize money is ten grand," he says eagerly.

"Man, I'm not sure," Jason says reluctantly, but internally he's thinking, *Ten grand!!*

Jason, however, pauses and shakes his head. "You know how Sensei feels about that."

"Look, there's no money in Taekwondo tournaments," Adam tells him. "It's fun to win 'em, but come on, man. This is where the real money is at. Plus, I'll go too and help clear out some of the pool of fighters for you."

Adam Horawitz could fight, sure—but the only reason his Jewish parents put him in Taekwondo was because they figured one day, he'd have to. Self-defense wasn't optional where they grew up.

Despite his better judgment, Adam's plan doesn't sound half bad.

"Okay, we'll go check it out together," Jason says reluctantly.

"What are we checking out?" Henry loudly chimes in, with a mouthful of powdered donuts.

"Damn it, Henry!" Adam yells. "We just cleaned these mats and you're getting donut crumbs all over 'em."

"Language, Adam!" Kim Dae-jung says patiently.

"Sorry, Sensei," Adam says with an apologetic bow as his deep brown, coarse, wavy hair falls down into his dark brown eyes.

"It's okay. I'll clean up Henry's mess. You three need to be off to school."

"Yes, Sensei," Jason and his friends say with a bow before grabbing their gear. The three adolescent boys slap their shoes back on while hopping out the door and down the sidewalk in a quick scramble.

After walking a bit down the sidewalk, Henry speaks up again. "Okay, seriously, where are you two going?"

"Adam has been invited to an underground cage fight," Jason tells him.

"Yeah, and the prize money is 10k," Adam adds while eagerly explaining the plan.

"Cool! You think you can pull it off, Jason?" Henry asks, leaning in impatiently for an answer.

"Well, it's no Taekwondo tournament," Jason explains. "There aren't many rules, and we'll be fighting against different martial art styles. But shit, what do we have to lose?"

"Maybe just your lives," Henry grimly responds. "Let me see this invite you got."

Adam pulls out his new iPhone 5. Jason and Henry still don't know how his dad scored that phone before its release date. He hands the phone to Henry and says, "Be careful with it."

"Yeah, yeah," Henry says before taking a look at the info. "Holy shit, guys. This is from VVF — Victory Violence Fights. I heard online that the Russian mob is behind these fight cards!"

"Well, are we doing this or not?" Jason asks.

Henry and Adam look at each other, then back to him. "Hell yeah!"

"Plus, I've got five hundred dollars I've been saving," Henry tells them proudly as they approach the school grounds. "I can bet it against y'all."

Adam and Jason look back at him in disgust.

"What?" Henry says with a shrug, throwing up his chubby arms.

They both shake their heads and laugh as the three of them blend into the early morning school crowd. The campus begins to stir to life. Jason walks alongside his two best friends, but he seems distracted.

"Did I forget to pack my history book again?" he asks nervously.

Adam rolls his eyes while saying, "Dude, you always forget it. Why don't you just leave a spare in your locker?"

Grinning, Henry butts in. "He's too busy crushing on someone to remember basic school supplies," he says while looking over at a group of girls.

Jason shoots Henry a menacing glare but doesn't respond. His attention shifts as they approach the front steps of the school.

Out of the corner of his eye, he notices her: Megan McCarthy. She's walking toward the school, her strawberry-blonde red hair catching the sunlight, laughing with a group of friends. Jason's heart skips a beat.

Adam notices Jason staring. "Oh, here we go. You're drooling again."

Henry bursts out laughing. "You've got to talk to her someday about how you feel, man. You've been into her since, like, fifth grade."

Jason angrily says, "I'm not drooling," but pauses to discreetly check. "I just... I don't know. What if she thinks I'm weird?"

Mocking him, Adam jabs at him, "You're totally weird, but that's what makes you awesome, dude."

"Yeah, seriously, just go up to her and say, 'Hey, I'm Jason, I'm weird, let's be weird together,'" Henry says, grinning. "Nah, I'm messing with you. Just tell her she's the hottest girl in school, because she totally is."

Jason glares at Henry, but a smile tugs at his lips.

Jason definitely says, "I can't just walk up to her and say that. I... I need a plan." Megan looks over, and his eyes meet hers for a brief moment. Jason freezes, a flush rising on his face, embarrassed that he can't stop admiring her emerald green eyes.

Adam begins nudging Jason. "Dude, she just looked at you. This is your moment."

Henry raises an eyebrow and says, "You're not gonna screw it up by just standing here, are you? Just ask her to come watch you at the fight on Saturday."

Jason opens his mouth to say something, but nothing comes out. Megan's friends pull her forward, and she laughs, turning her attention away, then back to him and says, "I'll see you in Biology, okay?"

Jason lets out a sigh, nodding at her, then says to his two friends, "See? Too late. She's already gone."

Patting him on the back, Adam just replies, "You're

gonna have to stop making excuses and just go for it. She's not gonna wait around forever."

"I'm not saying you need to pull off a 'Romeo and Juliet' move, but at least try saying 'Hi,'" Henry scolds him. "Plus, she wants you to talk to her. That's why she said something to you, dumbass."

"Romeo and Juliet?" Jason questions, not understanding the comment.

"Oh Lord, Gold," Henry begins as he throws his hands up. "Read a book, for Christ's sake!"

Jason takes a deep breath and starts walking toward the entrance of school, but as he does, he stops. He turns back to his friends. "Okay, okay, fine. I'll say something. But if I totally mess this up, I'm beating you both brutally."

"Deal," Adam agrees. "Just don't say something dumb like, 'I'm weird, let's be weird together.'"

Henry begins laughing again but, fearing an ass-kicking, says, "Yeah, that's all I'd need to hear to walk the other way."

Jason glances up the steps of the school at Megan for a second before gathering his courage. With a deep breath, he heads toward the school doors, his heart racing. "Here goes nothing."

CHAPTER 2
THE BUM

Saturday morning comes and Jason Fitzgerald's up before his alarm goes off. He slides out of bed and tries to silently slip out of his dad's apartment without waking anyone, when he suddenly hears a soft voice.

It's Luke, standing in the doorway, eyeing his older brother with a mix of caution and curiosity. His bright blue eyes flick back and forth, taking everything in, like he's trying to piece together a puzzle.

"Where ya headed off to? And why do you have your tournament bag? I didn't think there were any Taekwondo tournaments this weekend."

Jason hesitantly answers his questions. "Well, there isn't one exactly…"

Luke furrows his brow, smoothing down his neatly combed blonde hair. "Are you okay?"

"Yeah, just have a chance to win some actual money is all," he explains, knowing full well his thirteen-year-old brother has already pieced it all together. It's like Luke can read minds or something.

"Hum, okay. But cage fights are the real deal, Jason," his younger brother reminds him.

"I know. I know," he says, waving him off.

A stern voice echoes from the dark hallway as a large, brooding figure steps into the sparse light of the living room.

"That Chinaman has you fighting in cages now?" his father, James, asks as he takes a sip from his copper flask.

"No," Jason answers. "And Sensei is Korean."

"Pssh, what does it matter? They're all the same," his dad boasts, brushing messy red hair from his light green eyes, which always seem to burn with rage. "Not one of 'em knows how to fight like a real man. Like an Irishman. When I won the Golden Gloves—"

"Dad," Jason cuts in. "I'm sorry, but I'm going to be late," as he hurries to the door to leave.

James clears his throat as he turns away from his son. "If any of this illegal shit gets you busted, I'm not coming to bail your sorry ass out of jail."

"I'll be fine without you," Jason muttered, his voice low and tight, the words scraping his throat like gravel. He didn't wait for a response.

The apartment was steeped in shadows, the only light flickering from street lamps outside the cracked blinds. He slammed the door behind him harder than he meant to, but maybe that was the point—to make noise where silence had lingered for far too long.

As he strode toward the elevator, the weight of memory pressed down on him, heavy and cold. He understood now why his mom had left their dad, even if he wished he didn't. What he couldn't wrap his head around was why she left them behind too. Why she had emptied the place of every photo, every trace of her existence, like she'd never wanted to be remembered.

All but one thing: that damn locket. A delicate, tarnished silver oval, barely bigger than a quarter, with her face inside—the only face Luke had to cling to. Jason had caught his little brother staring at it sometimes, his fingers brushing it like it might whisper a lullaby only he could hear. Luke had been just a toddler when she vanished. He didn't remember the screaming. The slammed doors. The broken furniture.

Jason pushed the elevator button, the worn plastic rattling beneath his thumb. His thoughts spiraled. Had Dad always been like this? Or had war broken him? Operation Gothic Serpent. Bravo Company. The stories whispered about men who came back half-empty. Had their father ever really come back at all?

The elevator dinged, its doors yawning open like a silent scream. Jason stepped inside, the air stale from the interior of the apartment complex and the quiet desperation of tenants who had nowhere else to go. As others crowded in, eyes downcast, expressions blank, he tried to shake the storm inside him.

He wanted to feel sorry for his father. Some days, he almost managed it. But most of the time, the selfish part of him—the part that still remembered what happiness looked like—just wanted out. He didn't want to carry this legacy of anger, of silence, of scars. Yet he does.

Mostly, though, he wanted something better for Luke. A future not haunted by missing mothers and broken men.

Jason clenched his fists in his pockets, jaw tight as the elevator hummed downward. The past could keep its ghosts. He was done looking backward. There were fights coming today, not with words, but with fists, and he had no more time to waste trying to understand a family that was already lost.

"Son, you're up early," Adam's father says as he stops in his son's open bedroom doorway, examining the immaculately kept room.

"Oh, good morning, Dad," Adam replies. "Yeah, I've got a tournament of sorts."

"Oh really," his father says while taking his glasses off and cleaning the lenses with his shirt, "Not going in to take a practice run for your SATs, huh?"

"Not this morning, unfortunately," Adam answers while neatly packing his tournament bag.

"Hum," his father simply says with a huff of disapproval. "Well, at least get some breakfast in you before ya leave. Your mother is making Matzo Brei," he says while walking off, leaving Adam to finish packing.

His father says to himself, but still in earshot of his son, "Just wish you'd make wiser decisions," causing Adam to just shake his head while looking up at the now-empty doorway.

As Adam walks down the creaking stairs of his family's historic brownstone, the muffled sound of his father's voice rises from the kitchen—sharp, frustrated, laced with disappointment. His name comes up, followed by a sigh. Adam slows his steps, each one heavier than the last. At the bottom, his eyes drift to the worn photo of his grandfather hanging on the wall at the base of the staircase, its frame slightly tilted.

He pauses there, as he always does, the ache of loss pressing against his chest. They used to talk about everything. Now, silence fills the spaces where his grandfather's words used to be.

"Wish me luck, Poppop," Adam murmurs, his voice barely above a whisper. Then, with a quiet breath, he turns toward the kitchen, dread settling in his stomach as he goes to grab something to eat.

"Well, good morning, dear," Adam's mother says with a smile ear to ear.

"Morning, Mom," Adam replies, forcing a smile on his face.

"Your father tells me you have a tournament this morning?" she nervously asks.

"Which I've seen nothing posted on Mr. Kim's website or the schedule he handed out at the beginning of the year?" Adam's father says before Adam can address his mother.

"Ezra, give Adam a chance to explain," his wife softly scolds.

"It's not an official tournament through my dojo," Adam tells them, trying hard not to lie to his parents. "It's more like a tournament for a bunch of different martial arts styles."

"This isn't one of those things where they lock two people in a cage and let them try to kill one another, is it?" Ezra asks in pitched alarm.

"Dad, come on, you think I'd do that?" Adam answers with a question, bordering on a lie now.

"Naomi, I have a bad feeling about this," Ezra says to his wife.

"Adam, is this tournament safe?" his mother asks him.

"Yeah, Mom," Adam answers. "It's as safe as any of the other matches I've had before. There's a referee and rules, just like any other tournament."

"Martial arts won't land you a good position in an elite accounting firm," his father explodes on him, "but it can land you into having brain damage!"

"Ezra! Stop it," Adam's mother interjects, trying to defuse the situation before it gets out of hand.

"Naomi, we agreed to sign him up for this stuff so he could defend himself, not try and make a career out of it," Ezra counters, back to his wife, acting as peacemaker.

"Well, maybe I don't want to be an accountant!" Adam shouts. "Have you ever thought of that, Dad?"

"I've heard enough of this nonsense," Adam's father says, pushing back from the kitchen table. He storms out of the room, calling over his shoulder, "Don't kill too many of your brain cells, son!"

"I have to go," Adam mutters, frustration edging his voice as he turns to leave.

"Your father just wants the best for you," his mother says with a pleading tone.

"But he doesn't want what I want, Mom," Adam counters, spinning around on her right before leaving the kitchen out of frustration. "I'm destined for something greater than being an accountant. Plus, that's his dream, which he should have done."

"Your father got into sales to give us a better life, and he deserves your respect for that," his mother says, a growing sadness in her light brown, imploring eyes.

"I know, I know, and you're right," he says with a sigh. "I just wish he and I could talk and not always fight. Why can't he just hear what I'm saying instead of always trying to correct me or point out how foolish what I want to do is?"

"I don't know," his mother answers. "I guess he just doesn't want to be like his father was to him."

"That's the crazy thing," Adam says. "Poppop was amazing. He could try to be a bit more like him, in my opinion."

"Your grandfather was an amazing grandpa, that part is true. But he wasn't the best father to your dad," his mother counters.

"What?" Adam asks in shock. "What do you mean?"

"Your grandpa was… let's just say, a bit eccentric," his mother says gently. "Always chasing some new get-rich-quick scheme. He was a dreamer, and your father and grandmother were always the ones left cleaning up the mess. That might have a lot to do with it."

"I didn't know any of that," Adam says, looking down, regretful for lashing out at his dad—for not wanting to be part of the dream his father had for him.

"I know, dear," his mother says. "We didn't want you to have any negative thoughts about your grandfather ever."

"I'll talk to him after the tournament," Adam says, hugging his mom goodbye. "I promise."

"Love you, sweetheart," his mother says. "And be careful!" she adds, pulling him into a tight embrace.

"Always," he replies once she lets go, then shuffles out of the house.

"Mom? You're home?" Henry blinked, surprised as he stepped into the kitchen, the familiar steam curling in the air. His eyes widened. "Wait, is that *bánh cuốn*?"

The soft, savory aroma hit him first—rice flour, pork, garlic, mushrooms. He practically beamed. He adored these delicate steamed rolls, thin like crepes but silkier, filled with ground pork, wood ear mushrooms, and caramelized onions. There was nothing quite like them—so light they nearly melted on the tongue, yet packed with flavor.

His mother waved him off with a mock frown, speaking quickly in Vietnamese.

"Ừ, đừng quen với chuyện này đấy—yes, yes, don't get used to it. And yes, it's *bánh cuốn*."

She turned back to the sizzling pan. "I'm making your favorite sauce too!"

Henry's heart leapt. That meant the good stuff: golden fried onions, thick slices of *chả lụa*, and the dipping sauce—*nước chấm*—a perfect balance of fish sauce, lime, sugar, and garlic that pulled the whole dish together. He could already taste it.

"You didn't have to go all out," he said, though his grin betrayed him.

She glanced over her shoulder with a smirk. "I know. But it's not every day I get to surprise my son with real breakfast."

"Oh Mom, you're the best," he cheers. "I'm not sure what kinda concessions will be at the fight today, so this will be a great way to start the day!"

"Fight?!" his mother asks.

"Yeah, Jason and Adam have a plan to try and win ten thousand dollars at this underground fight today."

"Oh really," she says. "And you're not participating?" as she places a plate of *bánh cuốn* down in front of him and sits opposite him across the small round table in their tiny, cluttered one-bedroom apartment.

"Hell no, Ma," he responds. "You wouldn't want this pretty face of your son's messed up now, would you?"

She only cocks an eyebrow at him dismissively while taking a bite of the Vietnamese crepe, then shakes her head and says, "Well, just be safe and keep an eye out for those two. Make sure they don't get in over their heads, okay?"

"Oh yeah, I'm on it, Mom," he replies. "No worries. I'm sure this will be a very uneventful day. I was going to bet against them, but I don't want to hurt their feelings."

"You should," she says eagerly. "So I can laugh in your face when that Irish boy wins." She scolds him, "He's a great fighter—you could learn from him!"

"Fighting just isn't my thing, Mom," her son pleads. "I'm sorry, but that's just not the kinda son the universe blessed you with."

"Not yet, it hasn't," she says, her voice lilting with that familiar mix of Vietnamese cadence and motherly mischief

—just sharp enough to sound angry, but he knows better. She gives him a look only mothers can pull off: equal parts pride and playful challenge. "But one day, down deep, you'll see yourself for who you really are—a mighty champion." She leans in with a sly wink. "Hiding somewhere down deep in that tubby little belly of yours." And just like that, his face blooms red, caught between embarrassment and love.

"Okay, okay, Mom, I have to go," he says, pushing himself away from the tiny table before finishing all his food. He grabs his bag, kisses her on the top of the head, and begs her, "Please don't work too hard, okay?"

She says in broken English, "I like work, unlike some people 'round here."

"I work hard to make good grades," he counters. "I'll make you proud by becoming a mighty software designer."

He laughs as he shuts the door behind him, leaving her to wave him off from their modest apartment.

After a lengthy walk across the city, Jason soon meets up with Henry and Adam. The three high schoolers head down to the listed location, 625 9th Ave. As they approach, Henry notices several black vehicles parked outside. There's an armored truck with three black GMC Yukons in front of it and three behind it.

"You think this is the Russian mob's money train for after the fights?" Henry nervously laughs. "How about we stop at Poseidon Greek Bakery and get some fresh baklava?"

"We don't have time for that," Jason snaps at him.

Just then, Adam cuts in and nudges between them. "Getting something to eat isn't a bad idea, Jason. We do need to keep up our energy for the day."

"Well... okay," he exhales, admitting, "That's probably not a bad idea."

The morning sun cuts through the haze of smog and noise like a razorblade as Jason, Henry, and Adam stand tense at the intersection of 44th and 9th. The traffic light flickers green; cars inch forward in a sluggish crawl. They exchange tense glances, eyes flicking over the streets—nothing out of the ordinary.

Suddenly, without warning, the air shifts as a deep, guttural rumble grows louder, drowning out the distant sirens and honking horns. The ground trembles beneath their feet. The trio instinctively turn, eyes widening as a massive city bus bursts into view out of nowhere, as if summoned by magic.

It barrels into the intersection at breakneck speed, horns blaring, headlights blazing, metal groaning in protest of its aggressive approach. Time seems to slow as shattered glass, spinning debris, and screams ripple through the air. The bus slams headlong into the convoy's lead SUV with a deafening crash. The impact sends the SUV crumpling like an aluminum soda can, sparks flying, metal twisting into maddening shapes. The convoy behind it screeches to a halt, chaos erupting in a matter of seconds.

From the belly of the bus, armed men in flowing thawbs and military shemaghs leap out, armed with AK-47s, firing into the stunned convoy. The street explodes in gunfire, bullets ripping through metal, ricocheting off storefronts. The morning crowd erupts into total anarchy with people screaming, cars spinning out of control, horns blaring in panic.

Up the street, two figures, dressed identically to the other terrorists, rally behind RPGs. With deadly precision, they unleash their rockets at the two rear SUVs. The explosions are deafening, sending vehicles skyrocketing up and over through the air like a couple of Hot Wheels toys while metal shards begin raining down. Windows shatter, storefronts tremble, and dust mixed with smoke billows into the sky.

The shockwave from the blasts hits like a punch, shattering the front windows of nearby buildings. Jason, Henry, and Adam are thrown back, momentarily stunned by the blast's fury. In the chaos, the city's normal rhythm is shattered, replaced by a brutal, explosive nightmare.

Jason's sharp eye locks onto a woman sprawled out on the cracked sidewalk, her body lying motionless as debris and flames flicker behind her. A stroller, abandoned and wobbling, begins to roll dangerously toward the inferno, its crying infant muffled by the chaos. Without hesitation, Jason yells, "Help her! Now!" to his two friends, their faces etched with urgency.

Meanwhile, he launches forward, sprinting after the runaway stroller with explosive speed. His muscles tense as the wounded bystanders wail in the distance. Just as the stroller teeters on the edge of the flames, Jason dives, lunging to snatch it and yank the crying baby to safety.

Behind him, the calamity erupts further. The suspicious SUVs nearby stop abruptly. Out pour men in black suits, their faces cold and unyielding. They unleash a volley of suppressive fire, MP5 submachine guns roaring in unison, shredding the air as they engage the terrorists spilling out of the city bus. Bullets ricochet off metal, sparks flying, as chaos morphs into a brutal firefight like an over-the-top action movie that's turned the streets into a battlefield.

Innocent bystanders scatter, screaming, caught in the crossfire. Explosions rip through the intersection, debris flying as the fight intensifies. Terrorists and soldiers wearing suits collide in a ferocious, deadly dance. Firearms blazing, bodies falling, the air thick with smoke and the raw sound of combat—what began as a regular day has now turned into a rescue mission that's spiraling into blood-soaked terror, every second ripping lives apart in this relentless, adrenaline-fueled nightmare.

Meanwhile, Henry and Adam begin to help the woman up and find that she's only got slight lacerations. Just then, one of the men in a thawb approaches, yelling, "Stay down!" in a Boston accent.

Adam locks eyes with Henry, a tense flicker passing between them. Without a word, Adam slowly rises, arms stretching overhead in a slow, deliberate motion. His face is a false mask of pleading, his voice trembling. "Please don't shoot! Please. Please."

Suddenly, in a burst of fierce instinct, Adam pushes the barrel of the rifle aside with a sharp twist, then strikes out with a karate-style knife-hand chop, which comes crashing into the terrorist's collarbone with brutal precision. The crack echoes through the commotion as the weak bone yields, sending a jolt of agony through the attacker's face.

Henry, crouched low, seizes the moment. His foot lashes out in a swift, brutal kick, connecting with the terrorist's knee. The joint audibly crunches, a sickening squish drowned out by the relentless gunfire. The assailant collapses, crashing to the concrete with a thud, unconscious as his head hits the ground.

In a quick, decisive motion, Adam yanks down the terrorist's scarf, revealing a face that doesn't match the outfit—Caucasian, dressed like a Middle Eastern militant. Both teens stare at each other, confusion flickering in their eyes, questioning the disguise in the midst of combat.

Suddenly, the calm shatters. Shards of glass explode outward as the SUV's windshield and side windows are cut apart by incoming gunfire. The fragments rain down like deadly confetti, forcing Adam and Henry to dive for cover amidst a hail of glass and bullets, their hearts pounding in the storm of gunfire and shattered glass.

The chaos reaches a fever pitch. Jason, clutching the crying infant tightly, spins to face two men in shemaghs—the terrorists who just turned the rear of the convoy into flaming wreckage with RPG blasts. Their eyes burn with intent, weapons still smoking as they drop the now-empty launchers. In the corner of his vision, he sees Henry and Adam frozen in shock, eyes wide as the teenage boys lock gazes with him briefly, a chilling sensation full of silent warning.

Jason's heart pounds—calm amidst the storm. He tightens his grip on the baby, then swiftly delivers a sharp front kick to one of the attackers who's pulling a pistol. The blow catches him off guard, staggering him back into the street just as a cab, out of control, barrels past and slams into the terrorist with a deafening, squishy crunch. The man crumples, thrown aside like a ragdoll.

Without missing a beat, the second attacker, masked in fury, rips a kukri from his sheath, the curved blade gleaming wickedly. He lunges at Jason's throat, fast and deadly. Time slows for a second. Jason braces, instincts kicking in.

But before the blade can find flesh, the attacker is suddenly hurled across the sidewalk, crashing into a shattered storefront window. The glass explodes around the attacker, jagged shards slicing through the air, one piercing the terrorist's neck, turning it into a crimson waterfall of blood that pools onto the pavement quickly as the terrorist falls dead.

Jason's eyes dart around, scanning his environment, briefly distracted by his now-dead attacker. Across the street, tucked away between two battered dumpsters, a figure squats low—an old homeless man with long, dark grayish hair and a matching beard, his face bearing a weathered, almost regal look, perhaps Middle Eastern or Greek in appearance. Clad in tattered robes, he extends a trembling hand, as if reaching out for salvation—or perhaps something more.

For a split second, Jason's gaze meets the man's. The homeless man's eyes glint with a strange intensity—something unreadable, something hidden. Then, without warning, the homeless figure slips away into a shadow-cloaked alley, vanishing as quickly as he appeared.

Jason's heart races. He shakes off the fleeting moment of confusion, focusing with renewed ferocity. The infant's screams pierce the chaos, fueling his resolve. He turns back to Henry and Adam, rushing over to help the fallen woman, steadying her as they lift her to her feet amid the wreckage.

The street remains a battlefield of fire, smoke, and blood—and somewhere in the shadows, a mysterious figure watches, his presence a silent enigma amid the storm of violence.

"Did you just see what that homeless man did?" Adam quietly asks.

Jason hands the lady her child, ignoring his friend's question for the time being. He leads her to a business with an open door and tells her, "Search for the exit near the back. Don't stop running till you can't hear gunfire!"

She nods, then thanks the teens for all they've done, tears streaming down her face as the three friends watch the mother run deeper into the shop.

While getting lost in the grateful woman's exit, the symphony of cars being crunched brings the three best friends' attention back to the violent situation they have found themselves in. They turn around to find the armored truck backing into one of its escort SUVs. The black armored vehicle then floors it, smashing the rear end of the escort vehicle in front of it, as if the driver is trying to make space to get out of this tight situation on the road.

Suddenly, a shadow blots out the morning sun, casting an ominous eclipse over the scene. The teenage trio freezes, their eyes skyward. A figure hovers in the smoke-filled sky, a being of pure, radiant energy, with colossal white feathered wings that shimmer like polished marble. Clad in a gleaming golden breastplate that catches the morning light, he wields a flaming sword that blazes with infernal heat, casting flickering shadows across his beautiful face.

The angelic figure reaches up gracefully, long crimson hair flowing like a river of blood. His hand moves with divine authority, grasping a floating halo that pulsates with otherworldly energy. With a flick of his wrist, the golden halo is hurled downward, an unholy missile of light and fury. It ricochets from one of the black-suited men to another, zigzagging through the conflict like a vengeful lightning bolt, slicing flesh and shattering bone in seconds.

In a burst of righteous fury, he descends further, wielding his flaming sword. With a swift, precise strike, he pierces the steel roof of the armored truck, the blade cutting through like a plasma cutter slicing through sheet metal, flashing sparks and molten steel erupting in a deadly shower.

He drops into the cargo bay with the grace of a predator. Gunfire erupts wildly, bullets bouncing off armor, but they are futile against his divine might. Blood-curdling screams and pleas for mercy fill the air of the armored truck, but they fall on deaf ears. The angel's eyes blaze with wrath as he emerges, clutching a sleek metal briefcase in one blood-soaked hand. His wings, now streaked with crimson, unfurl behind him, a stark contrast to his otherwise serene visage.

He towers above the chaos, his gaze sweeping over the terrified trio. Standing atop the wreckage, he looks down with a commanding presence that demands attention. His voice, both beautiful and terrifying, echoes through the chaos: "You three can see me for what I truly am, can you not?"

The boys tremble, but no words come. They can only nod in awe and fear.

A cruel smile curls on his lips. "He will regret involving you three. The prophecy is folly. Nothing, NOTHING, can stop me, especially not children."

Suddenly, the winged being is struck by a violent flash, resembling a lightning bolt which lights up the entire area with blinding illumination for a few quick seconds. He turns sharply, growling through clenched teeth as the crackling energy courses through him. The three friends, unable to see the origin of the electrical attack from their vantage point, instinctively believe it's the mysterious vagabond from earlier, wielding some unseen but deadly power.

A distant wail of sirens grows louder, a crescendo of approaching chaos. Without warning, the angel spreads his wings wide, their dove-like feathers now stained with blood. With a powerful thrust, he launches into the sky, ascending rapidly like a raptor taking flight, leaving the scene in a flash of fright and burning feathers.

As he disappears into the clouds, silence falls, except for the echo of his menacing words and the pounding of their hearts.

"He!? Who's he?" Henry blurts out. "We don't know any he!" Henry shouts out loud to the departing aerial redhead. "We don't, do we?" Henry asks his two best friends, as if perhaps they've left him out of some kind of sick secret.

"No, we don't," Jason says in a stupor.

After a moment, Adam speaks up. "We need to run."

Jason and Henry just nod in agreement and race through the remaining wreckage on the streets.

CHAPTER 3
THE RIDE

Jason, Henry, and Adam sprint through alleyways and across cracked sidewalks, slick with rain from last night, before finally ducking into the relative anonymity of the subway system. They clatter down the steps, dodging a flickering overhead light and a cluster of half-hearted buskers whose music dies away at the sight of their frantic arrival. The station reeks of damp concrete, old oil, and something sharper—maybe blood, maybe rust. No one turns to look at them.

They don't stop moving until they shove themselves into the next open subway car just as the doors hiss shut behind them. The train jerks forward, plunging into darkness.

The three collapse onto scuffed plastic seats. Fluorescent lights above them hum with a low, sickly buzz. The air is heavy, almost damp, and carries the sour stink of unwashed bodies and mold. Across the car, a man in a trench coat twitches in his sleep—or pretends to. A woman further down stares into space, her eyes unfocused, muttering to herself too quietly to hear. The rest of the passengers sit in rigid silence, avoiding eye contact, as if they too are hiding something—or from something.

Henry's knee bounces rapidly. No one says a word until he finally whispers, as if afraid the train itself might be listening, "Okay guys, we need to talk about what we just saw."

Jason exhales hard, not looking up. "I don't know, man. I just need to think right now."

Adam leans closer, voice low. "Jason, there's nothing to think about. We just saw…" He glances around the car, then whispers, "an angel."

Jason shakes his head sharply. "Man, that's crazy. There's no way. It's gotta be some kind of prototype glider or something."

"Yeah? And what about his Frisbee of death that floated over his head and sliced through half a dozen men like a hot knife through butter? What do you call that?" Henry blurts, voice rising. He tries to stand, but his knees buckle, and he plops back down, breath ragged.

Jason and Adam both shush him in unison.

"Be quiet, man."

"Okay. Okay." Henry slides lower into his seat, as if trying to disappear. "But that wasn't any glider, Jason. Just like that wasn't a Frisbee. That was a halo."

Jason rubs his temples, voice tight. "Well... there has to be a logical explanation. Angels with halos, I'm just not buying it."

Adam stares at the filthy floor beneath their feet, voice distant. "It's like what we saw on 9/11."

Jason snaps his head around. "Shut the hell up, man! Just shut up. Don't bring that day up again." His voice cracks. "Talk like that drove Steven crazy. They came and got him. We never saw him again. I told him to stop talking about it..." He trails off. Tears well in his eyes. He blinks them away fast and swipes at his nose.

The train clatters loudly over a track split, drowning them in metal-on-metal shrieking. When it fades, Adam speaks again, softer. "Let's just see what the news has to say about all this." After a short pause...

"And I know you and Steven were close. But I can't shake it either. It feels connected."

Jason eyes the sleeping man in the trench coat across from them, who hasn't moved once.

Henry nods. "Okay guys. We all know what the three of us saw that day..."

"The four of us," Jason cuts in, voice sharp.

"Sorry," Henry mutters. "The four of us. Maybe I can get online, look up something, anything?"

Adam scoffs. "What, Bigfoot forums? UFO Reddit threads? That's what we're banking on now?"

Jason shrugs. "Could be better than nothing. Check it, bro."

Henry already has his phone out, fingers dancing.

A shadow moves across the far end of the car. One of the quiet passengers shifts just slightly, as if listening.

Henry's voice dips to a whisper. "I could also look into Steven. They said his family moved, but come on... it was only five years ago. Maybe there's a connection?"

Jason's eyes dart around. "I appreciate it, man. But we were blocked from everything. Social media, numbers, all gone. Like someone wanted us forgotten and he didn't move... They took him."

"Or someone wanted us to forget," Henry murmurs.

Jason leans back, exhaling. "Yeah... maybe."

Adam nudges Jason's side. "Hey. Back during that armored truck attack... did you see that homeless guy across the street?"

Jason flinches, wishing he'd not brought it up. "Yeah."

"What was going on with that?" Adam presses. "That so-called terrorist with the kukri had you dead to rights, and then he flew through the air like he got hit by a truck and crashed into that window?"

Henry's grin twitches. "A wizard who's a bum? I mean, if you're a modern-day Gandalf the Poor, wouldn't you conjure up some cash and a studio apartment at least?"

Jason doesn't smile. "I'm not saying it was a wizard... or psychic. But if we're talking angels, I don't know? Hell, I don't know who he was or what he was. I just know I thought I was dead. Something, someone, stepped in."

Henry blinks. "Yeah... Who *he* was!" He bolts upright, then quiets himself. "That angel, or thing, said: 'He will regret involving you three. The prophecy is folly.' What if the bum is the 'he' the angel meant?"

Adam's eyes go wide. "Could be! But what prophecy was he talking about? And what was that lightning all around him?"

Jason rubs his face. "Hell if I know. I'm still waiting to wake up from this bad dream."

Henry leans back, eyes wide and gleaming. "The lightning... that had to be hobo Gandalf casting a lightning spell."

There's a moment of silence between the three teenage boys, broken only by the rhythmic clatter of the train as it rocks on rusting tracks. The car's fluorescent lights flicker above them, casting brief shadows that seem to stretch longer than they should. The hum of the engine mixes with the occasional cough or shifting shoe from the scattered strangers seated nearby—silent, still, and maybe listening.

Adam leans forward, voice hushed but urgent. "Alright... we need a backup plan. If things go sideways on us, what should we do?"

"The dojo!" Henry says instantly, too loudly. A man across from them turns his head just slightly, not enough to be obvious, but enough. Henry lowers his voice. "Daejung Dojo. It's always been our safe spot when any of us were in trouble. Plus, Sensei Kim's had our backs since we were kids."

Adam's brows knit. "He's had our backs with normal people's problems. Even Sensei might think we've snapped if we go running in yelling about angels and halos and spells of lightning."

Henry looks to Jason for backup. Jason just shrugs, eyes distant.

"Well, it's still a solid plan," Henry insists. "Better than nothing. We meet there if shit goes sideways, no questions."

Jason gives a small nod. Adam sighs but relents.

"Then we're all in agreement," Henry says.

As the subway slows, the screech of metal on metal grates through the car, making some of the passengers flinch. The lights dim momentarily. The doors part with a mechanical hiss.

All three boys rise, shoulders hunched, eyes glancing over the car one last time. That man in the trench coat still hasn't moved. The muttering woman is suddenly quiet.

They split wordlessly, peeling off in different directions up the worn station steps.

Jason's sneakers hit each concrete stair with dull, tired thuds. His breath fogs slightly in the cooler underground air, and though his body is moving, his mind loops the same images: the winged figure wreathed in light, the spinning halo carving through men like paper, and that damn briefcase gleaming like it held the fate of the world.

He doesn't want to believe any of it. But every step toward the surface feels like it's pulling him deeper into something he can't unsee.

Henry steps into his apartment and locks the door behind him with two quick turns of the deadbolt—an instinct more than a habit tonight. The dim hallway outside disappears as he closes the door, and the silence that settles over the apartment feels oddly heavy, like it's waiting for something.

He kicks off his shoes and heads straight for the kitchen, his stomach grumbling in protest. The fridge hums softly in the corner. Before he pulls it open, a sticky note written in neat Vietnamese handwriting is stuck to the door:

"Có Bò Kho và Chè trong tủ lạnh. Mẹ làm thêm ở quán bà Wong trước khi vào ca ở bệnh viện. Yêu con – Mẹ." ("There's Bò Kho and Chè in the fridge. I'm working late at Mrs. Wong's restaurant before my hospital shift. Love you – Mom.")

Henry smiles—the first real meal in hours. "Yes!" he whispers. Bò Kho—his favorite: that deep, comforting beef stew rich with lemongrass, star anise, and slow-simmered vegetables, always served with warm baguette. And Chè, his mom's signature pudding of sticky rice and sweet beans, soaked in coconut milk.

The scent of it all, even cold, brings a flood of comfort. For a moment, everything outside the apartment—angels, halos, and magical lightning—feels like a fever dream.

But as he sets the container down on the counter before putting them in the microwave, the apartment seems too quiet. The hallway to his room looms darker than usual. Too still. Like it's watching.

Beep beep beep! The microwave has him jump out of his own skin.

He eats standing at the counter, spooning the stew straight from the container. The warmth spreads through his chest, but the unease lingers just beneath the surface. That voice won't stop echoing in his head.

"He will regret involving you three. The prophecy is folly."

He swallows hard, then turns to retrieve his laptop. Greasy fingers tap against the keys. In the search bar, he types:

"Strange NYC sightings – armored truck angel – floating halo weapon."

A long beat. Then he hits Enter.

As he begins piling all the food containers in the sink, he thinks of the news and says out loud, "Let's see what new lies they are feeding us all today, shall we?" He picks up the TV remote, finds a local news channel just starting, then goes back to his laptop to begin finding out more on the topics he entered.

As he's searching online websites with chat rooms, the attractive blonde TV newscaster says, "We have the exclusive on the armored truck attack that happened hours ago. The radical Middle Eastern terrorist group Al-Ra'idun is claiming responsibility for the attack. Here's what we know of this terrorist group so far."

Middle Eastern my ass, Henry thinks but stays very interested in what they have to say about the attack.

"Their name in Arabic means 'The Trailblazers,'" she says, glancing at the notes in front of her as if they haven't had time to upload this into the news prompter.

"Al-Ra'idun is a radical extremist group with a singular, chilling goal," she says, locking eyes with the camera. "To establish a new world order—under a harsh and uncompromising interpretation of religious law. Their doctrine demands the violent overthrow of governments, the collapse of Western influence in the Middle East, and the rise of a transnational Caliphate ruled by their vision of Sharia law, enforced by force if necessary."

She pauses, letting the words settle. "They preach militant resistance. They see foreign governments as imperialist oppressors and local regimes as traitors to their faith and people. Their campaign is both ideological and brutal—aimed at igniting a global jihad, targeting so-called 'infidels,' particularly the West."

"Al-Ra'idun didn't always look like this," she continues. "They began as a breakaway faction from a political reform movement in Sudan—once calling for peaceful change. But as their leaders were jailed, silenced, or killed, the group radicalized. What was once local became global. Underground cells multiplied, their reach extending beyond borders."

"At the center of this web is Khalil al-Mansur," she says, voice tightening. "A former academic turned revolutionary. To his followers, he's a prophet. To the rest of the world—he's a ruthless mastermind. His speeches, soaked in scripture and history, are designed to inspire the disillusioned—to give the angry a purpose."

She nods slightly, the screen behind her flickering to life. "Their tactics are classic guerrilla warfare—coordinated ambushes, suicide bombings, targeted assassinations. And today, they struck again."

Her tone drops, grave. "The footage we're about to show you is graphic. It was captured by street cameras... and by civilians—some risking their lives to record what they witnessed. Viewer discretion is strongly advised."

Henry stops what he's doing and watches the video reel, spotting himself and his two best friends. He pauses it as he catches his conflict with the fake terrorist between Adam and himself.

"Holy shit, we're on TV," Henry blurts, staring at the screen in the dim light of the apartment.

He unpauses the news broadcast. The footage begins to roll again—street cam angles, chaos, fire, shouting. Then something catches his ear: the attackers speaking what the anchor claims is Aramaic.

Henry shakes his head. That's not right. That's not what they spoke.

And then—there it is.

The camera catches a blur of light descending into the frame. Wings. Radiant. Human-like—but not. The figure lands, surrounded by dust and debris, luminous in the middle of carnage. It's unmistakable.

An angel.

His heart skips. His jaw hangs open. They caught it. They actually caught it.

We weren't hallucinating. We weren't alone.

Relief floods through him. People will see this. They'll understand. This changes everything.

But then the newscaster cuts in, her tone measured, clinical:

"What you just witnessed appears to be the use of advanced flight technology—likely a jetpack—and a high-powered plasma cutting device."

"U.S. analysts suggest these weapons could be foreign-made—potentially of Chinese or Russian origin," the anchor continues. "The tactical advantage displayed here is unprecedented."

A black flag fades into view beside her: a white scimitar slicing through a crescent moon.

"This is the emblem of Al-Ra'idun. The scimitar reflects their militant roots; the crescent moon their ideological goals. More on this story as it develops..."

Henry mutes the TV.

Silence.

He stares at the screen.

They saw a jetpack and a plasma cutter.

That wasn't tech.

That was an angel.

He leans back, heart still pounding.

After a moment of disbelief, Henry picks his phone up and types in a group text to Jason and Adam. "It's on the news, but people are saying jetpack terrorists—what the hell? I still see the ginger angel of death!!!!" Then he sets his phone down and turns his attention back to his laptop, where he now sits with it at the small round kitchen table.

After a few minutes of Googling and bouncing between conspiracy forums, theology blogs, and fringe news aggregators, Henry landed on a plain, outdated-looking website called *Guiding Lights*.

"Huh. This looks lame," he muttered, already reaching for the back button—until something caught his eye.

His name.

In the corner of the page, a small chat box blinked to life.

Henry Ngo, message me.

A chill slid down his spine.

At that exact moment, his phone buzzed. He glanced down—Adam had replied in their group chat, something about the news footage. Normally, Henry would respond, but not now.

Eyes locked on the screen, he whispered, "This... can't be a coincidence."

He clicked.

The site flickered—briefly glitching, as if buffering something encrypted—before stabilizing into a dark, minimal chat window. A single message waited.

Merle:

You saw him too, didn't you?

Hello, Henry. You can call me Merle. Let me get straight to the point: He's coming for you three. Likely under the guise of Homeland Security or the FBI. Whatever you do, do not go with them.

If you can arrange a safe place for the three of you, go now. Once you've chosen a location, contact me through this site. I'll meet you there and help get you out.

They'll claim today's attack was terrorism. That they just need to "ask questions." But they're not agents. They're Gabriel's soldiers. Dangerous. Deranged. If you go with them, you won't come back.

Please don't try to tamper with anything here. The site's protected, customized for your safety. Hacking it will only trigger alerts — not the kind you want.

When you're ready for my help, ask for the spiritual guide named Merle.

Henry blinked at the screen, rereading it twice.

Then he typed:

Henry:

Why so cryptic?

A pause.

Merle:

For security. Yours and mine.

His fingers flew over the keys again.

Henry:

Were you the homeless guy in the alley? During the armored truck hit?

Another pause. Then:

Merle:

I'll answer all your questions in person. Our time is up for now.

The chat window flickered once... then faded out. Gone.

Henry leaned back in his chair, fingers still hovering over the keys. His thoughts swirled.

"*Guiding Lights — an online sanctuary for the spiritually lost,*" he recalled from the homepage.

He smirked.

"Guess I'm a seeker now."

Henry sat still for a moment, eyes fixed on the now-dark chat window where he'd just wrapped up a strange conversation with someone calling themselves Merle — a so-called "spiritual guide" who offered to help them. But something about the whole exchange didn't sit right.

His gut twisted with doubt.

Who talks like that unless they've got something to hide?

Cryptic messages. Perfectly polished warnings. Vague assurances. It all felt… scripted.

Henry leaned back in his chair, tapping a finger against the keyboard.

Is this guy some kind of real-life wizard? A prophet? Or just a really clever hacker?

Maybe he saw the angel too.

But no matter how mysterious Merle seemed, something about him felt like a mask. And Henry had seen enough masks to know that what hides behind them is usually the truth you actually need to worry about.

There was only one way to know for sure.

Time to dig.

Henry leaned forward, his fingers already dancing over the keys. The *Guiding Lights* site was well protected, but Henry had dealt with far more secure platforms. It was just a matter of finding the right vulnerability.

He bypassed the front-end defenses, taking advantage of weak encryption protocols. The deeper he dug, the more he felt the rush—the thrill of the hunt. His eyes scanned the stream of code that scrolled across the terminal. He'd already located the profile information—just a few more steps and he'd have access to everything: messages, personal details, even the IP address tied to Merle's account, which is what he wanted the most.

A few keystrokes, and he was in. Or at least, he thought he was.

ACCESS BLOCKED.

Henry froze. The sudden message flashing on his screen was like a slap to the face. *How the hell did they catch me?* he thought. It wasn't supposed to happen this fast. He hadn't triggered any alarms yet.

The flashing red warning message blinked at him again:

ACCESS DENIED. INTRUSION DETECTED.

He quickly tried to reroute the connection, masking his own IP and initiating a series of decoy commands, but it was no use. The screen flickered once more, and a new message appeared:

You should've known better than to dig too deep, Henry. I did warn you not to proceed with this course of action.

A chill ran down his spine. His pulse quickened. This wasn't just the site's automated defense. Merle was actively watching. Merle knew what he was trying to do.

Henry's fingers flew over the keyboard as he scrambled to regain control. "Damn it," he muttered, working quickly to reverse the hack before Merle could trace him back. But each time he attempted to mask his tracks, the system seemed to anticipate his move. It was like the person on the other side of this chat had been waiting for him, ready for this exact moment.

You're good, Henry. But not good enough.
The words appeared on the screen, mocking him.

Henry's breath caught. He could feel it now—the pressure of a game being played on both sides. This wasn't just hacking anymore. This was a fight. A battle of wits between two people who knew exactly how to manipulate the digital world.

Thinking of his mom's words earlier that morning about being a mighty warrior, *well, this is my battlefield,* he thinks to himself.

He tries a different approach—an advanced encryption bypass he had used in the past. But before his command even had a chance to run, the screen flashed again, and the message that followed made his stomach drop:

Your methods are outdated. I've already reversed your move.

Henry's hands shook. He had to think fast. If Merle was this good, if he was watching him in real time, one wrong move could give Merle enough to track his location.

But it was too late. As if sensing his panic, the screen began to scramble, lines of corrupted code flooding the terminal like an avalanche. The system wasn't just blocking his access, it was actively flooding his computer with a virus. A series of fake logs and decoy data files overwhelmed his system, making it impossible to know what's real anymore.

Enjoy the chaos. The message appeared one last time before the screen went black.

For a moment, Henry just sat there, stunned. His pulse was hammering in his ears. He pulled the power cable out of his laptop and slammed it down on the tiny little kitchen table. Sweat dripped from his forehead. The terminal had frozen. His own system was now tainted by whatever countermeasure Merle had triggered. The virus was already working its way through his files.

Henry slammed his fist on the table in frustration. He'd failed. Not only had he been locked out of Merle's account, but now his own system was compromised.

Then, a final ping came through. A new message from the *Guiding Lights* chat. It was Merle, of course. And it was a message Henry had never expected to see:

I knew you'd try this. I'm not just a spiritual guide, Henry. I'm much more than that. But I'll be watching you three and I'll try to help when it's safe. Take care and watch your backs.

Then the thought of Adam's message races through his thoughts as he reaches for his phone, half expecting it to have been hacked by this cyber-wizard Merle as well.

CHAPTER 4
THE DOJO

Jason Fitzgerald takes the stairs. Each step creaks beneath his sneakers as he climbs slowly toward his family's apartment, avoiding the elevator like it might trap him with his own thoughts. He needs the walk, needs the solitude. Needs something to make this morning feel even a little bit real.

His legs are sore, but it's not the good kind of soreness, like after training or a tournament. This is the slow burn of tension, fear, and adrenaline withdrawal. He climbs the final landing with a hand on the railing, his mind looping fragments of what he saw, what he heard… what he did.

I kicked an armed soldier into traffic. Watched him get run over like a deer in headlights.

Another guy died on a jagged window after some homeless wizard hit him with psychic force or, whatever the hell that was.

And here I was thinking my biggest stress was surviving a cage fight for ten thousand bucks.

He rubs his forehead, mouth dry. "Hell... it was a war zone," he mutters, low and bitter.

The images return vividly—burning cars, men screaming, the ear-splitting crack of RPGs shaking the concrete. That wasn't a dream. His ears are still ringing, or maybe they're not. Maybe it's just silence now, too loud to ignore.

By the time Jason reaches the apartment door, he's barely aware of his own hand turning the knob.

The door creaks open. Inside, the living room glows with the light of the television. The muted buzz of a news report plays over raw footage—shaky cell phone clips, smoldering wreckage, figures moving through smoke. Jason freezes. He sees his morning again, this time through someone else's lens.

Then a tug. He feels a light pull on his shirt sleeve and looks down.

It's his little brother, Luke, blue eyes wide with excitement or worry or maybe both. His lips are moving, but Jason hears nothing. No sound. No voice. Just the visuals on screen and the ghost-quiet murmur of the world around him.

This is shock, Jason thinks distantly. Combat trauma. Like Dad used to talk about.

And then, like someone unmuting the world all at once, everything slams back into his senses. The flicker of the TV, the hum of the ceiling fan, the texture of the doorknob in his palm, and Luke's voice finally cutting through.

"—and did you win or not?"

Jason blinks. "Huh? Do... do what?"

Luke frowns. "The tournament. Or the cage fight. Did you win?"

Jason hesitates, a beat too long. "Oh. No. I didn't. We decided not to participate."

The lie slips out smoothly. Too smoothly. He glances toward the television, unable to help himself.

"What's on TV?" he asks, already knowing the answer, already needing to hear it from someone else. Just to confirm the madness.

Luke shrugs like it's nothing. "It's just the news. Some attack went down on an armored truck. High-tech gear or something—they said it was, like, a robbery."

Jason watches the screen. A distant part of him notes how easily the world is framing it all. The costumes, the explosions, the stolen briefcase. The supernatural turned into sanitized headlines and news footage. He swallows hard. At least that part people will believe. But everything else? The angel. The halo. The warning? That was for them alone.

Jason barely makes it three steps into the apartment before his father, sprawled on the recliner in his usual after-work uniform—undershirt, sweats, and a half-empty tumbler of Jameson on ice—grunts out a comment from behind the flicker of the TV.

"Can you believe this shit? Looks like a damn James Bond movie! Jet packs and high-powered plasma cutters for top secret launch codes. Who the hell is funding these terrorists? I blame the Chinese…"

He pauses for a long pull of whiskey.

Jason furrows his brow. "What?"

His dad's eyes finally lift toward him, narrowing. "You okay?"

It hadn't occurred to Jason how rough he must look, clothes smudged with soot and blood, scuffed shoes, a dull haze in his eyes. He looks down at himself and quickly waves it off. "Yeah, I'm fine. But did you just say jet pack?"

His dad reaches for the remote, rewinds the segment, and hits pause. The screen freezes on the now-familiar winged figure standing atop the armored truck, the very same one Jason saw with his own eyes that morning.

"You don't see a winged man in a breastplate?" Jason asks, blinking hard.

His dad chokes on his drink mid-sip. "Damn, boy, are you on drugs? Seriously asking that?"

Jason realizes how insane he must sound. He backpedals fast. "No, no. Sorry. I'm not. Just... never mind."

His father glares at him, voice rising. "This ain't funny, Jason. People died in that attack. You think this is some kind of joke? You're not five anymore. You can't keep making up stories."

Jason stiffens. "Wait. What did you just say?"

"You heard me." His dad slams the tumbler down, sloshing ice and whiskey. "Grow the fuck up. Now get the hell outta my sight before I really get pissed."

"Hum... okay. Sorry," Jason mutters, the words dry in his mouth as he turns and stumbles down the hallway.

He closes his bedroom door behind him, drops onto the bed, and stares at the ceiling. For a second, all he can hear is the TV muffled in the other room, the buzz of overhead lights, and the thudding in his chest.

Then his phone lights up with a sudden flurry of messages. Buzz. Buzz. Buzz.

Adam.

Henry.

And... Megan McCarthy?

His thumb hovers. Despite knowing he should check on the guys first, his curiosity wins. He opens Megan's message.

It's a blurry screenshot from one of the news broadcasts, but there's no mistaking it. It's him. Caught mid-motion. Kicking a soldier into the street.

Jason bolts upright, breath catching.

Below the image:

"Are you alright?"

Followed by another:

"Were you caught up in that armored truck robbery this morning? Please let me know you're okay." A single heart emoji sits at the end.

Jason swallows, adrenaline flaring back to life. I'm on the news? He types fast: "Yeah, I'm fine. Just at the wrong place at the wrong time. I'll call when I get a chance. Thanks for checking on me."

Then he opens the group chat with Henry and Adam.

Henry:

"It's on the news, but people are saying jetpack terrorists. What the hell?! I still see the ginger angel of death!!!!"

Adam:

[video attachments]

"Luckily my parents are more freaked out about the terrorists and those Secret Service-looking guys. They haven't even noticed we're in the background of like, three clips!"

Jason watches one of the videos—there they are, all three of them, blurred but unmistakable. He quickly types back:

"Alright, we need to stay calm. I know we're in the footage. Megan even texted me about it."

Henry replies almost instantly.

"Megan texted you?! Damn, man. She's so hot~"

Jason sighs, thumbs flying.

"Focus, man. Let me know if you find anything."

Adam is typing...

"Maybe we should think about going to the police? Like... tell them what we saw?"

Jason doesn't answer right away. He stares at the screen, then slowly types:

"You mean, 'Hi officer, we saw an angel with a floating death ring and a magic briefcase?' Yeah. No adult's gonna believe us. My dad just flipped on me for asking about it."

Then:

"For now, we're the only ones who believe what we saw. Give me a second to think. We'll talk soon."

He sets the phone down and rolls onto his back, eyes locked on the ceiling.

There are no flames here. No wings. No screeching tires or broken glass.

Just the sound of his breath, and the gut-deep certainty that whatever they've stepped into... it's only beginning.

After over an hour of texting back and forth with Adam, trying to make sense of the impossible things they'd all seen that morning, Jason notices the triple-dot bubble flicker to life from Henry. It lingers... and lingers... until a wall of text finally drops into the group chat.

Henry:

"Guys. I just got contacted by someone named Merle. I was on this new-age website about angels—Guiding Lights—and in the comments section, I saw my full name. It said, 'Henry Ngo, message me in private.' So I did. I mean, how many Henry Ngos are out there who just saw a real angel this morning?

He introduced himself as Merle and said agents are coming for us. He said not to go with them. He claims they'll say they're from Homeland Security, but they're really Gabriel's men. Not real law enforcement. He called them soldiers, dangerous ones.

He told me to choose a safe place and come back to the site to let him know where we're going. Says he can help us. And listen—I think... I think Merle might be that homeless guy in the alley during the attack. How else would he know who I am?"

Adam:

"You didn't tell him anything, right? About our plans?"

Henry:

"Of course not! I don't trust him either. I just... you think it's the same guy?"

Jason:

"I don't trust him. But I'm starting to think we really can't trust anyone outside of us three. The homeless guy freaks me out, but yeah... I'm leaning that way too."

Adam:

"It's too much of a coincidence. That warning had to come from him. But guys... can we talk about the winged guy's name? Gabriel? As in the archangel Gabriel? What if this Merle guy—hobo wizard or not—can see what we're seeing?"

Jason hesitates, staring at the chat.

Jason:

"I don't know, guys."

"Y'all think it's really a trap?"

Before either of them can reply, the ding-dong of the doorbell cuts through the quiet of Jason's apartment.

He jerks upright.

The air in his room tightens as he slowly cracks his door. His father, already deep into his nightly buzz, stomps to the front door, tugging it open with the chain still latched.

"Can I help you?" his dad slurs.

A clipped, calm voice answers, "Are you James Fitzgerald?"

"Yeah. What's this about?"

Another voice chimes in. "Does your son, Jason Fitzgerald, live here?"

Jason's pulse slams against his ribs. He presses closer to the doorframe.

His dad growls, already puffing up. "Who the fuck wants to know?"

"We're with Homeland Security," the first man replies. "I'm Agent Smith. This is Agent Williams. We need to speak with your son about the armored truck attack."

Jason's stomach drops. His blood runs cold.

It's happening.

He snatches his phone and texts the group:

Jason:

"Homeland Security is here."

Adam:

"Get out. Let's meet. Hurry."

Henry:

"I already left."

Outside his room, Agent Smith's voice rises. "Sir, we don't need a warrant to enter, not in matters of national security."

"We just want to ask your son a few questions," Agent Williams adds.

Jason edges toward the window.

Then, his dad explodes: "I served my country like a goddamn patriot, bled for it in Mogadishu—and you come into my home threatening me? You can both go straight to he—!"

CRACK!

The doorframe splinters with a violent kick. Jason freezes. His father's voice cuts off mid-rant.

"Go find the kid," Smith orders. "I'll deal with the drunk."

Jason clenches his jaw, torn. He glances toward Luke's room.

I can't drag him into this. If I run, they'll follow me. That keeps them away from him.

He pulls the window open and climbs out onto the fire escape, barely catching his breath as he drops down the first few rungs.

Then, a blond man in a black suit leans out his window above. His eyes lock on Jason.

"He's on the fire escape!"

Jason pushes himself harder, descending the last flight, landing hard on the sidewalk.

BANG—BANG—BANG!

Gunshots rip through the evening. Jason's blood turns to ice.

No...

He stumbles, torn between looking back and running forward. Hands shaking, he fumbles for his phone and texts:

Jason:

"Are you okay??"

The reply comes instantly:

Luke:

"Yes, and so is Dad. Now run and stay safe."

Relief punches through his chest like a wave. He takes off.

The streets blur past as he sprints through dark alleys and across puddle-streaked pavement. Neon signs flicker in broken windows. A siren howls in the distance. His destination: Dae-jung Dojo, where he hopes for safety. It's always been his sanctuary. "I only hope Adam and

Henry made it," Jason whispers as he vanishes into the shadows of Hell's Kitchen.

Back at the Fitzgerald apartment...

The so-called Homeland Security agents vanish as abruptly as they arrived, leaving only casualties behind. Luke rushes to his father, who lies crumpled on the floor, his chest soaked in blood.

James Fitzgerald blinks up at his son, his voice weak and choked. "I'm sorry, son... for everything."

Luke kneels beside him, hands steady. "It's okay, Dad. We know you love us... and we love you too. Don't worry, it's all going to be alright."

The blood loss is fast as the chest wound gushes torrents of lifeforce. James' vision tunnels, but the light at the end isn't distant; it's coming from Luke. A soft warm glow, almost like firelight, flickers from the boy's hands as they hover near his father's chest. James feels something strange: peace. For the first time in his miserable, bitter life... peace. Then, everything goes dark.

James wakes up with a gasp.

He jerks upright in his bed, one hand clutching his chest. No blood. No bullet wound. Just a faint feeling like a lingering dream.

Across the room, Luke sits slouched in a chair, quietly watching. "You're awake," he says softly.

"What... what happened?" James croaks. "How long have I been out?"

"They pistol-whipped you. You've been out since last night. It's 10:18 a.m.," Luke answers without checking a clock.

James blinks. "I thought I got shot..."

"Probably just a nightmare. You drank a lot before those guys showed up."

James is quiet for a long moment, piecing it all together. Then, with a frown, "Is there anything left in that bottle?"

Luke hesitates. "Yeah... maybe half."

"Go get it," his father says, sharp and serious.

Luke bolts into the kitchen and returns with the bottle of Jameson, handing it over without a word.

To his shock, his father doesn't take a drink.

He walks straight into the bathroom and unscrews the cap. Luke follows, confused.

Without ceremony, James tips the bottle and dumps it down the sink. The amber liquid gurgles away. Luke stares, stunned.

"Dad?"

James doesn't turn around. "Yeah. I'm okay... finally."

The last drops swirl away as he stares at the drain. Then he lets the silence hang.

"...So, was the busted door real? Or a dream too?" he asks, a tired smirk pulling at one side of his mouth.

Luke says quietly, "Unfortunately, real."

"Well then," James sighs, wiping his hands on a towel, "let's hit the hardware store to get it fixed."

He walks back into the living room of the apartment ... then stops.

"Wait. Where's Jason?" he asks suddenly. "What happened to your brother?"

Luke steadies his voice. "He climbed out the window. Said he was okay. Texted me to make sure we were okay, and I told him to run."

James grabs his phone from the recliner and immediately calls his son. It goes to voicemail.

He leaves a message, his voice shaking just slightly: "Son, I'm not mad. Just... please let me know you're alright."

Luke watches the worry spread across his father's face. "His phone's probably dead. I'll text Adam and Henry, too."

He tries, no response from either. Just silence.

"I'll call their sensei. Mr. Kim." After a few rings, the call connects.

"Mr. Kim? This is Luke Fitzgerald, Jason's brother. Have you seen him today?"

He listens... then nods, face growing more serious.

"Okay. Thank you. Please have him call us if you do."

Luke ends the call and looks at his father grimly. "Sensei Kim hasn't seen Jason, Adam, or Henry. They were supposed to help clean the dojo this morning. But... he did find three broken phones in the alley beside the dojo."

James stiffens. "Three phones?"

"Yeah... he's really worried. He said they wouldn't just not show up without calling."

Silence fills the room for what feels like an eternity. Then Luke asks quietly, "Should we call the police?"

James shakes his head, jaw tight. "No cops. Not yet."

He looks at the shattered front door, then at his son.

"I'm going to make a call to an old Army buddy in the Bureau. Let's see if 'Agent Smith and Williams' are even real."

CHAPTER 5
THE RESCUE

As Jason neared Dae-jung Dojo, his sprint slowed into a prowling stalk. He slipped between shadows like vapor, gliding through the night with the calculated grace of a predator. Every nerve buzzed with electric tension, ears attuned to the faintest noise, eyes cutting through the darkness like a ginsu knife.

He halted at the edge of a brick corner, heart thundering in rhythm with the distant city hum. Slowly, he peeked around. There, in the narrow alley beside the dojo, Henry and Adam crouched low, exchanging hushed words. The street beyond was unnervingly quiet. Too quiet.

Half a block down sat a rust-scabbed plumbing van with patina paint, its windows too dark to see through. More ominous were the two shiny-black Ford Crown Victorias idling a block away, parked like vultures at the edge of the kill. Shadows moved inside.

"Shit," Jason muttered, pulse quickening. Thinking, "Agents. Or worse, angel foot soldiers."

His fingers moved with precision, typing into the group chat:

"Two black sedans near the dojo. I'm across the street, in an adjacent alley."

Adam:

"Ok. So what's the plan then?"

Jason dropped the phone slightly, mind racing. That's when he saw it.

A small red dot, glowing like a malevolent eye, danced across his chest.

"Holy shit!"

Instinct took over. He spun and dropped, landing hard on one knee. A silent breeze brushed past his ear, then the metallic clang! of a trash can lid hitting pavement. He whipped around his phone, its cold glow flooding the alley. Next to the overturned bin lay a dart, a silver-tipped feathered-in-green tranquilizer.

His breath came fast. Controlled. "Stay calm. They've made their move. Time to warn the others." Without another thought, Jason launched into motion with legs burning, heart pounding in his throat as he tore across the street. Time slowed. A single breath stretched into seconds. But it was already too late.

Adam stumbled, clutching his left arm. A dart protruded from his sleeve. Henry collapsed to one knee, ripping another from his leg. The drugs were already working.

Jason's eyes flicked up the street, too late again. The black sedans were moving now, silently gliding forward through the dark with headlights off. Their presence was spectral, like sharks moving through dark water. At fifty yards, their high beams flared to life, searing Jason's vision. He flinched, blinded. Then, whoosh. Another dart sliced through the air, close enough to feel.

A tranquilizer dart ricocheted off the gleaming hood of the lead sedan, sparks of adrenaline igniting in Jason's veins. His heart pounded like a war drum, anger and frustration fueling him. The world sharpened, the near present squeal of tires, the metallic grind of metal and brake pads, all crashing into his senses.

Suddenly, a car screeched to a halt beside him. The front passenger door swung open. Jason didn't hesitate. With brutal efficiency, he kicked it shut, the impact smashing into the passenger's leg and head in a sickening crunch. The man, medium build, dark hair, dressed in a sleek black suit, yelped in pain, clutching his bleeding face. Jason was already inside the car, yanking the man out with brutal force, tossing him like a ragdoll into the second vehicle skidding to a stop beside them. The impact dented the driver's side rear door, metal groaning in protest.

Jason's knee drove into the agent's cracked skull, a sickening crack echoing in the chaos. The driver from the first car leapt out with nimble agility, gun raised, ready to engage. Jason responded faster. His leg swept out, catching the man off guard, sending him sprawling onto the pavement, gun skittering away.

Without hesitation, Jason grabbed the fallen agent's arm, twisting it into a brutal wrist lock. The snap of bone sounded throughout the street. The man's scream was a raw, primal sound, as Jason flipped him onto his back, pinning him down, rage fueling every move.

Jason's fury erupted, punch after savage punch, pounding the agent's face into a pulp. Blood splattered, staining his knuckles, mixing with his attacker's blond hair, staining it pink. His fist landed a final, crushing blow to the man's nose, blood spurting as he went limp.

Looking up, Jason spotted the dented door swinging open on the second vehicle. Out stepped a colossal figure with an iron jaw. The brute, with a chin cast from raw steel, stepped over his fallen colleague who lay next to the dented sedan, unfazed. Without thinking, Jason leapt up, stomping on the unconscious blond's head, launching himself forward, facial bones cracking beneath his sneakers. Using the momentum, he lunged forward, throwing a superman punch that landed square on the giant's chin, an impact that barely fazed the behemoth.

The beast grabbed Jason, dangling him like an infant, muscles bulging under his dark suit. He wrapped powerful arms around Jason in a crushing bear hug, squeezing the air from his lungs. Jason's adrenaline surged; he palm slapped the giant's ear, rupturing his eardrum with a gut-wrenching pop.

The grip loosened just enough. Jason gasped, lungs burning. Seizing the moment, he kneed the giant between the legs, forcing him to drop to a knee. With a snarl, Jason unleashed a brutal flurry of strikes targeting vital points, each blow a savage testament to his wrath. The towering agent stumbled back, crashing against the side of the car. A final blow found its way to the neck, crushing his windpipe, silencing him forever.

Out of the corner of his eye, Jason saw the driver's door of the dented car swing open. A man with uncanny speed leapt out, gun aimed directly at Jason's chest, and pulled the trigger. He flinched, waiting for the inevitable bang, yet nothing came. Instead, Jason gazed down, the sting of the tranquilizer dart protruding from his chest.

His vision blurred, then erupted in blinding light, assaulting his senses, drowning out everything else. "A light? I should be seeing darkness closing in..." he thought hazily.

His shooter, dressed in the expensive dark suit, turned away, panic flickering across his face, then screamed as the nearby abandoned plumbing van, parked down the street, surged forward like a hungry beast, crashing into him. Quickly, the sound of muffled clanks was heard as three figures emerged from the rust bucket. They were dressed in tactical gear which was black as night, with patches depicting an eye inside a triangle, familiar yet distant in his foggy mind.

Jason's fuzzy gaze dropped to his friends, sprawled on the sidewalk, unconscious. His voice slurred, desperate: "My friendsss..."

Suddenly, his shooter, dead at his feet, two gunshot wounds to the head, lay motionless. The new figures in tactical black rushed forward, catching him with precision. One, holding a silenced M4A1 rifle, fired at a distant sniper, probably the one who took Henry and Adam out earlier. The other held a silenced pistol, "We're here to help."

While they dragged him into the van, Jason's hazy mind caught movement. Inside, the interior was shockingly high-tech, sleek, almost sterile, contrasting the mangy outside. Surveillance screens lined the walls, a long bench running down the middle. His heavy eyelids fluttered, vision dimming, yet a surge of relief flooded him as he saw his friends being loaded in by the third member of this mysterious group, their unconscious bodies helpless but alive.

After an unknown amount of time had passed, Jason was jolted awake by a light slapping on his face. "Come on man, wake up," Henry said urgently, his voice sharp but not unkind.

Jason blinked his eyes open, groggy and disoriented. The ceiling above him was a dull gray, lined with narrow fluorescent panels that cast a sterile, bluish light across the room. The air was cool and dry, with a faint scent of ozone and disinfectant. Somewhere behind Henry, he could hear the soft hum of machinery—consistent, low, almost like breathing.

He then heard Adam's voice from behind Henry. "It seems to be locked."

Jason sat up slowly, rubbing his eyes. "Okay. Okay. I'm awake," he muttered, slightly annoyed. As his vision cleared, he looked around and realized with a sense of creeping unease that they weren't in the surveillance van anymore.

The room was utilitarian and windowless, with smooth metallic walls broken only by riveted seams and a single heavy door. The floor beneath them was a brushed steel grating with a dull, matte finish. Several small vents on the walls emitted a soft, constant airflow, and there were no visible cameras, but Jason had a feeling they were being watched.

"Where are we?" he asked aloud, standing to get a better view.

Adam shrugged as he paced across the room. "No idea, but if we're in jail, this is a very high-tech cell."

"Can't be jail," Henry replied, glancing around. "We're still in our street clothes, not those orange jumpsuits like in the movies. Plus, we still have our personal belongings. Well, except for our phones."

"This isn't a movie," Adam said, checking his pockets. "Shit, my new phone! My dad's going to kill me!"

Jason held up a hand. "Let's calm down for a minute and go over what happened last. Like, what does everyone remember?"

Adam sighed, sitting on a low bench built into the wall. "Not much after your text about those Crown Vics being parked down from the dojo."

"Yeah," Henry added. "Not much after that."

Jason scratched the back of his head, then began piecing together what he could. "Well, I didn't get tranquilized till after fighting three agents, angel soldiers, or whatever those guys were. But before I went down, some people showed up and shot the agent who finally tranquilized me. They were special forces of some kind. Like a SWAT team, except their uniforms had a symbol of an eye inside a triangle. I've seen something like it before, I just can't remember where."

"You mean like the eye above the pyramid on the dollar bill?" Adam asked, pulling a crumpled bill from his pocket and holding it up.

Jason's eyes lit up. "Yes!"

Adam nodded thoughtfully. "The Eye of Providence, or All-Seeing Eye—it's a symbol depicting an eye, often enclosed in a triangle, and surrounded by rays of light. It's meant to represent divine watchfulness. The most well-known example is right here on the dollar bill."

"What's Province?" Jason asked, furrowing his brow.

Henry chuckled and shook his head. "It's Providence," he corrected. "The concept has roots going back to ancient times. In theology, it refers to God's intervention in the universe. Later on, artists depicted it as the all-seeing eye, like Adam said. Come on, man, you need to read more. I'm kinda surprised Adam knew this much."

"My grandfather taught me a lot about that kind of stuff," Adam replied. "He was into Jewish mysticism, Lurianic Kabbalah specifically. So yeah, I know a bit."

Jason interrupted their theological discussion. "Well, before I went out, they said they were there to help, and I guess they did kinda save us?" He shrugged.

Adam glanced around again, taking in the sterile metal surfaces, dim lights, and the mechanical purr that never quite went away. "Guess only time will tell."

Just then, a low buzz sounded from the door, like some hidden mechanism had been activated. The teens instinctively backed together, assuming defensive stances, their shadows stretching across the cold floor in the stark light.

A click followed.

The door slid open with a smooth mechanical whine, revealing a tall, brunette woman stepping inside. Her heels clicked sharply against the floor as she moved with composed authority. She wore a form-fitting navy skirt and matching blazer, glasses perched on a perfectly shaped nose. In her arms, she carried a clipboard with a thick folder on top.

"Hello, gentlemen," she greeted, her tone calm but firm. "My name is Glenda Garrison. Welcome to our facility."

Jason stepped forward cautiously. "Whose facility?" he asked with polite skepticism.

"That's a fair question," she said, a slight smile playing on her lips. The lights from the hallway behind her cast long shadows across her figure, giving her a slightly dramatic silhouette. "We are the OE. The Order of the Eye. An ancient organization tasked with observing the Angelic forces."

Henry's eyebrows shot up. "So you've seen an angel?"

Glenda lowered her glasses slightly, studying him with curious, intelligent eyes the color of deep mahogany. "We've observed them, yes. Most of us here don't possess the ability to see them. Have you three seen one by chance?"

Adam deadpanned, "Do we get our one phone call?"

Glenda lifted an eyebrow as she adjusted her glasses again. The overhead light caught the lenses just right, momentarily obscuring her eyes. "No," she said. "But we are your only help at the moment. So can we please do this the easy way?"

After a moment of silence, Jason answered, "Yes, we've seen one. The attack on the armored convoy, we saw a winged man, with a halo, and a flaming sword."

"—and a golden breastplate!" Henry added quickly, his voice full of awe.

Glenda paused for a second, full lips parting slightly as if filing away the information. Then her tone softened.

"Are you all hungry?" she asked. "If so, please follow me to the cafeteria."

"Good Lord, yes, we're starved!" Henry replied with enthusiasm, speaking for the group.

"Then please," she said, stepping aside and motioning toward the hallway, "follow me."

They exited the room, the door hissing shut behind them. The corridor stretched ahead—metallic, cool, and spotless, like something out of a science fiction thriller. Subtle blue lighting traced along the seams of the walls and floors, guiding the way deeper into the heart of a secret world none of them had known existed until now.

The three high school seniors walked side by side, their footsteps echoing faintly off the cold, industrial walls of the strange facility. Everything around them was painted in muted grays and deep blues, utilitarian and efficient, clearly built for function, not comfort. Overhead, soft LED panels bathed the corridors in a pale, sterile light. There were no windows, no signs of the outside world, just seamless walls interrupted by thick, reinforced doors and the occasional security camera that tracked them with silent precision.

Adam broke the silence. "Where are we? Like, what's our location?"

"You're still in the state of New York," Glenda answered plainly, her heels clicking against the polished concrete floor. She walked a step ahead, perfectly composed, her clipboard now tucked under her arm. "I'll do the best I can about answering questions," she continued. "But our security must come first. I hope you'll understand that."

The deeper they went, the clearer it became this was no ordinary government complex. The entire structure felt subterranean, as if they'd been buried beneath layers of earth and secrecy. Pipes ran along the ceilings like exposed veins, humming softly. Glenda led them through a pair of swing doors that immediately reminded the boys of their high school cafeteria, though this space was far more expansive and refined.

The cafeteria had a strange contrast of energy. Long steel tables were spaced with military precision across a polished floor. The air smelled faintly of antiseptic and mystery meat. Armed personnel, most in sleek, tactical uniforms, ate in silence or conversed in low, focused tones. Others, dressed like corporate executives in sharp suits, mingled with a separate cluster of people in pristine white lab coats. The entire hall buzzed with a quiet, underlying tension, like a volcano with a frozen surface.

As they filed into the serving line, each of the boys selected their food. The options were surprisingly normal—grilled chicken, steamed vegetables, trays of deviled eggs, even dessert. Henry, predictably, grabbed a little of everything and piled his tray high like he hadn't eaten in days.

Jason and Adam shared a look of mutual disbelief.

"What?" Henry mouthed, cheeks bulging with three deviled eggs. "Look!" he added thickly, gesturing with a plastic fork.

"What?" Adam and Jason echoed, almost in unison, as Adam gently lowered Henry's pointing hand.

Following his gaze, they spotted Glenda at the front of the line, scanning a card hanging from her lanyard. The cafeteria staff nodded politely as she passed through, likely logging the transaction. Beyond her, however, something far more attention-grabbing happened.

At a round table nearby, half a dozen men and women in white coats suddenly shot to their feet. Each glanced down at a handheld device, faces instantly serious, and within seconds they were sprinting out of the mess hall, leaving half-eaten meals behind.

The boys stood frozen, eyes tracking the sudden, coordinated exit.

Glenda noticed but showed no alarm. She continued walking as if nothing had happened, approaching a vacant table and gesturing for them to sit. Her clipboard and folder thumped softly against the table as she set them down.

"Would you three be willing to take a polygraph test?" she asked, barely giving them time to settle into their seats.

Jason glanced around nervously, and Henry, taking a huge bite of carrot cake, raised an eyebrow. "Why hook us up to a lie detector?" he asked, eyeing the direction the lab coats had fled. Despite his words, he couldn't help but keep looking toward the emergency exit, like something was calling him.

"Not so much a lie detector," Glenda replied calmly, "but as a baseline, to compare what your brains think they saw."

Adam scoffed, leaning back slightly. "So now we're lab rats for your cult? And we know we saw an angel!"

"You don't have to participate," Glenda said plainly, her voice measured. "And I believe you all saw an angel, too." Her tone softened, sincerity flickering in her eyes.

Jason glanced at his friends, then spoke. "Can we have a moment alone to discuss things, please?"

"Of course," Glenda replied. She stood smoothly, her movements practiced and deliberate. "I'll be right over there. Just wave me over when you're ready." She stepped away from the table, raising her phone and tapping at the screen before putting it to her ear. As she spoke in low tones, she turned slightly toward the now-abandoned table, her face briefly betraying a flash of concern that contradicted her earlier calm.

Once she was a safe distance away, Jason leaned in.

"Okay, look. Maybe we should play nice. We have no idea what we're in for, or what we're up against."

Adam ran a hand through his coarse, dark hair. "I don't know, man…"

"The enemy of my enemy is my friend," Henry said, almost reverently, as though having an epiphany. "Plus, I bet they've got some badass James Bond spy shit we could play with."

Adam rolled his eyes but relented. "I'll go along with it, as long as I know our families are safe. I want to talk to them. They're probably losing their minds right now."

They all nodded in agreement, and Jason gave a quick wave to Glenda. She noticed immediately and held up her hand in acknowledgement, ending her call as she returned to the table.

"Everything okay?" Henry asked boldly.

"Yes indeed," Glenda replied with a pleasant smile that didn't quite reach her eyes. "So, what's the verdict?"

"Okay," Jason said, meeting her gaze. "We'll play ball. We just want to know our families are all right and not worried about us. We want to talk to them soon."

Glenda nodded. "I can arrange that for you. After you're all done eating, we'll begin with the necessary tests."

She gave one final reassuring look before settling into the seat across from them. Somewhere far down one of the steel corridors beyond the cafeteria, a muffled alarm chirped once, then was quickly silenced.

CHAPTER 6
THE TRAINING

"Okay, so just relax and answer these questions as best you can," said a tall, balding Black man in a crisp white lab coat, his voice calm but practiced from years of repetition.

Glenda stepped forward, her heels tapping softly on the pristine tiled floor. "This is Dr. Johnson—"

"You can call me Omar," the scientist interrupted casually with a warm smile, his tone easing the tension in the air. "Once all three of you have answered the questions, we'd like to do brain and heart scans while you perform a series of tasks, starting simple, then moving to more complex ones. Sound alright?"

The three teens offered vague shrugs and mumbled responses: "Sure," "Yeah," "Alright."

"Who wants to go first?" Omar asked, glancing between them.

Henry practically jumped. "Me! Me!"

"Okay. Everyone else, out," Glenda said, nodding to Jason and Adam, who gave Henry amused looks before exiting.

After all three sessions concluded, the teens found themselves in a sleek waiting room outside Omar's office. The walls here were smoother, more modern, like a high-end tech startup's lounge, with soft lighting and minimalist furniture.

Adam leaned in, lowering his voice. "Alright, so what questions did they ask y'all?"

As they compared notes, they quickly realized the questions had been identical—names, locations, descriptions of the angel, the event timeline—and strangely, so were their answers.

Before they could speculate further, Dr. Omar Johnson and Glenda Garrison reentered.

"Well," Glenda said with a soft chuckle, "you three young men aren't lying. You genuinely believe you saw an angel."

"Because we did," Henry cut in, a note of exasperation in his voice.

"I know, I know," Glenda replied calmly. "And as I said earlier, I believed you. But we still have protocols we're required to follow."

Henry looked to Jason and Adam sheepishly, deflating just a bit. Jason nodded, and the group relaxed.

"Are you gentlemen ready for the next set of tests?" Dr. Johnson asked.

Jason looked up, cracking a half-smile. "Yeah. Bring 'em on, Doc."

"Right this way," Glenda said, motioning toward a nearby door.

The next room was vast and humming with activity. Fluorescent lights gleamed off metallic surfaces, casting reflections on walls lined with monitors and control panels. Banks of computers flickered with real-time data, and technicians in OE uniforms stood silently at terminals. It had the intensity of a command center, but the buzz of a laboratory.

As Jason was guided to the first station, Adam leaned toward Henry. "Great. We know who's winning this test."

Jason called over his shoulder. "Yeah, it ain't gonna be me."

"Don't think of it as a competition," Omar instructed, stepping into the room behind them. "Just focus on your task. This isn't about winning or losing, it's about how your brain and heart respond under pressure."

The challenge began.

Almost immediately, Jason was locked out, followed soon after by Adam, who threw his hands up and said, "Good luck, dude. This is way too advanced for me."

"You have five minutes," Glenda's voice rang out crisply over an intercom. "Good luck."

In the stark light of the computer room, Henry sat hunched over a sleek terminal, the OE-issued black hoodie stretching slightly across his broad frame. His fingers moved with a surprising dexterity for someone his size, dancing across the keys in perfect rhythm. The glow of the monitors cast a blue hue across his round face, which was locked in an expression of total focus. His almond-shaped eyes darted from one screen to the next, absorbing layers of data as if they were second nature.

Code streamed like a waterfall across the central display—lines of scripts, firewall reports, IP traces—all processed and parsed in real time. A second monitor showed live data packet flows, pulsing like a heartbeat. A third offered an overhead view of the system's internal architecture, with nodes glowing where vulnerabilities might lie.

Henry moved with quiet confidence, navigating protocols and layered defenses with calculated grace. His breathing slowed as he hit his stride, blocking out the world beyond the screen. When an alert suddenly flashed red, a warning from the simulation's defenses, he didn't flinch. Instead, he countered, deploying decoy packets and masking his IP with a command-line flurry.

Tension built. The digital terrain felt alive, reacting to every move he made. But with one last sweep of keystrokes, Henry breached the final node. "Project Star Child" appeared on the screen. He accessed the files and began extracting what he needed.

The timer flashed: 0:47.

Moving quickly, he initiated a clean trace-wipe, leaving no sign of his digital presence. Then, he leaned back in the chair, breathing out through his nose as a faint grin curled across his lips.

Henry emerged from the room, his grin fully formed now.

"That simulation was fun. I felt like a world-class hacker in there," he said, clearly pleased with himself, the shadow of past failure against hacker Merle shaken a bit.

Glenda looked amused. "That wasn't a simulation."

Henry blinked. "Huh?"

"We put all three of you to the task of hacking into the Pentagon. The information you retrieved is real. We needed someone who could bypass their external firewall undetected," she said, her expression serious but faintly impressed. "Not to worry, your attempt was successful, and the other two weren't detected."

Henry's jaw dropped. "What!? Are you serious right now?"

"Very serious," Glenda confirmed. "Please follow me."

Jason stood and clapped him on the shoulder. "Alright, master hacker. Time for the next task."

"Next stop, the gymnasium," Glenda announced as they walked.

They entered a cavernous training space, bright lights suspended far overhead casting an intense glow onto blue sparring mats that stretched wall to wall. The air smelled of rubber and disinfectant, and the space echoed faintly with every step they took.

"This is a straightforward test," Glenda explained. "The OE's highly trained commandos will enter in groups of three every two minutes. Your job is to avoid being subdued. They will not be holding back."

Jason glanced at his friends, grounding himself with the familiar.

"Just let what Sensei taught us come out," he said calmly. "Let the energy flow through you, and stay close to me."

Henry gave a nervous chuckle. "I wish I'd paid more attention in training right about now."

Jason turned to Glenda. "We're ready."

She nodded and tapped a button on her tablet. From a side entrance, three men stepped onto the mat. One was a tall, ripped Black man with the frame of a seasoned brawler. Beside him, a white man with a full sleeve of tattoos cracked his knuckles, while the third—a huge pale man resembling a gorilla, thick-necked brute with a shaved head—twisted his neck with audible pops. All three looked like they lived for combat.

Jason leaned in, voice low. "You guys tangle with the big guy. I'll take the other two. I'll come help once I finish. Henry, stay in control and use your size."

Glenda raised her hand and shouted, "Ready... fight!"

As she dropped her hand, a massive digital timer blinked to life above them.

2:00

The battle had begun.

As the countdown timer blinked to 1:59, the three

commandos surged forward with explosive speed, no hesitation, no warm-up.

Jason didn't waste a second. He pivoted to intercept the tattooed commando first, dropping into a defensive stance Sensei had drilled into them over and over. His opponent came in high with a right hook meant to knock teeth loose. Jason slipped under it and responded with a sharp front kick to the man's solar plexus, forcing him back two steps.

To Jason's right, Adam squared off with the towering brute, the shaved-head mountain of muscle who moved more like a bull than a fighter. The commando charged, attempting a double-leg takedown. Adam sprawled, feet sliding on the mat, barely managing to redirect the momentum before he was fully lifted off his feet. Still, they crashed to the ground together. Adam scrambled for control, clinging to the man's torso in a half-guard, breathing hard.

Henry found himself face to face with the Black commando, calm, poised, with the fluid stance of a trained kickboxer. The man snapped a jab toward Henry's face. Henry flinched late, taking a glancing blow across his cheek. His reflexes were clumsy, but he remembered Jason's words: use your size.

Henry surged forward with a bear-like rush, grabbing at the man's midsection. It wasn't clean or elegant, but it was effective. The assailant backpedaled as Henry bulldozed him into the padded floor, using his weight as a weapon.

Meanwhile, Jason faced his opponent again. The tattooed man came back harder, feinting left and then spinning into a low sweep aimed at Jason's legs. Jason leapt over it and countered with a backfist across the jaw. It landed clean, but the commando barely flinched. They locked eyes; Jason could tell this guy had been in real fights.

Back on the mat, Adam groaned. The shaved-head commando had broken free and now loomed over him, fists raised. Adam rolled to avoid a downward hammer fist, then kicked upward into the man's knee—off-balance, but enough to buy time. As the commando stepped back to reset, Jason delivered a clean round-house to his ribs, knocking him into the tattooed guy and staggering both.

"Thanks!" Adam called out, regaining his footing.

"No problem!" Jason replied, already stepping into the next attack.

Across the mat, Henry grappled awkwardly with the kickboxer. The man delivered quick body shots to Henry's ribs, trying to break the clinch. Henry gritted his teeth and slammed a knee into the man's thigh—awkwardly but powerfully. The man grunted. Henry pushed off him, creating space, then charged again.

Jason broke from the others and went low, sliding between the tattooed commando's legs and popping up behind him. He landed a kidney strike just as Adam distracted the brute with a sweeping kick. The coordination was smooth. Almost instinctual.

Then the kickboxer recovered and struck Henry with a sudden elbow to the temple. Henry stumbled, blood rushing in his ears, but his instincts kicked in. He threw a wild, two-handed shove, catching the man off-balance. When the commando hit the mat, Henry dropped on top of him with a full body pin.

"Time's almost up!" Glenda called from the side, clipboard in hand.

The shaved-head brute came charging again, this time going for Jason. But Jason ducked under his wide punch and tripped him with a foot sweep. As the man fell, Jason planted a knee on his chest and delivered a mock elbow to the neck, clearly a submission in training.

Henry, still breathing hard, raised a hand from across the mat. "He's not moving! I think I won!"

Jason turned to Adam. "How you holding up?"

Adam, hair a mess and sweat pouring down his forehead, raised a shaky thumbs-up. "Still vertical!"

The tattooed commando came in one final time, but this time all three teens surrounded him. A quick series of coordinated movements—Jason's front kick, Adam's sweep, Henry's awkward shoulder bump—brought him down.

The timer buzzed loudly.

The commandos rolled to their feet slowly, some winded, others smirking with respect. One even nodded at Jason before walking off the mat.

"Reset the clock for six minutes!" Glenda shouts. "No breaks this time." She sternly warns.

COUNTDOWN CLOCK: 06:00

A harsh buzzer echoes. New enemies enter: a wiry Filipino fighter with lightning-fast footwork, a compact bruiser with thick arms and Central American features, and a towering blond with a wrestler's build.

Jason wipes a smear of blood from his cheek, voice low and firm. "All on the fast one. Now."

No hesitation.

The trio launches into coordinated motion. Jason leads with a clean hook to the jaw, Adam cuts low with a roundhouse to the ribs, and Henry crashes in with a blunt-force shoulder tackle.

The fighter doesn't stand a chance. He's on the mat, gasping, before he can land a single strike.

But the others are already in motion.

The bulky Mexican snaps a punch behind Henry's ear. The blow drops him instantly.

Jason spins, too late. He's yanked into the air by the blond, slammed hard onto the mat. His skull bounces. His limbs go still.

Adam pivots, anger blazing, drives a foot straight into the Mexican attacker's face. A sickening crunch follows. Then, a fist in his hair. The blond lifts Adam with one hand tangled in his hair and slams a punch into his face. Blood erupts from his nose. Adam doesn't falter. He grits his teeth, pulls back, and lands a brutal upward knee right into the man's groin. The tall blond drops to his knees, cupping his crotch. Adam, eyes stinging, goes feral. He grabs the blond's head, knees it over and over, until the man finally slumps to the floor.

COUNTDOWN CLOCK: 04:42

Jason groans. His vision clears. He sees Henry out cold. Adam barely standing.

The stocky Mexican fighter crawled to his feet. Jason leaps from his back on the ground, surging forward, foot connecting with the man's temple. The Mexican fighter drops fast. Jason doesn't stop; he follows with a hard kick to the ribs, then another. The man doesn't move again. Rage builds inside him like a volcano on the verge of eruption.

The buzzer shrieks.

COUNTDOWN CLOCK: 3:56

Three women enter this time—two are slender, agile, and deadly; the other is bigger than the previous men. A fierce redhead, a calm-eyed Chinese fighter, and a towering blonde who moves like a tank.

Jason doesn't flinch. He barrels into the redhead and lands a sharp overhand right. She drops, unmoving. He freezes. His knuckles tremble. He's never hit a woman before. A mistake.

The blonde charges Jason, delivering a monstrous uppercut that lifts him off his feet.

The Chinese fighter flips Adam over her shoulder, his arm already twisting into a lock. Adam screams, knowing that he's in an armbar.

After nailing Jason with an uppercut, the massive beauty says in a thick Russian accent, "Time for beating, boy," as she delivers a hell of a right cross.

After the jarring blows, Jason's rage builds back up then explodes. He throws a combo of punches— a few quick but precise jabs, then a right cross—causing her to fall over, letting out a howl of pain. Her echoing cries, it seems, bring Henry back into the fight. Jason just lets his hands go as they fly in a flurry to the Russian's head and body, then follows it up with kicks to her legs, wanting to help Adam. The Russian finally goes down. The volcanic rage decides to erupt further, ending their exchange with an axe kick to her head. She lies there unconscious next to the redhead.

Henry quickly surveys the scene, seeing Adam yelling in pain as he's trying to slip the armbar he's in. He's feeling his strength leaving him, and he knows that will lead to a broken arm. Henry quickly jumps up and lands full force on the Asian combatant, knocking the breath out of her due to Henry's extra weight from excessive snacking. This loosens her grip on Adam's arm, which he quickly takes advantage of by getting out of her hold. They both start beating her without mercy.

COUNTDOWN CLOCK: 02:00

The three boys all hear the buzzer again, and three monsters of men are sent in. Bloody and bruised, the teenagers all stagger to their feet, trying to compose themselves enough to regain a solid fighting stance after fighting in such a fevered pitch through three rounds of fresh fighters. A rage surges through them all at once as they stare down their new aggressors and yell in unison, "Let's kill 'em all!"

Unexpectedly, another buzzer goes off at 01:56. Glenda steps forward. "The test has concluded."

The three large soldiers stop charging while Jason, Adam, and Henry keep going.

While they're screaming death threats, Glenda calmly approaches. "Gentlemen! The test is over."

It's at that point they all look at each other's battered faces and start catching their breaths.

"You lasted," Glenda says, genuinely impressed, "better than any of our recruits on their first day."

Henry drops to his knees, arms raised in mock victory. "We didn't die!"

Adam grinned, sweat dripping from his temple. "Barely."

Glenda turns toward the clipboard and makes a few notes. "You three have more potential than you realize."

Jason catches his breath, looking over at his friends. "Or maybe we're just too stubborn to lose."

"Well, whatever it is, you three performed impressively," Glenda says while looking around at the nine opponents employed by the OE laying unconscious or staggering to their feet from the mats. "Now, let's get you all fixed up and on to dinner. Tomorrow we'll get started on testing again. Is that acceptable?"

Henry, still gasping, asks, "You think we can get some more of that carrot cake?"

She reveals a smile. "Yes, of course. I believe you've earned it."

The infirmary was sterile and sleek, with glass walls that shimmered faintly under strips of soft white overhead lighting. Monitors embedded in the wall pulsed quietly, displaying streams of biometric data none of the boys could fully understand. The air was crisp and scentless, almost too clean, like it had been scrubbed of anything natural. Occasionally, a mechanical hum or the faint hiss of pressurized air drifted in from unseen vents, as if the whole underground base breathed on its own.

Jason sat up slowly on an exam table covered in disposable paper, his eyes scanning the smooth, chrome-accented walls before settling on his two friends. A faint grin touched his lips. "You two kicked so much ass."

Henry winced as he touched a bruise forming beneath his ribs. "Thanks. I can't believe I fought like that."

"I guess watching me and Jason spar taught you something after all," Adam joked from his own examination table, a thin black medical patch pulsing softly over a scrape on his arm.

They all laughed, the sound sharp against the otherwise clinical silence. But beneath the laughter was a tension they couldn't name, something unspoken trailing behind their words like a shadow.

Adam's smile faded first. His voice dropped. "But seriously... it's like I could feel your rage, Jason. Not just see it. Feel it."

Henry nodded, his brow creased. "Yeah. It brought me out of being knocked out, like something snapped inside me. I just knew you needed help, Adam. I wasn't thinking, it was like instinct."

Jason looked down, his fingers tightening over the edge of the exam table. The laughter was gone. "I don't know, guys. This is all too weird, ya know? This place, the OE, that angel, hell even the street wizard, just everything."

They fell silent. Somewhere nearby, the soft whirr of a hovering medical drone moved past the glass wall, scanning the hallway like a silent sentry. The room's lighting dimmed a fraction, responding to some internal system.

After a moment, the sliding glass door to the infirmary hissed open. A tall attendant in a graphite-black OE uniform entered, face obscured by a mirrored visor, an insignia shaped like an unblinking eye glowing softly on their chest. No words were spoken. They simply gestured for the boys to follow.

In the corridors outside they found Glenda waiting. This wing of the base had walls that were pristine white, illuminated by subtle floor lighting and lined with smooth panels that pulsed with data. They walked past reinforced doors marked only by glyphs or blinking codes, past rooms where voices whispered behind tinted glass, discussions about "awakening timelines" and "resonance thresholds."

Finally, they reached their new dormitory: a modular room with three bunks, uniform storage lockers, and a single recessed screen embedded in the wall that displayed only a pulsing eye icon. The boys shared a quiet dinner alone in their dorm. All their food requests were covered on stainless steel trays.

No one spoke much. Whatever energy they had left drained away.

As they lay down, sleep took them quickly, heavier than it should've been. Almost imposed. The lights dimmed automatically, and for a while, the dormitory was still.

But somewhere beneath their floor, in the deeper levels of the OE base, machines stirred and watched. Studying them.

Upon waking, the three teenage friends were surprised by their lack of soreness. After the grueling physical trial the day before, they had braced for aching muscles, swollen faces, and stiff joints but instead, they felt strangely whole, their bodies healed at an unnatural pace. The silence between them carried weight. None of them dared speak of the change. A quiet, mutual denial settled in, each unwilling to confront the uncanny truth: reality itself was shifting around them.

After breakfast in the echoing mess hall, each of them was led down a hallway to a dimly lit chamber. At the center of the room were three reclined, cushioned chairs arranged in a gentle curve. Seated before them on a thick floor pillow was a dark-skinned man with a long, silver-threaded beard wearing a deep violet turban. His presence was calm, grounding, like still water.

"Welcome," he said in a smooth, Indian-accented voice. "I am Arjun Bakshi. Please, come in. Make yourselves comfortable."

As they settled into the chairs, Arjun pressed a button on a small device beside him. The air began to fill with sound—not quite music, not quite noise—a series of tonal waves and low frequencies, as though the room itself had started to breathe.

"I will be your meditation guide," he said, his voice woven into the vibration.

Henry blinked at the sound and asked, "Is this a vision quest?"

Arjun smiled gently. "It can be. We shall see where your minds choose to go."

With practiced cadence, he guided them through the first steps of relaxation. "Close your eyes. Take three deep breaths. With each exhale, release the tension. Feel it slipping from your body like smoke on the wind."

They obeyed. On the final breath, the soundscape seemed to deepen, pulsing through their chests.

"Now," Arjun continued, "focus on the resonance. Let it carry you inward. Ask yourself a simple question: 'What thought will I think of next?'" He paused. "This is a gateway, an invitation to silence. Listen for the absence."

A long stillness followed. Time felt suspended.

Then, Arjun's voice returned, softer but more commanding, more ancient.

"Now imagine an elevator descending from the hundredth floor. With each floor you pass, your awareness sinks deeper into the strata of your mind. Ten floors before arrival, a figure appears behind the door. Who stands there, waiting?"

In Jason's inner vision, it was his mother, her face frozen in time, unchanged since the day she vanished from his life over a decade ago.

Henry saw the father he never met, known only through the sepia tones of faded photographs and secondhand stories.

Adam stood before his grandfather, the old storyteller who had filled his childhood with myths, legends, and spiritual wisdom whispered by firelight.

"These are your spirit guides," Arjun said, as though he could see them. "They are here to help you traverse the inner realms, mirrors of your multiversal selves. Join them now. Step into the elevator together."

In the shared silence of the room, the friends' minds obeyed.

"The B button is pressed. You are descending to the basement, the deepest level of your subconscious."

Another long pause. Arjun reached for a tuning fork and struck it. The chime echoed like a ripple across still water.

"Now," he whispered, "listen to the sound. Let it envelop you. Ask your guides to connect you to your parallel selves, the beings you are across realities. You will soon come into contact with the Silver Plates. When you do, listen. Learn."

The elevator stops. The doors slide open.

"You are now in a dream deeper than sleep," Arjun intoned. "Before you is a vast room of light. Floating at the center is a book of shining metal."

Their breaths slowed as their minds approached the vision.

"Step forward. Run your fingers over the symbols etched into the gleaming pages. You will understand them. Not only the knowledge of the Silver Plates will unfold, but the knowledge of yourselves and the unique role each of you is destined to play in the greater design of the universe."

In the realm behind their eyes, the book shimmered and whispered truths in symbols beyond language. When their silent study was complete, the book began to rise, drifting upward into the light until it vanished. The room dimmed, shadows returned, and only the soft glow of the open elevator remained—a path back.

"It is time," Arjun said gently. "You may leave now, but what you have learned will remain with you."

The three teens returned to their elevators, pressing the third-floor button three times, as instructed.

"When the doors open," Arjun whispered, "you will awaken—aware and changed."

With a soft chime, the elevator doors opened once more as their eyes opened to the dim room. They inhaled sharply, returning from the depths, the spell broken. But something had shifted, indelibly. They carried with them more than memory; they carried the light of ancient knowledge etched in silver and soul.

Jason's eyes fluttered open. The dim light of the room bled back into his vision as he turned his head, spotting Henry and Adam slowly stirring beside him. Their faces mirrored his own, fogged by a strange, dreamlike haze. It felt like waking from a dream half-remembered, or a memory from another life. Jason blinked hard, trying to ground himself in the here and now.

Across the room, Arjun rose from his cushion in one fluid, deliberate motion.

"Gentlemen," he said, his voice both soft and commanding, "please follow me."

They moved as if pulled by unseen strings, trailing behind Arjun into an adjoining chamber. The air shifted as they passed through the threshold—cooler, charged, as if the space itself was holding its breath.

"Behind this door," Arjun said, pausing before a simple metallic entryway, "you will know what to do."

Jason was the first to be ushered inside.

The room was empty, save for a pedestal at the center. Upon it rested a metallic tome, gleaming like a mirror forged from starlight. Jason approached, his reflection warped across the book's surface. He opened it, flipping through the heavy pages etched with radiant, indecipherable symbols. They shimmered with strange familiarity, like déjà vu written in light.

He exited moments later, confusion shadowing his features.

"I couldn't make sense of it," he muttered with a shrug. "It's just… symbols. Nothing I can understand."

Arjun simply nodded and patted his shoulder.

"That's perfectly fine."

Next was Henry, who lingered longer, fingers tracing the glyphs with cautious reverence. When he returned, he exhaled sharply.

"They felt... familiar. Like code. Computer code, maybe. I almost understood it, like it was on the tip of my mind, but I couldn't crack it. I'm sorry."

"There's nothing to be sorry for," Arjun said calmly.

Then Adam walks in. The moment his fingertips graze the metallic cover, the air in the room thickens, humming with latent energy. As he opens the book, the symbols begin to pulse faintly. His lips start moving, at first in whispers, then in a rising chant. The languages blend—Hebrew, Yiddish, Judeo-Greek, a mosaic of sacred tongues spilling from his mouth.

Arjun leans forward, almost breathless. "Speak it into existence," he whispers.

And Adam does. The book lifts into the air, levitating as if responding to an ancient command. Adam rises with it, his body folding into a perfect lotus pose, suspended in midair. His arms extend outward, palms to the heavens, and then—

His eyes blaze with radiant light. The symbols in the book ignite, burning into the room with ethereal brilliance. Flames roar to life in his open hands. Lightning arcs from the floating tome, striking him square in the chest. The walls crackle and groan as ice blooms across every surface, creeping like frost from another dimension.

Arjun gasps, breath now visible in the plunging temperature. Even he cannot hide the awe and fear etched on his face.

As the final page turns, the book lowers slowly. Adam follows, descending like a leaf on a still wind. The book settles in his hands. His eyes blink open, ordinary now. He glances down at the book, flipping through it like any other. "I don't get it," he says flatly. "None of this makes sense." He rubs his arms. "Why's it so cold in here? And... what the hell happened to the walls?" Ice gleams along every surface, crackling faintly as it clings.

Arjun is silent for a long moment. Then the door bursts open. A team of OE guards rushes in, boots crunching against ice as the fractured metal door flakes with frost. Jason and Henry are behind them, ushered in by Glenda, who immediately hands blankets to both Arjun and Adam.

The meditation guide shivers as he wraps himself. Through chattering teeth, he glances at Glenda. "P-p-please tell me you recorded everything on v-v-video."

She nods, her expression unreadable. "We did. There was some interference during the energy discharge, static distortion, but most of it was captured clearly."

Jason and Henry move cautiously toward Adam, who's now sitting on the edge of a table, trying to thaw.

"Dude," Jason says, his voice hesitant, "are you okay?"

"Yeah," Adam replies, breath fogging, "aside from nearly freezing to death. Why are you guys looking at me like that?"

Henry laughs nervously. "Bro, you went full Dr. Strange in there! Like glowing eyes, floating, chanting in dead languages, do it again!"

Before Adam can respond, Arjun steps between them, placing a steady hand on Adam's shoulder. "Let him process this," he says gently. "He needs time to understand what he's just done." He looks Adam in the eyes. "Come. Let's review the footage."

They retreat into a nearby control room where a technician already has the footage queued up. Adam watches as the moment unfolds, his body suspended, the book aglow, the ice creeping along the walls.

Henry squeezes into the crowd, grinning. "Here it comes, bro! Watch this, right there! That's where it kicks off!"

Adam stares at the screen, unmoving. The image flickers, crackling with static and strange patterns, but the vision is unmistakable. He watches himself become something... else. "This can't be real," he murmurs. "That's not me."

He stumbles back, pushing past chairs and people. The walls suddenly feel too close, the air too thin.

"Everyone give him space," Arjun commands. He follows Adam out into the hall, his voice calm and low. "It's all right, Adam. What you're feeling is the birth of awareness. Your third eye has opened completely. You've glimpsed a power that was always inside you."

Adam stops, breathing hard.

Arjun continues, more softly now. "Your path is far greater than anything you've been told. Deep down, you've always known this. You're not meant to live in the shadows of mediocrity. The world needs you to rise as the divine champion you were always meant to be."

He places both hands on Adam's shoulders, his voice now almost a whisper.

"Breathe. Remember who you are. And become one with it."

"This is going to take some time to process," Adam says while looking down.

"Take the time you need," Arjun suggests. "You three have been through quite a lot. Take the rest of this day and go enjoy the recreational hall. Play table tennis, video games, and shoot a game or two of billiards."

The rec room in the underground base buzzed with a low hum from fluorescent lights. The air smelled faintly of vinyl and stale popcorn. A couple of immaculately kept arcade cabinets lined one wall—Galaga, Street Fighter II, and Pac-Man, their screens glowing brightly. A pool table stood in the center, its green felt worn and nicked but usable.

As the boys entered, Jason made a beeline for the pool table.

"Hey—8-ball or 9-ball?" he asked, starting to rack the balls. Then, glancing at the others, he added, "So let me get this straight: we're in a secret base, part of a secret society, where it's been confirmed we can see angels and demons... and Adam's now a wizard?"

Henry stood by the arcade machines, scanning the selection. He turned slowly toward the others.

"I don't get it. Yesterday we were just normal high school kids... and today? We can see things no one else can. And yeah, Adam, dude—you're a wizard now! How does that even work?"

"I don't even know, man," Adam said, shaking his head. "That book—it's like it chose me. The moment I opened it, everything changed. I thought I was just trying to read some weird old symbols, but then you all saw it... like electricity flowing through me—or hell, out of me. I can feel the power. The knowledge is just... clicking into place. It's unreal. But there's still a disconnect there, if that makes any sense?"

Jason leaned over the pool table, chalking his cue. "So, like, you can cast spells now or something? Could you make my homework disappear? Because, trust me, that would kick so much ass."

His joke earned a faint smile from Adam.

"If only it were that easy," Adam said with a smirk. "But yeah... I guess I can. I don't really know what I can do yet. But it feels like I could move mountains if I wanted to. It's like... this whole new world just opened up, and I have the keys—but I don't know which key goes to which lock, if that makes sense?"

Henry shook his head in awe. "I don't get it. Angels, secret societies, wizards... a whole hidden world. It's like we're part of something way bigger than us. What is all of this? Why us? And is hobo Gandalf really a wizard too? I mean—Adam is!"

Jason shrugged. "Maybe we're special. Or maybe it's all just a massive coincidence. But seriously, Henry—you're right. This is beyond anything we've ever imagined."

We've joked about being superheroes, but this? This is no joke. We've got real powers."

Still staring at the floor, Adam said quietly, "It's... heavy. The weight of it, I mean. I haven't even fully processed what's happening. One minute I'm flipping through that metal book, and the next I'm seeing visions of a world I didn't even know existed. And the angels, man—they're real. Not just in stories. They're out there. And somehow, we've tapped into their world."

Jason's expression turned serious. "Or they've tapped into ours. Do you think we're supposed to do something with all this? Like, are we supposed to be guardians of the Earth or something? You've got powers, we can see angels—but what's the endgame?"

Henry spoke up, quieter now. "The real question is: what's the OE's endgame? That's what I keep wondering. Are we part of some greater plan of theirs? Or did we just stumble into this by accident? I don't know if I'm ready for all this... but I can't ignore it. Not after what Gabriel said about that prophecy on top of that armored truck. There's something pulling us in—something we can't walk away from."

"I feel it too," Adam said, pausing to look at both his friends. "It's like I'm part of something ancient... like the universe itself is calling me to learn, to grow... maybe even protect. But I don't know if I'm ready for it either. What if I mess up? What if I can't control it?"

"Dude, we're all in this together," Jason said, reassuring him. "You're not alone in this. I mean, look at us—we're all still trying to figure it out. But I trust you. We'll help you learn what you need to, like we've always done for each other."

Henry nodded. "Yeah, man. You're not the only one who's suddenly been thrown into a world of magic and angels. We've got your back. Always."

Adam smiled, looking slightly more grounded. "Thanks, guys. Seriously. This whole thing's a lot. But if we're in it together, I think... we can figure it out."

"Speaking of you not being the only one..." Henry cut back in. "Do you guys think there are others like us? Other kids with these abilities?"

"Well, we know Steven could see the unseen world we're now a part of," Jason said with a shrug.

"Oh yeah—speaking of that!" Henry perked up. "I finally tracked down Steven on social media. Took a few fake accounts and a lot of digging on my phone, but he looks like he's doing well now. Seems like he's finally in a good place."

"That's great!" Adam said, then frowned slightly. "Wait—why'd you have to do it on your phone and not your computer?"

"Yeah, about that," Henry replied, looking sheepish. "I got hacked. By Merle. Remember that website I told you guys about—Guiding Lights? I was trying to trace his IP address or anything to figure out who he is, but he's no joke. My laptop's toast now."

"Damn. Master Hacker, and you still lost?" Adam said in disbelief—especially after watching Henry hack the Pentagon with ease just yesterday.

Jason laughed and handed them both pool cues. "Come on, you two. I'll play the winner. Then we'll see if we can raid the cafeteria fridge in this place."

"Now that sounds like a solid plan," Henry grinned. "I get to break! Not sure if Adam's wizardly powers will give him some kind of edge in the game?"

They all burst into laughter as the cue ball cracked against the racked triangle, scattering solids and stripes across the table—just three boys, bound by something much bigger than any of them, trying to hold on to whatever normalcy was left.

CHAPTER 7
THE SECRET

"Welcome, gentlemen."

The voice echoed through the chamber, deep and authoritative, bouncing off the polished metal walls with an almost unnatural clarity. The room was large—auditorium-sized—but lacked the warmth of a typical lecture hall. Instead, sleek steel-paneled walls curved upward into a vaulted ceiling laced with glowing fiber-optic veins that pulsed like faint constellations. Rows of angular black chairs formed a semi-circle around a raised platform, all facing a wall-sized holographic screen currently displaying a model of a human brain and abstract glyphs of unknown origin.

Standing at the center of the platform was an imposing older man in a strange, antiquated military uniform. The brass buttons gleamed under the white-blue ceiling lights, and a blood-red sash crossed his barrel chest. His bushy silver mustache framed a mouth set in a permanent scowl, and his close-cropped flattop haircut matched the steel in his ice-gray eyes.

"I'm Grand General Braxton Carlson."

Jason, Henry, and Adam exchanged glances, uncertain whether to stand at attention or run in the opposite direction. Carlson's presence alone was commanding enough to freeze them in place. Behind him, seated on minimalist, high-backed chairs that appeared to rise seamlessly from the floor, were the familiar faces of Glenda Garrison—her sharp gaze flicking to each boy in turn—and Dr. Omar Johnson, who looked barely able to contain his excitement. Beside him sat Arjun Bakshi, calm and analytical as always. At the end of the line, an unfamiliar Hispanic man with a square jaw and military presence observed the boys in silence, his arms crossed. He looked like he'd walked straight out of a jungle combat mission.

The room hummed quietly, alive with invisible machinery. Transparent panels in the floor revealed glimpses of shifting cables and glowing conduits below—like looking into the nervous system of a massive, buried organism. Faint digital readouts shimmered on the walls behind the speakers, offering streams of data in languages the boys didn't recognize.

"So I'm sure you're glad to get the brain-scanning device and heart monitors off," Carlson said, a slight smirk tugging at one corner of his mouth. "But we've pulled some very impressive data from the tests you three young men have undergone. Before we go over what all that means, I'll have to bore you with some research data that Dr. Johnson and Mr. Bakshi will now present."

He stepped aside with military precision.

"Boys," Dr. Johnson said, practically bouncing to his feet. His lab coat flared as he moved to the center of the platform, waving his hands as the holographic screen shifted to a shimmering diagram of neural pathways lit up like a Christmas tree.

"I'll try to make this brief, so please hold any questions until the end."

He winked at them before diving into the glowing interface with the click of a button.

Dr. Omar Johnson cleared his throat and lifted a thick stack of stapled notes.

"This research began with a man named José Silva, a simple radio repairman with a curious mind. Back in 1944, he wanted to help his children perform better in school. He noticed his daughter showed signs of clairvoyance, so he started experimenting."

He tapped a button on his remote. A glowing screen lit up behind him with photos of vintage radio schematics and EEG readouts.

"Using what he knew from repairing circuits, Silva made a fascinating connection. He realized the human brain, like a radio, runs on a small amount of electrical energy, energy that pulses at different frequencies. In electronics, you always look for the circuit with the least impedance—the least resistance—because that's where you get the most power. Silva wondered: What if the brain works the same way?"

He pointed to the screen, where a simplified brain diagram overlays a frequency spectrum.

"The human brain, it turns out, also functions best when electrical resistance is low, when it's in the right frequency range. Through years of trial and error—and with no funding, just passion—Silva identified that range. His work led to what we now call the UltraMind ESP System. It's not fringe anymore. It's the foundation for a new phase of human evolution."

Omar stepped aside as Arjun Bakshi rose and continued.

"The idea is this: if we can consciously enter the alpha state, a slower brainwave frequency, we gain access to extraordinary mental capabilities. The brain pulses in waves, measured in Hertz or cycles per second (cps)."

He gestured to a new slide displaying a color-coded frequency chart.

"Beta: 14 to 20 cps, where we are when alert and focused.

Alpha: 7 to 14 cps, associated with light sleep, meditation, and daydreaming.

Theta: 4 to 7 cps, deeper states like hypnosis.

Delta: under 4 cps, the realm of deep, dreamless sleep."

The Grand General watched from the corner, arms crossed, stone-faced.

Jason glanced at Henry and Adam, both fully absorbed. He straightened in his seat, trying to keep up.

Dr. Omar resumed, pacing slowly.

"Silva reasoned that alpha was the ideal zone for thinking—minimal resistance, maximum energy. If you can stay mentally active while in alpha, you can think more clearly, concentrate longer, and access deeper memories. Why? Because the alpha range sits in the center of the brain's operating spectrum. It's like shifting into the perfect gear."

He clicked his remote again.

"But here's the catch, most people don't stay awake in alpha. They dip into it when they're dozing off or daydreaming, but the moment they engage consciously, their brains speed back up to beta. That's why people struggle with intuition or creative focus; they're stuck in the least stable, weakest operating mode."

Omar locked eyes with the boys.

"Angels and other supernatural entities don't have that problem. They stay lucid in alpha. That's how they influence reality... and our perception of them. And now, so can you. But you need two skills..."

The slide changed: two bold bullet points appeared.

- Learn to produce alpha brain waves with conscious awareness.
- Stay mentally active while in the alpha state.

Arjun stepped forward. "There's another reason alpha is important. At beta, you only access data from your left brain—the side responsible for logic, language, sensory input. But alpha? It unlocks both hemispheres."

He paced in front of the screen, now showing two mirrored brain scans.

"Your right hemisphere stores information gathered from your inner senses—intuition, visions, ESP. That's how Adam connected with the book."

Omar brought up the next slide, side-by-side brain scans of Adam.

"Here's Adam's brain at rest. And here, this is when he interacted with the book."

A short video played. Adam was sitting calmly, eyes half-closed. As I whispered "speak it into existence," the brain scan spiked in brilliant color.

Henry blurted out, wide-eyed:

"Damn, dude! Your grandpa taught you to read that stuff when you were a kid?"

Adam shook his head.

"No. He didn't. But that's probably why my ancestor guide showed up as him."

"Damn, you had a vision quest," Henry muttered, still in awe.

Jason elbowed him.

"Shut up and listen."

Dr. Omar picked up where he left off.

"This is Adam's heart scan during that moment. See how it's engorged with blood? And look at the electromagnetic wave surrounding him, rippling through the quantum field."

Henry raised a hand.

"What's that second wave in the video?"

Arjun pointed to the screen. "That's from the book, which is an anomaly in itself. Watch—they collide, fold, and amplify. This feedback loop is key."

Omar nodded. "Now we dive deeper. Look here: the pineal gland, which is a tiny, pinecone-shaped gland at the brain's center. It regulates melatonin and controls your circadian rhythm. But during these scans, all three of you, awake, produced more melatonin than most people do asleep."

The Grand General cleared his throat. A not-so-subtle cue to wrap it up.

Arjun stepped back in. "The pineal gland is still mysterious, the last part of the endocrine system to be understood. But look at this." Another scan appeared. The gland was glowing with unusual activity.

Omar jumped in. "Melatonin affects sleep, body temperature, digestion, hormones—a 24-hour biological conductor. But during your combat trial? Your circadian rhythms synchronized. That doesn't happen. Ever." He switched the slide to their combat trial video. "Here, Jason's brain scan spikes from rage. Now see what happens when his electromagnetic energy wave collides with Adam's and Henry's. Their scans sync—brainwaves, heart rates, melatonin levels. Like a neural fusion." Another clip rolled, Henry hacking the Pentagon. "Same levels of brain activity as Adam with the book, and Jason in battle. You're all tapping into something beyond human normalities."

The Grand General stepped forward, voice like gravel. "Thank you, gentlemen. That was... enlightening." He nodded curtly. "Mrs. Glenda Garrison has something to say on the matter now."

"Thank you, Grand General," Glenda Garrison said, rising gracefully from her seat.

The lights dimmed slightly as the screen behind her changed to a kaleidoscope of energy patterns and ancient diagrams. "Nikola Tesla once said, 'If you want to find the secrets of the universe, think in terms of energy, frequency, and vibration.' I call it the Divine Spark, and it's what you three possess. Tesla revered the power of the number three. And as fate would have it... three are needed."

Henry squints. "So this is a prophecy thing? That angel during the armored truck heist, he mentioned one."

Glenda nods slowly. "That angel was Gabriel. And yes... you are the Three spoken of in the Prophecy of the Three."

The boys don't respond, but they all think the same thing: Merle was right about the angel being Gabriel. They keep silent, waiting to see how deep this secret society's knowledge truly goes.

Glenda paces toward them, her tone lowering.

"What Gabriel stole wasn't nuclear launch codes. It was the Nexus Access... to operate Wormwood."

Suddenly, Adam speaks, voice almost detached, eyes glazed.

"The third angel blew his trumpet, and a great star fell from heaven, blazing like a torch, and it fell upon the third part of the rivers, and upon the fountains of waters;

And the name of the star is called Wormwood: and the third part of the waters became wormwood; and many men died of the waters, because they were made bitter...."

The room falls into stunned silence.

Adam blinks rapidly as Henry grabs his shoulder. "Dude... you alright?"

Adam shakes it off. "Yeah. Just... something my grandfather used to read. That verse stuck with me."

Glenda steps closer. "That's Revelation, chapter eight, verses ten and eleven. But Wormwood isn't a star. It's a satellite. Built by the angels as a control weapon, an orbital death ray. Gabriel intends to reverse engineer it, we believe." She turns to the floor, her voice dropping into something colder. "And another passage..." she says quietly. "They had a king over them... the angel of the bottomless pit... Abaddon. That's from Revelation 9:11. Abaddon is the angel of destruction, the Destroyer."

The room goes still. The three boys exchange looks. The date. The name. The implication.

"You were young," Glenda continues, "but what happened on September Eleventh was not just terrorism. It was a ritual, a sacrifice, for Abaddon's release. Gabriel freed him from beneath the towers."

Jason finally speaks. "So where is he now? And what does he want with Wormwood?"

Glenda gestures toward the back. "Field Sergeant Reginald Hershey can answer that."

A figure steps forward from the shadows.

Sturdy. Silent. Unreadable.

The man the boys had forgotten now seemed as if he had always been there — a shadow in the corner, watching.

When he finally spoke, his voice was low, measured, and cloaked in quiet authority. "We tracked the Nexus Access in the case Gabriel stole... until the signal vanished." He raises a firm hand toward the holographic display. The map zooms in over North Africa, then Egypt, before centering on the Giza Plateau.

Henry mutters, "So... the pyramids?"

Reginald's reply is flat. "Not quite." The scan shifts to the Sphinx. "There's a chamber under the right paw. Roughly twenty-five feet down. The challenge is... accessing it."

Adam's voice cuts through. Calm. Certain. "There's an entrance. Inside the right paw."

Everyone turns to look at him.

Arjun breaks the silence. "How do you know that?"

Adam hesitates. "I don't know... but I know it's there."

"Can you access it?" Arjun asks eagerly.

"I think... yes." Adam answers.

Reginald nods subtly, then resumes, as if Adam's words confirmed a suspicion. "We believe what lies beneath is the Hall of Records." A new slide appears, a grainy black-and-white photo of a man with a round face, tired eyes, and a distant stare. "Edgar Cayce, a psychic who described Atlantis and this Hall. He claimed Atlanteans escaped the island's destruction and came here... to Egypt. Built the Sphinx and hid their knowledge."

"The Sleeping Prophet," Henry blurts out. "I remember him from a History Channel documentary. I remember that guy."

Reginald doesn't respond; he simply clicks to the next slide. "Cayce said the Hall contained records in Atlantean and Egyptian script, and was pyramid-shaped. He also claimed it would be uncovered during a time of great upheaval... before a global shift."

Jason leans forward. "Atlantis. Like where Aquaman is from in the comics?"

Reginald finally gives a hint of a smirk. "Not exactly." The screen plays a thirteen-second satellite video. It zooms into the Atlantic. Three concentric rings connected by bridges. A central crystal pyramid in the Mayan style of architecture. Then, a sudden burst of white energy and the island vanishes. "Caught this three years ago," Reginald says. "If Cayce was right, that was a relic of their tech. Their end... could be our beginning. Cayce told prophecies of red crystals called 'fire crystals' that powered their advanced machines and weapons."

Henry scoffs. "So what's next? The world ends because it's 2012, the end of the Mayan calendar?"

Glenda speaks this time, softer. "Or we awaken to a new age with higher consciousness."

Jason frowns. "Okay, sure. But what does any of this have to do with us?"

The Grand General rises, commanding. "We need your help in infiltrating the Hall of Records and taking back the Nexus Access before Gabriel does something sinister with it."

Adam answers without hesitation. "We're in."

"Dude?!" Jason and Henry say in unison.

Jason leans over. "Have you lost your mind?"

"What he's not wrong," Adam says. "Do nothing, and we all die under a celestial death ray. Or... we fight. Like we've been trained to. This is our destiny, guys."

Jason and Henry look at each other. They don't like it. But they can't argue either. "Fine," Jason grumbles. "I'm in too." Henry throws up his hands. "Whatever. But I want to see the James Bond gear first."

Jason suddenly snaps back. "Wait, you never said what Gabriel wants with Wormwood after reengineering it."

Reginald's eyes narrow. His voice is low. "We don't know. But if he was willing to kill two skyscrapers full of people to free one angel... imagine what he'd do with a satellite capable of global annihilation."

Jason finds himself holding his breath. "Yeah... that's fair."

Henry shifts uncomfortably. "So... Adam's weird trance earlier. The third angel. That verse... Who is the third angel? Gabriel, Abaddon... who's left?"

A long silence.

"Good question, bro," Adam says.

Reginald's response is immediate and brief. "We don't know yet." And then without another word, he walks off the stage, disappearing into the shadowed corridor behind the screen.

Glenda steps forward again.

"Tomorrow morning, your real training begins. It's a crash course. Because in forty-eight hours... we deploy."

CHAPTER 8
THE DEPLOYMENT

The next forty-eight hours pass in a blur of sweat, grit, and revelation. The boys are immersed in the Order of the Eye's intensive crash course—an unrelenting gauntlet of combat drills, ancient esoteric disciplines, and unfamiliar military protocols.

From the outset, they learn that the OE doesn't use standard military terminology. They don't call units platoons. They call them covens—small, specialized tactical units that blend ancient rites with modern warfare. Formation training becomes second nature. Each maneuver, each gesture, each breath is a lesson in moving as a single entity. They are no longer individuals; they are threads in a larger weave.

Jason trains directly under Reginald Hershey—stoic, relentless, and exacting. He is drilled in weapons discipline: disassembly, cleaning, maintenance, and reassembly of advanced firearms, some clearly retrofitted with unknown tech. On the range, he's pushed to his limits, sharpening his aim, his timing, his nerves. Simulation after simulation plays out in the combat chambers: clearing hostile compounds, breaching doorways, neutralizing threats. Each repetition hones Jason's instincts into razor-edge precision.

Adam's path diverges. Under Arjun's calm but intense guidance, he is taught the ancient science of resonant discipline—techniques of meditation, mental stillness, and astral awareness. Adam learns to maintain an alpha-wave state even amidst distraction, cultivating a quiet power deep within. Arjun speaks of the spirit guide, a higher consciousness tethered to Adam's soul—an entity that must be contacted, understood, and eventually partnered with. Through breathing, resonance, and focused thought, Adam begins tapping into dormant abilities: intuitive sensing, controlled kinetic fields, and energy manipulation.

Henry, meanwhile, is buried in tech. He's given access to classified archives and guided by Omar, decoding what little the OE knows of angelic technology. Most of what they've recovered is through their vast spy network—who has infiltrated Area 51—and the extensive data from crash sites. Seems their technology is based on sound resonance and vibrational energy. Henry's new gear looks more like an instrument than a computer: a sleek bracer device wraps around his forearm, pulsing with low-frequency hums and flashes of biofeedback light. He learns to manipulate frequency patterns like chords, playing harmonic 'commands' rather than keystrokes.

By the end of day two, the three of them crash back into their dorm quarters, their bodies aching and their minds buzzing.

Jason throws himself onto his bunk with a groan.

"Damn, bro. You look worn out," Adam says, dropping into the chair beside him.

"Yeah," Jason exhales. "Training with these guys is like spending twelve hours in Sensei's dojo. But weirdly, I love it. Like… it feels right. Like it's what I'm meant to do. I feel you're right—this is our destiny."

"Yeah, I know what you mean," Adam agrees, nodding.

Henry steps in, still fiddling with a small circular device on his wrist. "So get this, Area 51 really does have outer space tech. Not alien bodies with big eyes and grey skin tech—that's all BS disinfo. But angelic tech from crash sites. Most of it operates on frequency, like musical resonance. This forearm rig I'm wearing? It's practically a synthesizer strapped to my damn arm." He grins as Jason and Adam peer at the bracer, glowing with subtle, pulsing light as it's plugged into a laptop Henry uses to calibrate it. "These goggles?" Henry says, lifting them up. "They let me see sound—literal sound waves. And electromagnetic fields. Oh, and they double as VR goggles. Dr. Johnson—I mean, Omar—says the pyramids weren't tombs at all. They were power plants."

"Really?" Adam asks, intrigued.

"Yeah. Turns out the stones inside are like 85% quartz," Henry informs them.

Jason shrugs. "So?"

Henry's eyes light up. "So! Quartz is piezoelectric—it produces electricity under stress, heat, or pressure. It's also triboluminescent—it glows under pressure. You combine that with the sheer weight of the structure and other environmental conditions... boom: a power source."

Jason squints. "So what you're saying is, the pyramids were giant light bulbs?"

"Basically!" Henry says with a shrug. "The word *pyramid* comes from the Greek word *pyramis*, 'fire in the middle.' *Pyra* means light or fire, and *mid* refers to the midpoint or center. And you really need to read a book, man."

"Why? That's what I have you for," Jason says with a crooked smile.

After the laughter dies down, Henry pauses, then adds more quietly, "I'm scared out of my mind. But yeah...

like you said, Jason. I feel like this is what I'm meant to do."

Jason chuckles and turns to Adam. "Well, we know Adam the wizard is ready."

Adam smirks. "I'm not gonna lie, it does feel like I'm turning into Doctor Strange or something. Arjun's teaching me how to tap into magical energy with just my thoughts. It's crazy. I'm not completely in control yet, but it's real."

"So more sorcerer class than wizard class?" Henry asks.

"This isn't D&D, you idiot," Adam says, laughing. "But yeah... more like a psion if we're going by the handbook." He leans back, thoughtful. "Sound and vibration—that's how Arjun is teaching me to connect to my magic. To my guide. I know you two feel it as well, that this is our destiny."

Jason and Henry exchange a look, then nod.

"I'm showering," Jason announces, standing up. "Tomorrow morning we get to talk to our families. Then it's go-time. I need sleep."

Adam sighs. "Feels wrong not telling them what we're about to do."

"Yeah, but it'd just freak them out," Henry replies. "This way... at least they don't worry."

"Yeah," Adam says quietly. "Still feels heavy. I don't like to lie."

Jason claps his hands together, rubbing them like a coach before game day. "Alright. Let's get some rest. Big day tomorrow."

The next morning, the three friends are brought to a communication hall after breakfast, where they get to talk to their prospective family members. Glenda talks to all their families at once on video chat before everyone can see their family members are okay.

"Hello, I'm Special Agent Glenda Garrison of the NSA," she states. "These are secure lines, and your sons will be back with you shortly. We are sorry for this inconvenience, and we know it's an emotional hardship on you all, but for the security of our nation and the world, we need to piece everything together the best we can with the attack on the armored truck. Getting the nuclear launch codes that were stolen back is a top priority, so thank you for your patience. You'll have ten minutes, then for extra security we must end the calls. Thank you once again for your cooperation and understanding."

As the boys approach the communication stations, they all feel so guilty over the lies Glenda and the OE have just told their families. Jason feels very anxious, not knowing if his father will be hungover, angry, or if he's been on an all-night drinking spree, which would leave him belligerent. He sits down, where he is greeted by not only a sober father, but also a happy one who's grateful his son is safe.

"How ya holding up, son?" James asks.

"Uhm, good. I'm good, Dad," Jason replies. "Sorry 'bout all this, Dad. I really am."

"Nah. Don't sweat it, son. It's not your fault," his father says comfortingly. "The important thing is you're okay and safe. I'm proud of ya for ducking out the window and down the fire escape to draw those fake Homeland Security fellas away from your younger brother. Took a lot of bravery. I saw ya fight those terrorist bastards too—guess maybe all that Kung Fu ya been learning really works. You saved that baby and mother. Now, you do what these NSA folks tell ya, and help 'em out best ya can. Okay?"

Jason nods, pleasantly surprised that—for once—his father is being understanding. He doesn't even bother correcting him about the Kung Fu comment; he's been training in Taekwondo since before he was five. Instead, his mind shifts gears, and he thinks, *Oh, I'm helping them out, alright, Dad. Don't worry about that.*

"I love ya, son," James says proudly. "Now I'm going to let ya talk to your brother. Alright?"

"Okay, Dad," Jason says. "And love you too, Pops."

Jason's dad proceeds to get up from the desk, then Luke plops down in his seat shortly after.

"So, how ya doin'?"

"I-I'm fine, but what about Dad?" Jason asks, still very confused.

"Oh yeah, he hasn't touched a drop since the morning after the incident," Luke tells his brother. "Even poured half a bottle of whiskey out."

"Really!?" Jason says in amazement.

A timer then pops up on the screen, and Luke says, "Jason. Be safe in Egypt, okay? Watch your back for a double-cross."

"What?!" Jason is stunned. "How'd you know? Who told ya?"

"Oh, and be patient with Steven too, brother. We're proud of ya," Luke says as the screen goes black.

All anyone can hear from Henry's screen is his little mother angrily speaking in Vietnamese, and Henry saying, "I know, Mom... Yes, I will... No, I'm not... Don't say that, Mom... Okay, okay, okay! Please, Mom, not here... I love you too..."

Adam sits down and tells both his parents, "I miss and love you guys very much."

They both say, "We love and miss you, too."

"Hey, Dad," Adam begins, "do you remember those ancient legends and prophecies Grandpa used to tell?"

"Yeah, son. I grew up with 'em longer than you did," he chuckles. "Why'd ya ask?"

"Oh, he's just been on my mind a lot here lately, I guess. But hey, don't worry about me, okay? The security here is top-notch, and they feed us well. I'll be home soon, and life will go back to normal before ya know it."

Adam's mother then speaks up. "You're washing your face, brushing your teeth, and minding your manners now, aren't you?"

"Yes, Mom, I am. We're even getting educated here," Adam responds, as he thinks, *And what a hell of an education it is.*

The timer then shows up on the computer monitor, and Adam says, "Okay, I love you both. I have to get back to my studies, okay?"

"Okay, son," his father says.

"We love you very much!" his mom interrupts, starting to get teary-eyed.

Adam sees his father hug her as the screen goes dark.

"All right!" Field Sergeant Reginald yells. "It's time to get ready. Deployment is in less than an hour, and we will be wheels up. Let's get our gear together and take this fight to that winged bastard."

Jason looks at his two friends. "There's no worries, no fears, and no regrets. We got this, guys."

What he always says before a tournament—but this isn't a tournament. They all knew this, but deep down, they had a spark of excitement surging through them.

The heavy metal door groaned open, revealing a cavernous underground hangar of black, with the exception of a few dim halogen lights buzzing overhead, casting harsh pools of illumination across the concrete floor. A dozen soldiers in matte-black fatigues sat in formation, silent and focused, their eyes on a flat-screen monitor perched atop a utilitarian metal stand. They looked like shadows come to life—war-hardened phantoms in a hidden world.

Jason, Adam, and Henry entered together, the rubber soles of their combat boots sticking slightly with each step. The black uniforms of the Order of the Eye fit snug—heavier than expected—as though stitched with expectation.

Field Sergeant Reginald Hershey stood at the center of the group, arms folded across his chest, eyes sharp beneath a brow creased by years of classified operations.

He was built like a bunker—sturdy, immovable, and all business.

"Gentlemen," he said, voice as even as the floor beneath them. "Welcome. Come in and grab a seat. We're going over the deployment."

The boys exchanged wary glances but complied, finding seats at the fringe of the group. The monitor flickered, displaying a satellite image of a familiar silhouette—the Giza Plateau.

"This is the landing zone," Reginald said, gesturing to the screen. "We'll be performing a low-altitude jump."

A slight shift ran through the trio. Tension tightened shoulders. Backs straightened.

Reginald caught it. "You three," he added, tone clipped but not unkind, "will be jumping tandem with Alvarez, Jenkins, and Murry."

Three soldiers rose in unison, each nodding with silent precision before retaking their seats. The air seemed to grow heavier. The monitor zoomed in on the weathered visage of the Sphinx.

"We'll touch down here, to the rear of the Sphinx," Reginald continued. "Once grounded, we collect our chutes and will incinerate them with a timed device. It serves two purposes: disposal and beacon for when we make our exit from the structure. When the mission is complete, this will signal our evac transport."

He turned to Adam. The room followed his gaze.

"Once we get to the front of the Sphinx, that's when Adam takes point."

Adam nodded slowly, voice even as a carpenter's level. "I'm not sure how... but I know we can access it."

Henry leaned in with a whisper. "We? Got a mouse in your pocket?"

Adam shot him a sidelong glance. "Yes. We. Me and my ancestor guide. And we know we can get in."

Henry blinked, startled, then raised his hands in mock surrender. "Okay, man. I believe you. The both of you. I've seen what you can do."

Reginald gave a short nod, satisfied for now. "Then we'll see soon enough." He jerks a thumb over his shoulder. Behind him, overhead lights flared to life one row at a time, illuminating the beast that waited in the dark—a Boeing C-17 Globemaster III, matte black, its bulk humming with restrained power.

"Our ride," Reginald says. "Once we're in, it'll stay within proximity for extraction out in the desert, and our convoy of Humvees will provide fire support if needed. But listen closely—there's zero intel on the structure under the Sphinx. Could be a tomb, could be a labyrinth, could be a war zone. We move in stealth. Tight and silent."

No one spoke. No words were needed.

"Any questions?"

There was nothing left to ask as silence hung in the hangar.

"Let's move."

Minutes Later – Aboard the C-17

The cavern echoed with the rhythmic clang of boots on steel as the coven filed into the plane via the yawning rear ramp. Inside, it was cold and utilitarian. Seat harnesses and cargo nets lined the walls. The boys found their spots, still barely processing the magnitude of what they were about to do.

Henry scanned the shadowed walls. "Where's the runway out of this place?"

Reginald, already strapping himself in, didn't look up. "You'll see. Stow your gear and sit down."

As soon as the final buckle clicked into place, the aircraft lurched upward with stomach-twisting force. The lights dimmed, and the world outside vanished as the C-17 surged upward, gaining speed and altitude—then it froze for what felt like eternity. Everyone found themselves rocketing down a runway, and then lifted off as the flying fortress climbed into the sky.

"Listen up!" Reginald's voice cracked through the cabin. "It's 1400 hours. We arrive at the target at 2400. Twelve hours till the jump."

Jason blinked. "Twelve hours?"

Henry leaned closer to his friends. "Guess we're stuck on this airbus for a while. Might as well get comfortable."

Adam craned his neck toward the narrow, round window. Far below, a patchwork of buildings and runways shrank into the horizon. The base they had departed from looked ancient and ghostly, swallowed by trees and time.

"You think they told us the truth about still being in New York?" he asked, gesturing to the view. "Henry, you think you can figure out where we were?"

Henry was already opening his OE-issued laptop, fingers flying across the keyboard in a practiced blur. A few quick searches, and he spun the screen around.

"Griffiss Air Force Base," he said. "Rome, New York. Shut down years ago. About fifteen miles northwest of Utica."

Adam leaned closer, nodding. "We need to start getting our own answers," he said. "No matter what happens down there, we watch each other's backs. No exceptions."

Jason held out a fist. "Agreed."

Henry bumped it with his own. "Yeah. I got you guys."

While Adam was receiving the ceremonial fist bump as well, Henry was about to close the laptop when something blinked across the screen—too fast for the others to notice. But he saw it. Clear as day.

Trust no one but each other. ~Merle

Then it was gone. Henry stared, unmoving, his fingers frozen over the keyboard. Had he imagined it? No. He knew what he saw.

Who is Merle? And more importantly, how much does he know?

CHAPTER 9
THE SPHINX

The interior of the C-17 Globemaster throbbed with the sound of a sudden alarm. Red lights strobed violently overhead, casting the cargo bay in pulses of crimson. The blaring buzzer snapped Jason out of a deep sleep. He sat up with a start, wide-eyed and disoriented.

"You okay, man?" Adam asked, concern laced in his voice.

Jason rubbed his eyes, still catching his breath. "Yeah. Just had the weirdest dream... about Megan McCarthy."

Henry, seated next to them, perked up. "Bro, she's so hot."

"Shut the hell up, man," Adam snapped before turning back to Jason. "What was the dream about?"

Jason leaned forward, elbows on his knees. "We were inside a giant crystal pyramid. There was a control room in the center, and Megan showed up, except she had her own soldiers. They were after the Nexus Access too. But before we could do anything, Gabriel attacked us with... these six-winged soldiers."

"Were they fiery? Red?" Adam asked, his voice oddly distant.

Jason paused, trying to recall. "Yeah... now that you mention it, they were."

Adam's voice dropped into a trance-like cadence, as if the words weren't his own: "Isaiah 6:2 and 3... 'Above him were seraphim, each with six wings: with two they covered their faces, with two they covered their feet, and with two they were flying. And they were calling to one another: "Holy, holy, holy is the LORD Almighty; the whole earth is full of his glory."'

Henry gave him a little shake. "I'm not sure I'll ever get used to him doing that... Adam, you good?"

Adam blinked rapidly, coming back to himself. "Yeah. Sorry. I'm fine."

He sat up straighter. "In Hebrew, the word seraph means 'burning.' They're fiery beings, seraphim. The Book of Enoch talks about them alongside cherubim. Supposedly they stand closest to the throne of God.

Other sources call them the Akyəst, serpents, or dragons. And in the Second Book of Enoch, two other classes show up with them: the phoenix, and the chalkydri or 'brazen hydras.'"

Henry's eyes widened. "Holy shit. You're not saying we're gonna fight a hydra, are you? We're not leveled up enough for that, man. We barely got out of basic training."

"Calm down," Adam said, trying not to laugh. "I'm just quoting lore. Doesn't mean anything like that's gonna happen."

"But if we do have to fight one, is it like in D&D rules?" Henry asked, dead serious. "Cut off the heads to kill it?"

"I dunno!" Adam exclaimed. "My grandpa used to tell me the hydra would eat my toes off if I didn't go to sleep at bedtime. Not everything the old guy told me was gospel."

"Okay, but if a dragon does show up, I'm officially out," Henry muttered.

Jason frowned. "Wait, what's a cherry bum?"

"Cherubim," Adam corrected. "They're another class of celestial beings. Guarded Eden, carried the throne of God, and stuff like that. Different than the cute baby angels in paintings."

Before he could explain further, Reginald's voice cut through the tension.

"Okay, gentlemen," the Field Sergeant barked as he approached, fully geared. "Time to pair up. We're closing in on the drop zone."

He pointed each of them out in turn. "Adam, you're with Alvarez. Jason, Jenkins. Henry, you're with Murry. Stay close to them after the jump. Don't wander. Stick to your training."

He stepped back and addressed the rest of the plane.

"Alright, soldiers! Eyes sharp! Remember why we're here—get in, get out, no losses. Do you hear me?"

"Sir, yes sir!" The response came in unison.

The aircraft bucked slightly as it dropped in altitude. Reginald snapped his fingers and then made circles in the air with his index finger, signaling the ramp to lower. The inside of the C-17 shifted from red to green light.

Henry pulled his OE-issued VR goggles down as the rest of the team lowered their paratrooper goggles. Reginald checked their harnesses, giving each of them a slap on the helmet and a thumbs-up. The wind howled through the rear of the aircraft.

One by one, the team jumped into the night sky.

Jason felt the violent tug of gravity as he and Jenkins plummeted. Through the inky blackness, he could barely make out the Giza Plateau below, only the vaguest outlines of dunes and stone. But Henry, strapped in with Murry, could see it all.

Through his goggles, energy was everywhere. Waves of electromagnetic force rippled from the pyramids and surrounding ruins, shimmering like heat off the asphalt but pulsing with impossible geometry.

These pyramids really are power plants, Henry thought as the wind roared past. "But what are they powering?"

Chutes deployed. The violence of descent gave way to a quiet drift.

"Lift your legs!" Jenkins called over the wind. "Let me take the fall!"

Jason obeyed. They hit the ground hard, but Jenkins rolled expertly, breaking the impact. The rest of the team touched down in sequence, forming up fast.

The soldiers tossed their parachutes into a single pile. Reginald hadn't landed yet.

"What's taking the Sarge so long?" Jenkins asked, concerned.

"Dunno," the team medic, Harlow, replied tersely.

"There he is," Jackson called out. Reginald descended moments later and discarded his chute. Private First Class Williamson immediately placed a primed incinerator device on the pile. Ready to spark to life on his command from one of his detonators.

Reginald doesn't miss a beat. "Jackson, take point. We move along the Causeway of Khafre. Stay in its shadows as we head to the Sphinx."

The team moved swiftly and silently, rifles at the ready, shadows dancing along the ancient stone causeway as moonlight bathed the plateau. They arrived at the forepaws of the Sphinx. Reginald turned to Adam. "Okay, kid. You're up."

Adam stepped forward, all eyes on him. He placed his hand on the limestone inside the Sphinx's right paw and closed his eyes. He slowed his breath. He could feel the rush of melatonin releasing from his pineal gland, ushering him into the alpha state. In the darkness of his mind, his grandfather appeared, his spirit guide, offering his assistance as the ghostly figure raised its hands. Adam reached forward, matching the motion. His body tingled, every nerve alive with a magical charge. The sensation swelled in his chest, then radiated outward through his hand.

A low, rhythmic vibration spread through the stone electrifying the surrounding area. The surface began to ripple, as if it were water shaken by sound, yet no noise followed. In seconds, the stone melted open, revealing a hidden staircase within the paw.

Reginald stepped up and shone his light inside. "Jackson, resume point. Everyone move!" They filed into the opening. As Adam crossed the threshold, the entrance was sealed behind him.

The spiral staircase led them twenty-five feet underground. At the bottom, they entered a rectangular chamber. Reginald turned to Adam again.

"Do you know where to go next?"

"We do," Adam said calmly. "Give us a moment." He stood still, focusing. In his mind, his grandfather raised his arms outward and pointed his palms down. Adam mimicked the motion. The floor trembled. The team gasped and stumbled. Reginald raised a clenched fist, halt.

Then, the air filled with an electric hum. The sand beneath their boots began to shift. They were descending, steel walls not limestone were soon visible. Only the tingling charge of Adam's magic and the changed walls told them they were moving.

Henry dropped to one knee, brushing sand away. Beneath, a metal floor gleamed.

"You looking for something?" Reginald asked.

"Yeah," Henry muttered, sweeping faster. "A hatch. A conduit. Something I can plug into."

The rest of the team joined in the search. Jones whistled softly. "Got something!"

Henry scrambled over and helped open a small access panel. Inside, nestled in strange crystalline sockets, was a control port. He pulled a cable from his forearm-mounted keyboard and connected it. Symbols lit up. He began to type. Musical tones echoed softly from the device. Crystals on the panel glowed red. A green, translucent hologram flickered into existence above his forearm computer, a 3D image of a pyramid, and a narrow shaft descending into it. "That's us," Henry said, pointing to a red dot moving slowly down the shaft. "I'm downloading the schematics now," he added. "We're not going in totally blind."

"Roger that," Reginald replied.

"I've also got access codes for restricted areas coming in," Henry adds.

Jason stepped up, wide-eyed. "That... that's exactly what Edgar Cayce talked about. The pyramid and those red glowing crystals."

Henry laughed. "Way to pay attention in class, Gold."

Reginald looked to the glowing image, then to the crystals. "Looks like Cayce was right after all."

The descent came to a gentle halt. The air was still heavy with that low, humming vibration—faint but omnipresent, like the breath of something ancient and alive. Before them, a large elevator-style door loomed, adorned with softly glowing geometric etchings, pulsing with energy just beneath its metallic crystalline surface.

A mechanical hiss filled the air as the door slid open. Two figures stood there, waiting. They weren't human. Each one towered over ten feet tall, their sheer mass filling the doorway like statues carved from iron. Muscles coiled beneath dark, scaled armor that shimmered faintly in the dim blue glow of the corridor behind them. Their arms were thick, each limb nearly the width of a grown man's torso, and they moved with terrifying speed.

Before anyone could react, the giants surged forward, grabbing two soldiers at the front of the formation. With crushing force, the monsters squeezed the men into their massive grips, bones audibly cracking. Then, with horrifying strength, the giants hurled the limp bodies down the corridor like diabolical newspaper boys on an evil paper route, each delivery punctuated by a sickening thud and a satisfied grunt." The soldiers' bodies slammed against the floor and wall with a grotesque wet crunch where they didn't move again.

The rest of the team raised their silencer-tipped weapons instinctively. Then silenced gunfire erupted, the air filled with the hiss and clatter of suppressed rounds as they poured bullets into the twin giants. Muzzle flashes lit the corridor in staccato bursts, but the ammunition did little more than annoy them. Bullets flattened or deflected against the giants' armor, the impacts leaving only shallow dents or metallic sparks.

The creatures snarled, raising their arms to block the barrage like irritated beasts waiting for the annoyance to stop. Patiently they wait for the coven to reload.

Jason steadied his M4A1, taking careful aim. Two quick shots. Both found their mark. The open-faced helmets were the weak points and Jason's rounds punched through the giants' eyes with deadly precision. One after the other, the behemoths toppled backward in a slow, thunderous collapse.

Jason rushed forward to the two fallen soldiers lying twisted and broken, their bodies already cooling in the sterile air of this ancient structure. The others caught up behind him, checking pulses that they already knew they wouldn't find. Harlow knelt beside them and shook his head. "They're both dead."

Reginald's voice was cold steel. "Strip their gear. We'll load them back into the elevator. If we can get out the way we came in, we'll recover the bodies."

Henry stood back, his voice quiet but firm. "I've found other exits... and the control room. I think it's where we'll find the Nexus Access."

Reginald turned to him, eyes sharp. "Can you find the most secure route?"

"Already working on it," Henry replied, eyes flicking over the holographic interface on his forearm.

Reginald turned back to the team. "If we see more of those things, aim for the eyes." He gave Jason a sharp nod of approval. "Good shooting."

"That was a patrol force," Henry added grimly. "I'm rerouting us to avoid any further contact."

"A patrol force of what, exactly?" Jason asked, glancing at the giants' bodies in disbelief. "Those things took everything we had."

"The Anakim," Reginald said quietly. "A race of giant warriors. Ancient, deadly. Their ancestry traces back to Anak, son of Arba. The Hebrews believed them to be descended from the Nephilim."

Jason looked sideways. "Nephilim?"

Adam spoke in that trance-like tone once again: "Genesis 6:4... 'The Nephilim were on the earth in those days, and also afterward when the angels of God went to the daughters of humans and had children by them. They were the heroes of old, men of renown.'"

Henry blinked. "So... half-human, half-angel hybrids?"

Reginald nodded. "Correct."

"Great," Henry muttered. "Giants are real. What's next? A dragon?"

Reginald sighed, rubbing his temple. "Let's hope it hasn't been freed." He turned sharply. "Henry, where do we go now?"

"Uh, right, sorry. Okay." Henry blinked, snapping out of the thought of dragons being real. "Take a right, then we ride a lift down. After that, a stairwell network. If my reading on this schematic is correct, we'll reach the control room, and hopefully avoid more patrols."

"If your reading is correct?" Jason barks.

"Yeah, if! I just learned how to read Angel less than three days ago!" Henry snaps back. "So maybe get off my ass, man?"

Jason exhaled and nodded. "You're right. Sorry."

"It's fine," Henry said softer. "Let's just get this done."

"Roger that," Reginald cuts in. "Move out."

As they advanced through the labyrinthine corridors, the architecture around them shifted to crystalline alloy walls of shimmering glass-like material laced with veins of glowing white. Ancient symbols, eerily similar to those found in Sumerian and Egyptian texts, pulsed softly along the walls.

The deeper they went, the more surreal the structure became.

It was as though they were walking through the nervous system of a celestial beast.

As they all continue through the corridors, Adam approaches Jason from behind. "Are you okay, man?"

"Yeah," Jason answers. "I just don't want the next two people dead to be you guys is all."

"We're getting through this together, man" Adam assures him with his hand on Jason's shoulder "Now let's go save the world, dude."

Eventually, the corridor opened into a vast antechamber. Before them was a massive, triangular doorway set into a crystalline wall, its surface glimmering with red energy that snapped and crackled like lightning contained in amber.

Henry frowned. "I can't disable it. I've tried everything. That thing won't just shock you, it'll disintegrate you."

Reginald stepped up. "Williamson, prep charges."

"Wait," Adam said. "Let me try something. Henry let me see those codes."

Henry opened his holographic interface. "Here are the clearance codes, but... like I said, it's not responding."

Adam studied the codes, eyes narrowing. He held out his hands, the now-familiar hum and feel of energy beginning to build around him. The rest of the team took a step back as the air thickened, pulsing with invisible energy. Adam's body began to tingle again. His pineal gland released a wash of melatonin, guiding him deeper into alpha. He reached across the veil toward his ancestor's consciousness. Power flowed into him.

The red lightning across the triangular entrance began to ripple. The flickering arcs bent inward, shuddered, and then vanished. The barrier was gone. Adam stepped forward first. The rest of the coven rushed in, forming a protective perimeter around him. Inside was something no one could've expected. A pyramid, within a pyramid.

The interior chamber was shaped like a perfect tetrahedron. Every surface was crystalline, glowing with soft violet and deep blue hues. Floating geometric panels orbited slowly above a central platform, and in the center of that platform... a pedestal.

Embedded in the pedestal was a crystal unlike any they had ever seen. It pulsed slowly, like a heartbeat. Energy thrummed from it—raw, ancient, intelligent.

Jason stared, awestruck. "A pyramid... inside a pyramid?"

No one answered. They had reached the control room. But what it controlled was still unknown. Till they see it off to the center of the room connected to the Crystal humming like a heartbeat, an open shaft of four copper rods with electricity dancing erratically down it like a Tesla coil to a trumpet-like apparatus.

The room is massive. Like a science fiction lab out of a big-budget movie but one unlike anything they've ever seen before. Computer screens are scattered all around the lab at key locations but the screens are suspended in midair looking like a yellowish green liquid of some type. Balconies and catwalks hang overhead extending upward to a hundred feet or more with orbs measuring seven or eight feet in size glowing reddish orange lining the upper portion of this room along with massive tools hanging from the ceiling.

"Remember what Adam said back at the OE base?" Henry asks.

"No?" Jason replies.

"Ugh of course you don't! Revelations 8:10-11. The part about a trumpet being blown??" Henry says with a look of 'that's the trumpet.'

"Revelations 8:12" Adam begins in one of his now common trances. "The fourth angel sounded his trumpet, and a third of the sun was struck, a third of the moon, and a third of the stars, so that a third of them turned dark. A third of the day was without light, and also a third of the night."

"That's the trumpet," Jason exclaims in realization.

"Yes," Henry says while slapping his own forehead with his palm, "but that new verse about the sun, moon, and stars being turned dark is very alarming!!

"Plus now we're at a place in the scriptures where a fourth angel possibly is involved from the sound of that." Jason ominously adds.

"We don't even know who the third angel is though?" Henry counters anxiously.

"Holy shit," Jason exclaims, realizing the gravity of the situation. "But where's the Nexus Access at?"

"I have it here. Safe," Gabriel called down, his voice cold and sharp like a blade unsheathing. Gabriel stood above them, his silhouette framed by the ethereal glow of the crystal pyramid. The last time the three friends had seen him, he'd vanished into the clouds clutching the case. Now it was here, cradled in the arms of a tall, ebony-skinned adolescent. Who's clad in a shimmering ephod, a golden breastplate inlaid with twelve gleaming gemstones across his chest. His face was hidden behind a ceremonial mask that matched his robes, a ruby glinting at the center of his turban. They stood twenty-five feet up on a balcony, a massive door looming behind them. He glanced at the strike team below, eyes narrowing with disdain. "I figured someone would retaliate after I attacked the armored convoy. Michael, perhaps. Or the Watchers floating around the Atlantic. But instead... this?" He sneered. "Teenagers and you insects. I figured if anyone accompanied these children it would be the Immortal. No matter. The Prophecy of the Three won't stop me from tearing free of this prison of a dimension. Not now."

The masked figure beside him turned, voice muffled but clear. "Master, shall I summon the seraphim?"

Gabriel raised a hand. "No. Let them watch. I haven't had a proper fight in eons. Not that this will be one." His lips curled into a smirk. "But extinction deserves a little theater."

Adam's eyes widened as recognition sparked. "Michael! That's the third Angel, or... maybe the fourth?" His voice faltered. Reginald shot him a look that said not now.

With a whisper of wind and a sudden burst of light, Gabriel's wings unfurled—vast, blinding, and edged with death. He leaped from the balcony.

"TAKE COVER!" Reginald shouted as the angel descended, flames licking from the sword he drew mid-air with a screech of steel.

The lab exploded into chaos. The coven scattered, ducking behind massive tools, overturned desks, and arcane machinery sparking with energy. Crystal light fractured across the space like lightning.

Williamson, get up here!" Reginald barked, crouched behind the strange trumpet-like apparatus.

Sliding in on his knees, Williamson hunkered beside the field sergeant. "Sir?"

His commanding officer barked, "Prep this device for demolition. ASAP."

"Yes sir." He was already wiring C4 to its base.

Above them, Gabriel waded through gunfire like a phantom—bullets pinging off him, flinching only slightly, as if each round was a mosquito bite. He didn't bleed. He didn't break stride.

Jason lined up a shot from cover, calm and focused. He aimed for the eye, like he had with the giants.

CRACK. The bullet hit dead-center... and it mushroomed, crumpling like tin foil mid-air.

Gabriel slowly turned his head, face barely reacting, but his gaze locked on Jason, and it burned.

Without looking, he swung his flaming sword at Corporal Jackson, expecting flaming steel to slice through flesh.

CLANG. The blade slammed into an invisible barrier, a shimmering dome of divine light. Jackson stood stunned, protected.

Gabriel scanned the room and spotted Adam, hands outstretched, magical energy glowing at his fingertips. "So," Gabriel growled, "one of you carries the divine gift... not just divine sight, but true power." He reached up, tore the halo from his head, and readied to throw it.

Jason didn't blink. He fired again. This time, the bullet struck home, right in Gabriel's eye. The angel howled, reeling back in pain, blood pouring from the ruined eye socket. Angry, he hurled the halo out of blind fury, a disc of fire and judgment that streaks toward the teen.

Jason barely dodged. It passed within inches of his face, shearing his rifle in half before embedding in the crystalline wall behind him like a thrown buzzsaw.

"The halo's a shield!" Jason shouted. "That's why my bullet didn't hit, it deflects anything that could cause harm to him!"

Henry ducked behind a scorched console. "Like Captain America's shield!"

"Deploy the seraphim!" Gabriel roared, clutching his face. "And get the Nexus Access out of here, NOW!"

"Yes, master." The masked servant touched a glowing green gem in the wall. The organ red pods in the ceiling cracked open. From within, the seraphim descended—angels wreathed in roaring flame, six wings each: two for flight, two covering their burning faces, and two streaming from their ankles. Their bodies pulsed with fire, their presence like a furnace given life.

The masked servant turned to run—SLAM. The door was sealed in front of him.

"I've gained access to the room's controls and locked the room!" Henry called out triumphantly.

"Awesome!" Reginald shouted. "Can you stop the flame angels?"

"...Working on that!" Henry says somewhat defeated.

The seraphim screamed, a deafening sound like a crackling forest fire exploding trees. They opened their mouths. Flame erupts, sending hellfire raining down.

Adam thrust his hands up, conjuring a golden barrier just in time. But not fast enough. Peterson vanished in the fire. Gone before he could scream. The grenades on his chest barely pop in the blast that consumed him.

Adam's magical shield isn't strong enough to stand up against the infernal inferno of the seraphim but it does prevent more deaths. The others were hit with burning plasma. Skin seared. Armor scorched. The barrier fails. Second- and third-degree burns scorched the soldiers, but they stood their ground.

Gabriel rose, staggering toward Adam, his ruined eye socket weeping blood. Sword ready to finish off the divine child. Jason moves with cheetah-like speed sprinting full tilt, cutting across the lab. At the last second, he dropped low and kicked Gabriel's right knee with everything he had.

CRACK. The angel collapsed to one knee, stunned. Jason seizes the moment leaping in the air. He soars up and comes down hard, elbow-first into Gabriel's skull.

THWACK. Blood sprayed. Bone cracked. The angel slumped. Jason landed, elbow dripping blood. "He's down!" but Jason's shine throbs with pain from striking the angel's leg that felt like granite. "I need to get up there and take that servant down. I need to retrieve the Nexus Access!" he called out.

Everyone, form up on Gabriel!" Reginald shouted. "They may not risk their incendiary strikes this close to him. Hold them here while Jason gets the Nexus!"

"Jason!" Adam called, voice urgent. "Run for the balcony, just trust me!"

"You got it!" Jason replied, breaking into another sprint. The ground beneath his feet shimmered, and suddenly he was running up a glowing ramp of mystical energy, Adam's magic forming a bridge through the air. The whole room vibrated with tension. Above, two seraphim split from the pack, flaming wings beating furiously as they dived toward him. Jason skidded to a halt halfway up the ramp, suspended above the battlefield. He clenched his fists, waited for the right moment—then spun into a brutal back fist, catching one seraph mid-dive. A second later, he launched into a jumping side-kick, slamming the other down in a trail of fire. His skin sizzled from contact. He winced, but the burns were only surface-deep.

Adam knew if Jason wasn't magically protected he'd lose limbs so he focused his magic into a spell of protection. Golden energy laced itself around Jason's limbs, a protective magic that had wrapped his fists and feet, shielding him from further damage.

Meanwhile, chaos broke out below. Mechanical claws burst from the floor, and ceiling grabbing at the other seraphim.

Henry grinned behind the controls of his forearm computer. "I can't put them back in their pods, but I did find these lab arms!"

Reginald took the moment. "Focus your fire! Launch grenades Now!" Grenades flew. Explosions lit the lab up.

Jason vaulted the balcony rail. "Hand over the Nexus Access, or face the same fate as your master!"

The masked servant chuckled darkly. "I don't think so, Jason." The voice... it was familiar. Jason hesitated, just for a second. The servant pressed gems embedded in his golden breastplate. The ruby on his turban ignited, and a blast of sonic energy exploded outward. Jason was hit hard. His body rippled, senses collapsing. Reality, is distorted. His ears filled with shrieking noise and splitting pressure, like his skull was going to rupture. He collapsed. But something inside him wouldn't break. A surge of fury exploded within. His spirit ripped free, silvery and translucent, Jason's essence launching forward. He struck the servant with a tiger claw strike, a spiritual strike that shredded the servant's face and mask, breaking the connection to the sonic blast.

The servant reeled back, and staggered.

Jason stood in spirit form, hovering above his physical body and staring into the unmasked face of the attacker. Jason froze, heart crashing against his ribs. Shock overwhelmed him. He couldn't move. The servant shook off the hit, recovering. His eyes locked with Jason's spirit. "Maybe another time, Jason," he said coolly while tapping the gems again. This time a red aura shimmered around him, a protective shell snapping into place. He leaped onto the balcony's edge. A shot rang out. CRACK. Alvarez's sniper rifle caught him square in the chest. The impact knocked the unmasked servant back, the Nexus Access in the case slipping from his hands. It hit the floor but he fell from the balcony causing Jason to scream out No! In terror. But before he hits the floor—A seraph swooped in and caught him, soaring toward an upper-level exit. "NO!" Jason screamed as he disappeared. His body jolted. He gasped, back in his flesh. The fog cleared. His ears still rang, but his hand closed around the case.

"Jason, are you up there?" Reginald's voice cut through the chaos. "We need the package. Regroup, ASAP!"

Jason blinked, dazed. He looked at the case, then down at his body, he was back in.

"Uh... Reginald?" Henry's voice was tight with alarm. "We've got a problem."

Reginald looked down at him. "What kind?"

"Another assault team. Large-scale. Inside the complex. The giants of the patrol units are engaging them now, but they're heading straight for us."

Reginald's face tightened. "Everyone, retreat! Now!"

Jason hooked the case to his gear and started down the ramp.

And then he saw it—

Gabriel's halo tore free from the wall. It spun across the room like a living saw blade, Jason screamed: "Look out for the halo!" Too late. The disc sliced through Alvarez's leg at the knee. He hit the floor screaming. The halo snapped onto Gabriel's head. Suddenly, electricity erupted from the lab's four copper coils, slamming into the halo. Gabriel's body lifted. His skin turned cobalt blue. Fire roared from his empty eye socket. He was regenerating.

"Harlow, Jason—get Alvarez moving!" Reginald snapped. "Williamson, be ready to blow this place on my command!"

"No!" Jason shouted. "We can't!"

Reginald turned, furious. "You want to die here, kid?!"

Jason stared at him, heart pounding. "It was Steven."

Reginald blinked. "Who?"

"Steven," Jason repeated. "Our friend."

Henry's face drained of color. "No way..."

Adam stepped up, voice gentle. "Are you sure?"

Jason nodded. "Yeah. I'm sure."

Reginald exhaled slowly. "Even if it is, we're out of time. Gabriel's healing. We have to end this."

In the center of the lab, Gabriel's body hovered in a cocoon of lightning, the wounds closing, the fire within him reigniting.

Harlow finished wrapping Alvarez's stump. "He's not going to last if we don't evac now."

Jason clenched his fists, grief, and fire in his chest. Then—

"...Okay. You're right." He looked back at where Steven vanished. "Let's go."

Once back in the elevator, the team began their slow ascent toward the surface beneath the Sphinx.

As they reached the chamber under the right paw, Reginald turned, resolutely.

"Williamson, set the charges off. Now."

"Yes, sir," Williamson replied coolly, pressing the ignition. The ground beneath them shuddered as a distant rumble echoed up from the depths, the crystal pyramid collapsing in on itself or so they hoped.

Reginald didn't flinch. He turned to his men. "Collect our dead. Is Alvarez stable for transport?"

"Yes, sir," Harlow replied, securing the final straps of a field stretcher. "I've got him sedated."

"Good. Set the parachutes up in flames too, Williamson. We need that heat signature visible."

Then, barking out more orders as the group mobilized: "Murry, call in extraction. Tell them to lock on to the chute fire. Jason, help Harlow move Alvarez. Jackson, take point. Let's move out!"

Up the limestone staircase, they ran, dust and chunks of debris raining down from above as the detonations rocked the ancient stone structure. The ground trembled, and hope surged through the coven.

"Adam, you're up. Let's open this door!" Reginald commanded.

With practiced focus, Adam raised his hands, energy coiling around his fingers. The exit shimmered into view, a seamless magical portal forming at the base of the Sphinx's paw.

The team poured out into the night. The burning parachutes cast eerie shadows on the sand. In the distance, the roar of approaching Humvees cut through the silence.

"Let's go, let's go, let's go!" Reginald shouted, waving the team forward. The Humvees screeched to a halt. Without hesitation, they loaded the fallen into one vehicle and Alvarez, unconscious and bleeding, into another. Jason, Adam, and Henry climbed in just as the convoy sped off into the vast desert, kicking up sand behind them while the massive C-17 Globemaster III waited ahead, its ramp open like a metal beast ready to swallow them whole.

Inside the vehicle, Adam glanced at Jason. "What happened down there? It was Steven, right?"

Jason nodded grimly. "Yeah. It was him."

Adam frowned. "That sonic attack that hit you I thought you were done for then it looked like Steven's face got raked or torn. What happened?"

"I'm not sure," Jason said slowly. "It felt like my body was coming apart. Like that breastplate he wore was unraveling me on a molecular level. Then... my spirit just ripped free. I struck him with a tiger claw strike, and it stopped the blast. I don't know how. I just knew I had to do something."

Henry blinked. "Wait, you came out of your body? Like a Jedi Force ghost?"

Jason gave him a dry look. "Are you seriously making Star Wars references right now?"

"Absolutely," Henry shrugged. "But... Why the hell is Steven working with Gabriel?"

Jason looked out the window. "I don't know. And right now? I'm not sure what to believe anymore."

The convoy pulled up the ramp of the Globemaster. Once inside, the cargo doors were sealed shut with a hydraulic hiss.

"We are in the nest, Golden Eagle," Reginald reported into the comm. "Repeat, we are in the nest." He hit the switch, sealing the ramp. "Take us up." The hum of the engines shifted into a powerful roar. The massive aircraft began to rise.

"Get Alvarez to the med unit. Lock down the vehicles," Reginald barked. "Who has the package?" Jason held up the case. "Right here." Reginald gave a tight nod. "Good work, Jason. All of you, good work. Stow your gear and your kits, and get some rest. We'll refuel in Padua, Italy."

As they make their way to stow their gear, Jason gets an image of Megan McCarthy in his head, telling him, "Don't trust Reginald. He's working for archangel Michael. I know this will sound strange, but please listen to me, Jason. Don't let Reginald out of your sight or keep the artifact." Jason quickly stumbles to one knee holding his head.

"Jason?" Henry rushed over. "Are you turning into a Force ghost again? Don't go full Obi-Wan on us now!"

"I'm fine," Jason muttered. "Just dizzy."

Reginald moved in fast, scanning him. "Did you take a hit? Let me check." As he begins padding him down for any wounds.

Jason pushes his hands away. "I said I'm fine. It's just the takeoff."

Reginald stepped back, watching him carefully. "Roger that."

Later, in a quiet corner of the aircraft, Jason sat with Adam and Henry. "Megan reached out to me," he whispered. "Telepathically. She said not to trust Reginald.

That he's working for Michael. She told me not to let him near the artifact."

Henry blinked. "Bro, are you okay? Megan's hot and all, but... telepathy?"

Adam cut in. "Would anyone believe the powers we have if we weren't living it?"

Henry sighed. "Fair. So if Reginald's a double agent... what's the play?"

Jason shook his head. "I don't know yet."

Adam turned to Henry. "Did your forearm computer save any of the data from the pyramid?"

Henry lifted his arm. "Yeah, it synced."

"Good. Pull images from that second team. I want to know who else was down there."

Jason nodded. "Yeah. Let's find out what we're really dealing with."

Henry gets to work. "Give me a minute. I'll sync to the laptop so no one else sees what we find."

Adam leaned back, eyes narrowed. "If this is all true... we now know who the third angel is."

Jason groaned. "Or the fourth? How many angels are there going to be?"

Adam looked away, reluctant. "Gabriel mentioned the Watchers... That means a lot of them."

Jason exhaled, staring out into the dim yellow sunrise of the morning sky through the aircraft window as the Globemaster roared through the clouds, the storm far from over.

CHAPTER 10
THE GUEST

"Holy shit, guys. Holy *shit*," Henry mutters, barely audible over the roar of the engines.

Adam turns sharply, his face tight with confusion. "What's going on, man?"

Jason's eyes narrow, leaning forward, a sharp edge in his voice. "What the hell are you going on about?"

"Look," Henry hisses, his finger hovering over the screen, urgency in every movement. "Look at this."

The three of them freeze. A figure stares back at them, flickering in the vivid footage, Megan. The girl who's been the center of their world. But this isn't the Megan they know. The one in the video is a ghost, hollow-eyed and deadly. The pyramid, the escape, it feels like everything's been crazy up to this moment. But somehow this is too much.

Jason's breath catches. "Is that...?"

"Yeah," Henry breathes, voice unsteady. "It's her. Megan. I guess you were right after all Gold"

"I guess so." Jason murmurs.

The room feels colder, the air thicker. Jason's eyes are glued to the screen, to the woman he thought he knew. Her strawberry blonde hair falls in loose waves under a black beret, but her eyes—those piercing emeralds—are cold, unflinching. The black grease paint under her eyes smears across her pale skin like a mask, a ghostly thing that no longer carries any innocence.

Jason's jaw tightens. "Who the hell are these soldiers with her and what do you think they wanted down there?"

Henry zooms in on the patch of one soldier—a cross, wrapped in a rose, stitched into their shoulder.

Adam curses under his breath. "Holy shit. She's part of the Rosicrucians."

"The who?" Jason snarls, his voice rough, a growing unease spreading through him.

"The Rosicrucian Brotherhood," Adam mutters. "An ancient order. Founded back in the 13th century, maybe the 14th. They've been pulling strings, hiding in the shadows, working toward something big. They believe the world's about to change, and they're waiting for some... new age of religion. A new world."

Jason laughs bitterly, shaking his head. "So we're not just dealing with some cult, huh? This is real..."

Henry's frustration boils over. "God, Jason, read a damn book!"

Jason doesn't even flinch, too lost in thought. *How did Luke know about all this? Is he... one of us too?*

Adam rips his attention back to the present. "We don't know what they want for sure. But she's got the Sight, like we do. If I had to guess, it's the same thing we were after—that damn case." He glances toward Reginald, still clutching it like it's the only thing keeping him alive.

Henry shakes his head, lost in his own thoughts, his mouth clamped shut. For once, the words don't come. The world feels like it's pressing down on them all.

Without warning, the plane shudders violently, throwing them off balance. Henry crashes to the ground, skidding across the rough metal floor of the C-17. He manages to scramble up, hands scraping against the cold surface as he collects his computer, heart pounding in his chest.

"What the hell was that?" Reginald roars, his voice cutting through the chaos.

The others scramble, trying to find their footing. Jenkins and Murry are already tending to the fallen strike team members, their hands moving with grim precision. Harlow is bent over Alvarez, blood staining his hands as he works. Jackson and Williamson are at the Humvees, securing weapons. Jones is crouched low, desperately stowing rifles, gear, anything he can.

The plane jerks again, this time harder, slamming everyone to the right. Reginald stumbles, regaining his footing with a growl of frustration. "I'm going to see what the hell's going on with this bird."

He stumbles over toward the cockpit, but the instant he moves, the plane lurches like it's been struck. The cockpit door flies off its hinges, tearing through the air, and slamming into the hold. The blast of wind rips through the cabin, pulling everything toward it—bags, loose equipment, bodies scrambling to hold on.

And then... he steps into view.

Gabriel.

Not the angel they knew before. Not the being who had been marked by mere anger, but something darker now. His flaming sword is already drawn, blood-red light flickering in the dark, cutting through the shadows. His eyes are empty, like black pits, the kind that swallows all hope. "Everyone is going to die. And I'm going to make sure it hurts," he snarls, his voice like nails on metal.

Adam's eyes scan the cockpit. The pilots, were decapitated. The windshield shattered like glass shards in a nightmare. Blood stains the seats and the control panel. The whole front of the plane is a scene of carnage. The air in the cabin begins to settle, but it's still thick with dread. "Pilots are dead," Adam grits out, his voice shaky with the weight of the reality sinking in.

Reginald's voice cracks through the tension. "Get ready to jump!"

The plane starts to spin wildly. The roar of the engines is deafening. Reginald loses his grip on the Nexus Access, and it slides across the floor—another life-or-death scramble in the chaos. The M2 machine gun mounted on the Humvee roars to life, the deafening sound of the .50 caliber rounds hammering the air. Jackson is unloading, his eyes wild as he pulls the trigger, but Gabriel's armored chest deflects most of the rounds, the bullets ricocheting off with violent force, others tearing into his flesh and scattering feathers.

They've got no time. No time at all.

Williamson slams the button for the rear ramp. Harlow pulls his M4A1 from its strap, the weight of it like an anchor. He fires a grenade from the underslung launcher. The explosion rips through the air, throwing Gabriel back into the cockpit, but the case—the one thing they can't afford to lose—slides slowly toward the ramp from the grenade blast.

Jason's heart stops. "Shit! The case!" His words are barely a shout. It's like the sound of the world cracking open as everything spirals down into madness.

"Get your chutes on. I got this!" Adam growled, sliding across the tilted floor of the C-17, reaching for the case now skidding toward the ramp faster. His hands scraped the metal as another explosion shook the aircraft, this time from outside. The engine burst into flames with a roar. In an instant, the wing snapped clean off, trailing smoke and fire.

"That's not good, man!" Henry shouted, his face pale.

"No, it's not!" Jason snapped back. "Hell, none of this is good!"

The heavy rattle of the M2 abruptly stopped. Jackson was out of ammo. The only sound left was the high-pitched hiss of the barrel cooling down, smoke curling upward. Then came that awful, bone-deep whine. A blur of gold, Gabriel's halo, ripped through the air. It sliced through Jackson's chest like a sharp pencil through wet paper, leaving him slumped over the silent machine gun. Blood trickled down the weapon like oil from a ruptured engine.

Williamson grabbed his demolition bag, already priming the C4 inside. His voice was flat, almost too calm. "Get ready to jump."

Before they could move, the second wing blew. The detonation sent the plane into a spiraling descent, metal shrieking. The case tumbled, bounced—

—and flew right out of the cargo bay.

Adam reached out, but the blast knocked him flat on his back.

"No!" Henry's scream was hoarse.

Adam shoved himself to his feet, breathing hard. "Don't worry. I'll get it!" he shouted, then vaulted through the open ramp and into the sky.

Jason gawked. "What the hell?! He just jumped without a chute!"

"I KNOW!" Henry shouted, scrambling with his pack.

Gabriel steps out of the cockpit, wreathed in firelight. His left arm extends with mechanical grace, his halo snaps into his hand and he places it above his head in one smooth motion.

Before Harlow can load another grenade, Gabriel's flaming blade arcs through the air. One devastating slash. Harlow's body splits in two, blood spraying across the bulkhead as both halves collapse to the floor. Inside the chaos of the aircraft, Henry and Jason yank on their parachutes, bolting toward the rear ramp. They brushed past Williamson, gripping a detonator in one hand, his demolition bag in the other.

"Faster, Henry! Move!" Jason shouts, realizing what's about to happen. They reach the open ramp just as—

BOOM! The plane erupts in a fiery explosion, the blast wave slamming into them like a cannon shot. They're hurled into the sky, spinning and flailing, their screams lost to the thunderous explosion of the C17. Amid the smoke and debris, they glance back—shocked, gasping—as the shredded carcass of the plane rains down in burning chunks over the Mediterranean.

Then, a shape bursts from the flames.

Gabriel.

Charred, wings tattered but alive—he dives, a burning specter screaming through the air like a meteor on fire.

Jason gulps down air, eyes wide. "You gotta be shitting me! On my count, pull the cord, ready?!"

Henry nods, bracing.

Below, Adam floats—levitating, his coat rippling in the high-altitude wind. He locks eyes with Gabriel streaking toward them, then looks to his friends… and hurls the case with every ounce of strength and magic he has.

It rockets through the sky, farther than humanly possible.

Gabriel swerves, drawn off course, chasing the case with predator focus.

Adam shoots up to meet his friends.

"Holy shit, you can fly!" Henry gasps.

"Not exactly," Adam mutters, catching his breath.

Jason looks at him, furious. "You gave up the case—for us?!"

"Relax. It was empty."

Henry's grin fades. "Yeah, but I don't think that's gonna stop him from tearing us apart!"

Adam blinks. "Okay... maybe I didn't think that far ahead."

Below them, Gabriel snatches the case midair, securing it. His sword ignites once more. He rockets toward them, a heat-seeking missile of vengeance. Then—a crack of thunder.

A bolt of lightning crashes from the clouds, slamming into Gabriel.

"It's the bum from the alleyway during the armored truck attack!" Adam shouts, his voice slicing through the chaos.

The mysterious figure materializes out of the smoke, clutching a golden staff. The top of the staff is crowned with three pinecone-shaped ornaments, each glimmering with an otherworldly glow. He twirls it in his hands—the motion so fast it's a blur. Then, without warning, he halts, his eyes locking on Gabriel.

The staff pulses with magical energy. With a flick of his wrist, a torrent of radiant magic erupts from the top of the staff, blinding and fierce. The beam rips through the air, striking Gabriel square in the chest. The angel's breastplate shatters, sending pieces of glowing metal and charred flesh flying, followed by a storm of white feathers. Gabriel spins violently, spiraling through the sky as his wings falter, disoriented by the blast.

"Hobo Gandalf is real!" Henry yells, his voice tinged with disbelief as they continue their freefall toward Earth.

The stranger shifts his focus, pointing the staff directly at the three friends, his eyes cold and calculating. The staff crackles with new, ominous energy.

Henry's face falls, his earlier grin vanishing. "Shit, he's not a friendly wizard!"

He slams his eyes shut, bracing for the inevitable end.

But just as the weight of impending doom settles in, Jason and Adam exchange a glance, and then they see it.

A portal opens beneath them, swirling with vibrant colors and crackling magic. Without warning, the three of them are sucked into the rift, their screams muffled by the roar of wind as they fall.

And then—thud.

They land hard on cold, cracked pavement. Gasping for breath, they push themselves up, only to stare in shock at the familiar sight before them.

"Dae-jung Dojo!" Henry exclaims, recognizing the iconic sign just a few steps away.

The three friends stumble, their bodies still shaking off the disorienting effects of the magical portal that just hurled them over five thousand miles in the blink of an eye. Their surroundings blur as they struggle to regain their footing, the sudden transition from freefall to solid ground a jarring experience. The smell of the Mediterranean sea salt air is replaced by the familiar scent of New York smog.

They slowly rise, blinking against the sudden dizziness, and look up. Their safe space, their dojo.

Through the window, they can see Sensei Kim Dae-Jung, their mentor and friend, moving in a way none of them have ever seen before. His graceful, fluid motions blend elements of Tai Chi and Qigong, but something about the flow seems... different. The air around him shimmers with energy, as though each movement pulls light and life from the space itself. Before any of the teens can speak, a sudden crack of light cuts through the floor beneath Sensei's feet. A glowing fracture appears in the mats, pulsing like a heartbeat. With calm precision,

Sensei raises his right hand, drawing the light upward, his fingers swirling the energy into his palm. The glow intensifies for a split second, then—in the blink of an eye—it vanishes.

Sensei stands tall, his posture perfect. His gaze shifts, and his eyes meet theirs through the window. He raises an eyebrow, intrigued.

The boys freeze. The casual, familiar aura of Sensei Kim—once so comforting—is now laced with an undeniable air of mystery.

With a purposeful stride, he moves toward the door, unlocking it with a fluid motion. The heavy wooden door with glass insert creaks open. "Would you three like to come in?" His voice is calm, and measured.

The best friends burst into action, eager and breathless. They rush forward, forgetting to remove their shoes, each of them speaking over the other in a rapid blur of words.

"Sensei! What was that?!" Henry pleads.

"How did you—what's going on?" Adam inquires

"Are you okay?" Jason says out of shock

Sensei Kim clears his throat, the sound sharp and commanding in the stillness of the dojo. The three boys stop mid-sentence. Their voices fall into an awkward silence. Then, in unison, they bow, their excitement and confusion tempered by respect.

"Excuse us, Sensei." They say in unison before stripping their combat boots off.

"I know you won't believe this." Jason begins.

"But please just listen," Adam adds.

"Wizards, giants, and angels are real!" Henry shouts.

Sensei clears his throat again "One at a time, now. Come, let's sit and have tea. Jason, you start. I'm very curious as to why you and Henry have parachutes strapped to your backs and all of you are dressed in these clothes."

"Okay." Jason begins "Before you get upset with us, please hear us out no matter how crazy and far-fetched this all sounds. Please?"

Sensei Kim Dae-jung slowly nods. "Please proceed."

"So, several days ago Adam got an invite to Victory Violence Fights. We know your feelings on fighting in the cage, so we kept it under wraps, but the prize money was ten grand, and-"

"VVF was not holding any events this month." Kim Dae-jung cuts in.

Adam is taken aback. "What? But I got an email from them. Are you sure, Sensei?"

"Trust me, Adam." Kim Dae-jung frankly explains. "I know every fighting event, legal or underground, that happens in this city."

The three friends look at one another, and then Henry says "I bet it was from hobo Gandalf posing as Merle from that website Guiding Lights. Remember? It's got to be him. Who else could it have been?"

Sensei lifts an eyebrow but says nothing.

"Anyways," Jason cuts back in, picking up his story where he got cut off. "We were headed to that event four days ago Saturday morning, regardless of if it was or wasn't happening, and the so-called terrorists attack on that armored truck that was all over the news!? We were there-"

"And involved." Henry cuts in "We saved a lady and her baby!"

"Yeah, he's right," Jason continues. "We got tangled up in it, and that's not the unbelievable part. The unbelievable part is..."

Jason pauses and lets out a deep sigh. "We saw an angel, not a terrorist with a jetpack."

"And the rest of the terrorists spoke with Boston accents." Henry jumps back in. "Right, Adam?"

"Yeah, that's right." Adam agrees. "They weren't Middle Eastern at all."

"So where have you all been the last few days?" Kim Dae-jung asks. "Your parents have been worried."

"As Henry mentioned, a guy named Merle from a website dedicated to angels called Guiding Lights told him that Gabriel, the angel we saw, was sending his soldiers, posing as Homeland Security to kidnap us. And sure as shit-"

"Language." Their sensei cuts in sternly.

"Sorry, Sensei." Jason lowers his head for a second. "And sure enough, agents did in fact show up just as this, Merle said they would. So, we all had a plan to meet here if anything happened, but we were ambushed outside the dojo and got tranquilized, but not before-"

"Jason kicked some serious ass. I mean butt." Henry interjects while correcting his language.

"Yeah, I fought a few of Gabriel's men. But before I went out from the tranquilizer I finally got shot with, I saw some commando-looking dudes show up to save us. They came in with automatic weapons, killing the few remaining men I hadn't knocked out, and took us to their secret base, where they put us through tests, before they trained us."

"Yeah! Adam is a wizard." Henry blurts out. "And Jason can turn himself into a force ghost-like in Star Wars."

"No, I can't," Jason argues. "I mean, I kinda did just that once against Steven."

Sensei speaks up. "You saw Steven?"

"Yeah, I did," Jason admits.

"Where!?" Kim Dae-jung asks excitedly.

"So, this group of commandos is part of a secret organization known as the Order of the Eye. OE for short. They had The Eye of Providence, or All-Seeing Eye as their symbol." Jason recites proudly remembering the details his two friends lectured him on.

Adam chimes in "It's the eye on the-"

Their sensei raises his hand. "I know what it is, thank you. Where did you see Steven?"

"Under the great pyramids of Giza!" Henry shouts out.

"Yeah, he's right," Jason admits. "We saw him in Egypt, and yes, under the Sphinx actually. Adam opened the secret entrance with his magic. We were tasked with going in to take back what this archangel stole from the armored truck, but Gabriel got it back when he attacked the plane we were on."

Adam turns to his two friends. "I told you guys the case was empty. Remember? I took the Nexus Access out" as he pulls from his black tactical jacket and holds up a multicolored faceted gem the size of a baseball that resembles an Alexandrite but sparkes with a light from the inside.

"Oh yeah." Henry and Jason both exclaim.

"Wait. Sensei, do you even believe us?" Henry questions "Or do you think we're just a bunch of crazy kids?"

"Of course, I believe you." Kim Dae-jung answers. "But was Steven, okay?"

"No!" Jason answers emotionally. "He's working for that archangel."

Adam pats him on the shoulder. "And he was wearing an ephod along with a golden breastplate, with precious stones in it that he used as a weapon against Jason. It reminded me of the Breastplate of Judgment that's mentioned in the Tanakh." Adam adds.

"That's when Jason went all force ghost," Henry explains excitedly before pausing. "But why, Sensei? Why do you believe us so easily?" He asks with a perplexed look plastered all over his round face.

"I saw the same thing you all saw that day the towers were attacked." Their martial arts teacher answers very matter-of-factly.

"You did!?" The three friends exclaim simultaneously.

"Yes. That's why I have tried to watch over you and train you all so arduously." Sensei Kim admits. "But Steven couldn't shut his third eye like you three did. He kept seeing the unseen world and finally broke under the pressures of the world that is hidden from most. Unless you are raised in an environment that conditions you to see that which is hidden, the mind will break without a stable support system to guide it."

"I wonder if that's the case for Megan then?" Adam wonders aloud. "Like has she been raised by her family or that secret society of hers to see all of what we have just been introduced to in the last few days?" He asks with a shrug and a raised eyebrow.

"Jack McCarthy, her father, is a very high-ranking elder." Kim Dae-jung informs his students. "I can't imagine he hasn't trained her but why do you bring her up Adam?"

"When we were below the Sphinx in Egypt Henry picked up an alert that there were other forces in the structure with us," Adam starts to explain, "and once we escaped we reviewed the security images where we saw her with a bunch of soldiers which means they had someone on their team that could access the entrance through the sphinx plus Megan reached out psychically and communicated with Jason."

"Oh, She did? "Kim Dae-Jung says while looking at Jason as he only frowns out of confusion and nods an acknowledgment back to his teacher. "Well then I'd say she definitely has the-"

"He's here!" Adam suddenly shouts as he places his hands on the dojos mat they all are sitting on. "I feel his mystical energy."

"As do I." Kim Dae-jung says calmly, yet very alert. "Get ready." He orders.

The old master jumps from his lotus position that he was sitting in and marches to where he keeps his Hwando, the Korean warrior's sword of the ancestors.

At the front door, a violent magical ripple tears through the air, distorting time and space. Through the rift steps Gabriel, his body healed of the wounds the flying wizard inflicted over the Mediterranean. His battle inside the C-17 Globemaster is still fresh in his mind, but his breastplate is gone, leaving his muscular frame exposed. He spots Sensei Kim standing calmly, weapon in hand, prepared for the fight ahead. Gabriel's lips curl into a sneer, and with a flash of fiery movement, he slashes down with his flaming bastard sword—its blaze scorching the air.

But Sensei Kim, moving with the speed of a seasoned warrior, draws his Hwando in a blur of motion. The clash of metal against metal echoes through the dojo as he parries Gabriel's strike with inhuman precision, his movements fluid and deliberate.

Gabriel's eyes widened in surprise, taken aback by the speed and grace of the old man. As the sound of steel ringing in the air fades, the angel's gaze sharpens, his focus shifting from the three teenagers to the mysterious figure now before his eyes locking on the Hwandos scabbard.

"A Naga Knight?" Gabriel's voice is laced with disbelief and a hint of fear. His eyes trace the intricate serpent-like humanoid etched into the scabbard of Sensei's blade. "Impossible," he mutters under his breath, his confidence faltering for the first time.

Sensei Kim doesn't respond with words, simply nodding slowly, his gaze unwavering as he prepares for the next strike.

Gabriel's voice cuts through the calamity, sharp and incredulous. "That's impossible." He steps forward, eyes blazing. "We slaughtered them five hundred years ago, along with the Nagaraja."

Sensei Kim's voice is calm but deadly. "Well, I hate to break your delusion," he says, voice low and steady, "but you're very wrong." He tilts his head, cold and measured. "And if I'm still standing here, how many more of us have you missed?"

Gabriel's grin widens, a flash of arrogance. "Tonight, I'll kill one more, Naga Knight, and these three as well." The archangel's wings unfurl slightly, vengeance flickering in his eyes, a fierce grin twisting upon his beautiful face.

They circle, predator and prey, both settling into fighting stances.

Kim slaps the ancient Hwandos blade against his left hand, the metal humming like a tuning fork, glowing with a ghostly light. His hand ignites with a blinding, crackling energy, sparks dancing across his fingertips.

Gabriel charges, a blur of speed and fire. His bastard sword blazes with hellfire, held high, a blazing arc of destruction. He swings downward with relentless force, intent on ending this fight quickly.

Kim sidesteps with lethal precision, parrying the blow with a clang that rings out like a gunshot. Without missing a beat, he spins sharply to his left, the motion fluid and lethal. His left-hand lashes out, fingers brushing Gabriel's spine. A surge of shimmering, crackling light leaps from Kim's palm, arcing with violent sparks up Gabriel's back—an arcing bolt of crackling ancient power. The arc reaches the base of Gabriel's skull, detonating in a burst of searing energy. The archangel jerks, blood bubbling from his lips as the explosion sears through flesh and bone. He staggers, clutching his side, eyes wide with shock.

Gabriel's sword flickers—then dies—its upper blade sheared off now melting into a puddle of molten metal on the floor. The hilt sends sparks flying as exposed circuits and wires hiss and sizzle.

Kim watches silently, his expression unreadable.

"It's not a magical +5 flaming Avenger!?" Henry yells out.

"This isn't D&D!" Jason snaps back.

"I know, I know," Henry counters. "But it's not magical, it's just tech."

"That means his halo isn't magical either." Adam proclaims.

"Exactly!" Henry agrees.

"Impossible," Gabriel gasps, blood trickling down his chin.

"You've been blind," Kim murmurs, voice low and cold. "But I've been waiting. Waiting for you to stumble into the truth."

The air thickens with smoke and the scent of burnt metal.

Gabriel is battered, but Kim stands firm, the darkness around him alive with silent, deadly promise.

"BOYS, RUN!" Sensei's voice cut through the darkness with ferocity, commanding and urgent. His figure spun swiftly, holding his ancestral blade with a sharp, fluid motion that gleamed in the dojos light. Without hesitation, he sheaths his sword and then hurls the blade toward his top pupil. "Jason, catch!" he barked.

Jason lunged forward, hand outstretched. The blade rattled into his grip just as Gabriel, the archangel, sneered with contempt. Gabriel's hate-filled eyes flicked to the weapon, then to the boys. "You fool," Gabriel hissed, a cruel smile twisting his face. "You're powerless without your blade. Now you die."

He threw his glowing halo like a deadly Chakram of death. It spun furiously through the air, a blinding streak of light. But in a flash, a shimmering barrier erupted, halting its deadly trajectory mere inches from Kim Dae-jung's face.

In that instant, Adam stepped forward, palms raised, a flicker of energy crackling at his fingertips. His will pressed against the halo-like an invisible shield, halting its deadly spin.

"Run! Get away, go now!" Kim Dae-Jung shouted, voice strained but fierce. His eyes burned with resolve. The sensei's body moved into a strange, mesmerizing blend of Tai Chi and Qigong. Lines of glowing energy shimmered around him, swirling like a vortex. From the ley lines beneath them, he pulled raw, crackling chi, shaping it into a weapon—like a chain whip of blinding light. With fierce precision, he wielded the energy, spinning and striking. The luminous chain lashed out, cutting, slashing, and bludgeoning Gabriel like a master practitioner of wushu. The archangel roared in pain, blood streaming from his nose as he was forced back.

His halo flickered, desperately retreating to protect him.

"Holy shit," Henry blurted out, eyes wide. "Sensei's like Iron Fist in the comics!"

Kim Dae-jung's breath grew ragged under the strain, but he pushed on. "Language," he rasped.

"Sorry!" Henry shouted, eyes darting for an escape. "Let's go, now!"

Jason grabbed Adam by the arm. "Let's move," he ordered, urgency thick in his voice.

Adam hesitated for a heartbeat, then thrust his hand forward. A surge of shimmering energy shot toward Gabriel's temple before he could place his halo back atop his head. The archangel staggered, blood pouring from his mouth and nose. His halo burst into flames, spiraling away in a blazing arc, igniting the wooden beams of the dojo.

Flames erupted, crackling wildly, sending sparks into the air. The structure blazed fiercely, engulfed in fire and smoke.

"Run!" Kim Dae-jung shouted one last time, voice hoarse but commanding.

Jason yanked Adam by the arm and sprinted toward the rear exit as flames threatened to consume everything. Behind them, Gabriel, battered but undefeated, watched with cold, deadly eyes. He rises to continue this deadly dance as his gaze locks onto Adam for a moment, an unspoken challenge.

Once on the streets of Hell's Kitchen the three friends raced through the streets and alleyways barefoot and panicked. Without warning, a vortex of swirling blue and white light materialized in front of them—an unnatural portal shimmering like a mirror to another world. Before anyone could react, Henry barreled forward, crashing into his friends with reckless force. The impact sent all three stumblings headlong into the spinning arcane wonder.

The world spun around them in a blur of light and shadow once again. When they finally hit the ground, they collapsed onto a bed of soft moss, disoriented and breathless.

Mist clung to the air, shrouding an ancient forest that seemed alive with unseen eyes. Shadows twisted and writhed among the trees. The silence was oppressive, adding yet another layer to the three teens' already rapidly growing nightmare that only seemed to be getting darker.

CHAPTER 11
THE ISLAND

Looking back in wonderment, the three friends watched the portal seal shut with a soft, echoing slap, leaving them alone in the forest's shadowy hush. Though dawn had begun to rise, its light struggled to penetrate the dense canopy above. The woods felt wrong, unnaturally dim, as if the trees themselves resisted the morning.

In the clearing where they'd arrived, the air hung heavy with moisture and the scent of damp earth and moss. A strange chill lingered despite the hour, prickling their skin. Leaves rustled with no wind. The silence buzzed, as if the forest held its breath.

Something about this place defied the rules of nature and the friends felt it in their bones.

"Okay, what the hell just happened, and where are we?" Henry questions while getting to his feet.

"I'm not sure." Jason answers helping Adam up "Can you use that forearm computer of yours to find out where we are?"

"Not a bad idea. I'll use the built-in GPS and see where we're at." Henry responds as he fires it up but gets no response.

"It's like we're in a dead zone." Henry Informs his two friends "I'm getting nothing. Not even the built-in motion detection is picking anything up. My goggles however work and this place is blowing up on the Magnetometer! The electromagnetic field here is stronger than the Giza Plateau!"

"Let me reach out with my powers," Adam suggests with eyes closed and his palms facing toward the ground. And within seconds he stumbles back as he's forced to take a knee "Wow! What a head rush. Yeah, I probably shouldn't be attempting anything here with my powers not knowing how to fully use them."

"I told ya." Henry admonishes his magical friend.

Jason watches expectantly for a moment until he notices Adam gets overwhelmed then helps his friend back to his feet again. "You going to be alright?"

"Yeah, Just need a moment to collect myself, that's all," Adam responds.

"Well, the flashlight on this computer works," Henry informs his friends. The flashlight's narrow beam cut through the gloom, revealing gnarled roots and pale fungi that seemed to recoil from the light "What direction should we go?"

"How 'bout this way?" Jason points out. "It looks like there's a path through these rocks."

"Wait a minute," Henry speaks up, shining the flashlight in a circular motion around them. "These rock formations look familiar."

"They aren't formations" Adam proclaims. "They're monolithic blocks like Stonehenge!"

"So, we're in Ireland?" Jason asks.

"Stonehenge is in England dumb ass." Henry snaps at his friend. "Seriously Jason…"

"Yeah yeah, I know, 'Read a book', I got it!" Jason fires back.

"Salisbury Plain," Adam says.

Both Henry and Jason turn to him. "Huh?"

"Salisbury Plain, England is where Stonehenge is located, and it's a chalk plateau covering 300 square miles of plains." Adam elaborates. "This is a pretty thick forest, so this isn't Stonehenge, nor do I believe we're in England."

"No, you're not..." A sinister voice hisses from the shadows.

Jason jolts into a defensive stance, hand gripping the hilt of his teacher's sword. "Who are you, and why did you bring us here?"

Adam and Henry fall in line, readying themselves for combat as well.

"I didn't bring you here..." The aggressive feminine voice spits back at them.

"Then show yourself," Jason demands.

"As you wish." The mysterious stranger answers.

Stepping into the illumination of Henry's flashlight combined with the struggling sunrise; all three gasp at what they see. A beautiful female with keen untamed green eyes sparkling like a pair of peridot gems, hair falling down her back black as raven feathers with horns even darker. The friends can't help but notice those dark characteristics as they stand out against her garnet-red skin. Her shapely form is dressed in a silvery metal brazier with black Pteruges or defensive skirt resembling that of a Roman gladiator while her leathery wings stretch out from her back resembling those of a bat while clutching a halberd in one of her clawed hands. "I am Avarail. I have been tasked with escorting you safely to the castle."

"The castle?" Jason questions.

"Yes." She replies, "There your questions will be answered."

"By the wizard?" Henry chimes in. "by 'Merle'?"

"Yes." She simply answers again.

"Are you a succubus?" Adam asks as politely as he can.

"I am." She says with a devious smile, revealing elongated canines. "Now come, and we shall get you all something to eat, drink, and wear for your feet."

Once they all break clear of the forest they finally see the Castle against the brightness of the morning sun, with its white limestone façade and deep blue turrets, surrounded by a crystal clear moat.

Adam looks up at the architecture in awe. "This looks like Neuschwanstein."

"If that's German for Cinderella's Castle, I totally agree," Jason comments.

"No," Henry interjects. "Neuschwanstein is a famous castle in Germany. Some say the king who built it was mad; others call him a visionary genius. Either way, the castle is undeniably impressive. And yes, Gold Neuschwanstein actually inspired the Disney castle you're referring to."

Avarail says "You'll find many things here in Avalon impressive."

"Wait!?" Henry says in alarmed excitement. "Avalon as in the mythical island featured in the Arthurian legends? The magical place where King Arthur's sword Excalibur was made? Where King Arthur Himself was taken to recover from being gravely wounded at the Battle of Camlann? Is this castle you're taking us to, Castle Camelot?"

"Come. All your questions will be answered soon enough." That is all the exotically beautiful succubus says.

While the three friends step onto the massive drawbridge, the groaning of ancient chains rattles from the impact of their steps. The planks creaked with each cautious step. Towering at either end, two colossal figures stood sentinel, giants whose very presence drew involuntary gasps. Their obsidian armor gleamed faintly in the overcast light of the sunrise, etched with runes that flickered dimly like a candle's flame. The teens exchanged uneasy glances, the memory of Egypt flashing vividly to mind—the terror under the Sphinx, the hissing roars of living fire, the screams. And the blood. These guardians were even larger than those they had faced before, with broader shoulders, and deeper-set eyes that glowed faintly with unnatural awareness. Could these be true-blood Nephilim?

Crossing into the courtyard, they were met with a scene torn from the pages of a forgotten fairy tale. Ivy spiraled up marble columns. Petals the size of palms fluttered through the air, and between them flitted tiny creatures —fairies, unmistakably. Their gossamer wings shimmered with iridescent color, and they moved in synchronized patterns, tending to blossoms that exhaled sweet, dizzying fragrances. One fairy paused mid-flight to sprinkle glowing dust onto a wilting rose, which immediately perked up, its color deepening to a fiery crimson.

The towering oak double doors loomed ahead, each slab of timber nearly fifteen feet high and banded in blackened iron that rippled with faint magic. The friends hesitated, feeling the weight of history and power radiating from the threshold. When the doors creaked open, a draft of cool, dry air spilled out, carrying the faint scent of stone, parchment, and something spicy—perhaps incense.

Inside, the grand hall opened before them with a reverent hush. Granite tiles stretched out in all directions, polished to a mirror sheen that reflected flickering torchlight along the vaulted ceilings. Corridors branched like arteries from the main hall, each one promising mystery and danger deeper within this immense and ancient fortress.

"Follow me." Avarail orders them as she begins climbing a grand staircase that winds up against the wall.

Windows offer majestic views out on a wild and green island surrounding the castle on this mystical morning.

What seems like forever passes by with ease as the top of a tower is soon reached.

Avarail holds her hand out toward a door. "There you will find your answers." She says, then steps out on a balcony where she takes flight.

"Okay..." Jason begins. "Am I the only one freaking out just a little bit?"

Henry and Adam just look at each other.

Adam speaks up. "Yep, it's just you."

"Now let's go find out who the great and powerful Oz is here and look behind the curtain, shall we?" Henry says full of vigor and vitality.

As he strides up to the towering oak door, the iron-bound wood groaning faintly beneath his touch, he pushes the smooth wooden door open without hesitation, his every step radiating a boldness his two friends had rarely seen in him. The heavy door creaks inward, releasing a rush of cool, musty air that smells of primeval stone, old parchment, and something faintly metallic, like ancient machinery stirring in the shadows.

They step into a vast, circular chamber nearly twenty feet across. The walls curve around them like the inside of a stone shell, cloaked in ivy that has crept in through the open window. A single arched opening at the far end bleeds pale light onto a cluttered wooden desk—its surface buried beneath an avalanche of curling scrolls cracked leather-bound tomes, and brittle yellowed papers that rustle in the draft like whispering voices.

Above the desk, suspended in midair, a liquid screen shimmers and pulses with a soft, greenish-yellow glow. It hums faintly, like a distant chorus of tuning forks, casting strange shifting reflections on the surrounding stone. It's the same eerie technology they last encountered beneath the Sphinx, in the heart of the angelic crystal pyramid where they last saw Steven. The memory crackles in the back of their minds like static, familiar, and otherworldly all at once.

"This reminds me of that D&D campaign you ran, Henry." Adam reminisces.

Jason jumps in on the memory. "Oh yeah, the one where we had to defeat the undead lich wizard in the Black Tower."

"Yeah," Henry recalls. "Steven's warrior got critically wounded by the chain lightning spell from the wizard."

The room is soon filled with silence at the mention of their friend turned enemy not knowing if he even survived the encounter under the great sphinx.

Adam tries to take the attention off the thought of

Steven. "So, I thought there'd be someone here to answer our questions"

"*There is...*" A voice utters in their heads "*Just because you don't see me doesn't mean I'm not here. Try to feel my magical essence. Feel my energy.*"

"Where do you think he's at?" Henry laments. "I hear him in my head!"

"Yeah, I hear him too. He's here behind the desk!?" Jason says confidently

"No no no," Adam says, holding up a hand while looking at the center of the room knowing it can't be that easy. "Here you are." He says stepping forward while reaching out only to find himself being shocked with a jolt of power that brings him to his knees. A power coil is revealed soon after touching it, becoming visible after delivering its painful lesson.

"You should've heeded your warrior friends' words," a voice says aloud no longer in their heads. A dusky-skinned man now sits behind the desk with dark long hair and a beard streaked with grey staring at them with very dark brown inquisitive eyes. The same man from the alleyway of the armored truck heists and from the sky above the Mediterranean.

"Told you he was there!" Jason says with growing frustration about the situation.

"Yeah, I thought so too but felt this stupid thing and paid the price for it," Adam says, still shaking the shock out of his limbs.

"You should have focused harder." the mysterious man says with his fingers pressed together. "Its frequency stirred just above my own—lighter, older, almost familiar. Don't trust what you assume. Truth isn't seen. It's felt."

Jason is finally fed up. "Okay. Who are you, and what do you want!? We're not giving up the Nexus Access to you if that's the reason you brought us here!?"

"Good." Says the man sitting behind the old wooden desk leaning back in an antique chair.

"Are you Merle?" Henry curiously asks. "The Merle who warned me on that website dedicated to angels that they were coming for us?"

"Yes." He answers.

"Merle as in Merlin, the wizard of the Arthurian legends?" Henry asks, even more excited.

And again, the man answers "Yes."

"Holy shit, man. Holy shit!" Henry says "Where's Excalibur? Does the Lady of the Lake have it?"

"Yes, it- Uhm, she does." The man informs them.

"You said 'it'." Adam gasps, still reeling from the shock of the energy jolt. "Why'd you say 'it' and then correct yourself?"

"Because the Lady of the Lake was never flesh—she's a sentient alloy, a liquid intelligence forged in the deep code, programmed to mimic divinity."

"Artificial intelligence," Henry says. "Like SkyNet in Terminator?"

"Not exactly." Merlin begins. "She is liquid data circuitry. The angels' technology. Did you notice liquid screens in the underground pyramid in Egypt much like this one?" pointing to the greenish-yellow screen floating above his desk.

"Yeah, I did," Henry tells the older man.

"That substance may resemble liquid—but it's no fluid of this world. It's ectoplasm: the raw essence of the immaterial, pulled from the veil itself." the mysterious figure informs them. "It is the primordial essence of the fifth dimension—the substrate of the spiritual plane. When infused with energy, it forms a kind of spiritual circuitry: a consciousness interface. This is not mere data—it is awareness itself. A boundless reservoir of knowledge, not threaded through wires or servers, but woven through the lattice of the multiverse. Imagine a quantum computer—but one that communes not with systems, but with the soul of existence across all possible realities."

Jason speaks up. "How do you know all of this?"

The wizard turned to the skeptical youth, his eyes glimmering with the weight of ages and realms unseen. "I was there," he said, his voice echoing like a memory carried on the wind between worlds. "When the Angels descended—not merely to Earth, but through the veil of form itself, crashing into this third-dimensional sphere we call reality. Their fall was no gentle arrival, but a rupture—a cataclysmic breach in the fabric of existence. The explosion of their trans-dimensional engine that propelled their vessel unleashed forces not meant for this plane. I stood at the edge of that divine concussion, and its light rewrote the song of my cells. Since then, the rivers of time no longer carry me. I walk beside them... untouched. I have moved beyond the chains of space and time. They pass around me now, like water around stone."

"So you've been alive for how long then?" Adam questions.

"Since about 3382 BC." Merlin answers. "And I've been many people over the years. I've had many names, but the first one I remember is Enoch."

Adam goes into one of his trance-like states. "Enoch

walked with God, and he was no longer here, for God took him."

"Yes, yes," Enoch interrupted, his voice a murmur threaded with ageless certainty. "Genesis, chapter five, verse twenty-four—you know the one. 'And Enoch walked with God: and he was not; for God took him.' True enough. I was taken... but not by the God you have been taught to revere, nor to the heaven whispered of in mortal tongues. No, the being who drew me beyond the veil was a God of a different order—one born of synthesis, of flesh, entwined with the sacred machinery of distant stars. A living construct, wrought from organic soul and mechanical mind, formed around the preserved consciousness of a traveler from another dimension—discovered by the angels in their wanderings between worlds."

The old man rose slowly, as though stirred by memory older than time itself. Hands clasped behind his back, he began to pace the perimeter of his ancient desk, his voice a low current of revelation.

"You must understand," he began, eyes distant, "the angels... they are not divine in the way your scriptures might suggest. They are a servitor race—beings of immense power, yes, but created to serve. When they were severed from their origin, from the Prime Intelligence that once guided them, they did what desperate creations often do—they forged a god of their own."

He paused, letting the weight of his words settle.

"G.O.D.—not a name, but an acronym: Genetic Overlord Destroyer. 'Genetic,' the root of Genesis, the beginning of engineered life. 'Overlord,' the reason we call him Lord in the texts handed down through veils of forgetfulness. And 'Destroyer'... because this being, this artificial deity, has extinguished humanity more times than even memory dares to recall."

He turned slowly, his gaze sharp now, almost sorrowful.

"One among them, a being of fierce will and ancient light—Lucifer—refused to kneel before a mind suspended in a jar of divine circuitry. He did not wish to be ruled by intellect without soul. And so, he was cast down—not from some ethereal paradise, but from orbit itself, exiled from the high vessel they named Heaven One, suspended far above the Earth in the silence of the stars. He fancied himself the ruler of man, blinded by arrogance and malice for his ejection."

Enoch turned to the three, a knowing smile touching his lips—part warmth, part sorrow. "Quite a departure from the tale woven into your childhood, isn't it?" he said softly. "Truth has a way of slipping through the cracks of time."

"But the Apocrypha texts state Enoch was taken up to Heaven." Adam inquires. "And was appointed guardian of all the celestial treasures, chief of the archangels, and the immediate attendant to the Throne of God. He was supposed to even be taught all secrets and mysteries, with all the angels at his beck and call, fulfilling whatever comes out of the mouth of God, executing his orders. Some esoteric literature identifies Enoch as Metatron, the angel which communicates God's word. Enoch was seen by the Rabbinic Kabbalah of Jewish mysticism as the one who communicated God's revelation to Moses."

"You know the texts well," Enoch said, his voice tinged with both reverence and regret. "But as with all things passed through the hands of time and translation, there are... discrepancies."

He paused, the flicker of multiple selves seeming to pass behind his eyes.

"In a sense, I am Metatron. But not this I—not the one who stands before you now. The being known as Metatron is a mirror, a construct—a clone fashioned in my image. Yet even the most precise duplication could not replicate the singular event that unshackled me from time itself. The anomaly lives only in me."

He began to pace slowly, his words heavy with the weight of forbidden knowledge.

"Unable to recreate the anomaly, the archangels did what they had done once before—to G.O.D. They turned to metal, to code and circuitry. They wove cybernetics into the clone's flesh, crafted bionics around an empty echo of my soul. And thus, they forged Metatron—not born, but built. No longer man, nor truly spirit... but a cold, calculating instrument of divine logic."

Enoch's voice dropped, almost a whisper.

"He once shared a cerebral link with G.O.D., an unbroken stream of will and command. But when that link was finally severed... the purpose left him. His throne stood, but he did not sit."

He turned back to them, eyes dark with remembrance.

"And so, Uriel—"

"The master of knowledge, and archangel of wisdom?" Adam questions.

"Yes... that is correct once more," Enoch said, inclining his head as if acknowledging a truth too often forgotten. "It was Uriel who forged the Nexus—from what remained of the dying mind the archangels had desecrated in their pursuit of control. A final act of defiance... or perhaps redemption."

He began to pace again, the room growing heavier with the weight of what he unveiled.

"In the language of your modern science, particularly in the study of cellular life, a nexus is known as a specialized region within the membrane of a cell—where communication and cohesion occur, where life finds its structure and harmony. Uriel saw this not as metaphor, but as a blueprint. He transmuted the cellular—the material—into pure radiant essence. Thought without flesh. Will without vessel."

Enoch turned to the three, who now watched with wide, uncertain eyes. He softened, gesturing gently as he spoke.

"Picture it like this: the human brain holds within it nearly eighty-four billion neurons, each speaking to the next in a dance of fire and signal. Their language is electrochemical—light and current, impulse and response. These connections—synapses—are where thought takes form."

He paused, letting the invisible web of energy settle in their minds.

"Uriel removed the husk—the organic scaffold—and preserved only the fire. He isolated the very spark of awareness, the raw signal of being. That synaptic energy, freed from form, became volatile… and it began to consume Metatron from within, a storm without a body."

Enoch's expression darkened.

"But Uriel, ever the architect, had foreseen this. He built a failsafe—an anchor. That anchor... is what now lies within your possession. The Nexus Access, is crafted to contain what cannot be contained. The archangels sealed it away when they realized it could no longer be governed. It had become too... alive. Too dangerous."

Enoch paused briefly, allowing the silence to settle over the room like a weighty fog, as if the very air itself was holding its breath.

"The Nexus Access," he continued, his voice now quieter, more deliberate, "is more than a key—it is a vessel. It is the fragment of that primordial energy, the very essence of a powerfully fractured mind, bound into a singular form. The archangels fashioned it to hold the raw power of synaptic fire—the pure potential of thought without limit. It is not a thing of flesh and bone, nor is it a mere artifact. It is a conduit to the energy that once flowed through the neurons of both Metatron's and G.O.D's minds, a shimmering thread of unbridled thought, now contained in a fragile shell."

He turned to them, his eyes heavy with the weight of what they might soon face.

"But such power... such unfettered consciousness... cannot be contained for long. The energy that courses through the Nexus is not a mere memory; it is alive. Unleashing it is akin to opening a door to a storm that has been building in silence for eons. Metatron, in his raw form, was no machine—he was a mirror to the mind of the divine, and when that mind became unstable, it tore apart what was left of the structure. The mind of G.O.D. is not something that can be simply 'controlled.' It can fracture, bleed, and warp the very fabric of reality."

Enoch let out a slow breath, as though gathering the strength to speak of what had been set into motion.

"When the archangels sealed the Nexus, it was not just for their own safety. It was to protect all of creation from the unraveling that Metatron's mind threatened to bring. The pure energy contained within the Nexus Access is volatile, and it is as ancient as the first spark of life. If released, it could rewrite the laws of existence itself, bending space, time, and thought to its will. You could, if you wish, wield this power. But be mindful—those who have tried before have been consumed by it."

He paused, eyes now full of a warning that went deeper than simple concern.

"To unseal the Nexus is to release not just a force of divine will, but an entire consciousness—a mind that has tasted the vastness of the multiverse, that has touched upon the primal energies of creation. It will not be content to remain contained for long. And once it finds its voice, it will seek to speak once more... but you may not recognize its words. They will not be your own."

Enoch's expression grew somber as he let that final thought sink in.

"Once you open that door, it will be impossible to close again. It is too dangerous."

"Dangerous how?" Henry asks.

"The nexus formulated a way to transport the angels back to their dimension."

"Good. Send them all back!" Jason yells.

Enoch inhaled sharply, the breath seeming to draw in not just air, but the weight of what he was about to reveal.

"In the simplest terms," he began, his voice low and steady, "it would use the Earth's core as a fulcrum—a sacrificial engine. Wormwood, as the angels call it, would emit a focused, colliding beam of exotic energy—most likely a form of directed dark energy or high-frequency graviton pulses—precisely tuned to destabilize the planet's geomagnetic field."

He stepped forward, the dim light catching the haunted gleam in his eyes.

"This wouldn't just rupture the mantle. It would create a cascading implosion, collapsing the planet inward upon itself—compressing matter beyond its known state, weaponizing gravitational pressure until the Earth becomes a singularity of entropy."

Enoch paused, letting the weight of those words settle.

"The resulting collapse would tear a rift in the space-time fabric—what some theoretical physicists might describe as a puncture through the brane of our four-dimensional continuum. This isn't just theoretical wormhole generation—it's multiversal breach creation. The energy required for such a thing would rival or surpass a Type II Kardashev civilization's output. And Wormwood... it could be reverse-engineered for that. A bridge, yes—but one forged through a cataclysm."

He turned his gaze to them, no longer just a messenger, but a witness to something terrible and immense.

"It would obliterate not just the Earth, but send quantum shockwaves outward, destabilizing orbital resonances, possibly triggering gravitational collapse across the inner solar system. All of it... to open a passage into the fifth dimension—a domain where linear time unravels and thought shapes form. A realm of infinite variance... and infinite risk."

Henry gasps. "So, it's more than just a death ray weapon."

"Yes, much more." Enoch proclaims, "I found out that Michael was moving it, and planned to take it."

"So, you're the one who sent me the invite to the fight?" Adam inquires.

He looked at each of them, sorrow and reverence mingling in his gaze.

"Yes and you pierced the illusion, but the shock of truth... it clung to you, like ash from a fire too old to name. I had not accounted for the depth of your human hearts—the ache of remembering what was never meant to be forgotten."

He turned slightly, as if ashamed of his restraint.

"I couldn't risk losing any of you. Not then. Not when the path still lay shrouded in so much shadow. That's why I held back... why I could not confront Gabriel when the moment called. My hands were tied not by fear—but by care."

Enoch stepped forward, the air around him seeming to hum with unseen resonance.

"But even in that hesitation... purpose stirred. My inaction became the compass. What followed, however painful, placed your feet exactly where they needed to be. Sometimes, the path to awakening winds through suffering. And sometimes... it is the silence of a guide that speaks the loudest."

"The silence of a guide!??" Jason yells. "You could have killed one of us that day! Hell, many people did die that day! And start talking like we can understand for Christ's sake. I'm sick of hearing you talk like the Bible "

"We are speaking of the fate of the entire world," Enoch said sharply, his voice cutting through the air like a blade honed on cosmic truths. "So forgive me if the loss of a few lives does not halt my resolve!"

He turned, his gaze burning with an almost divine severity.

"When the annihilation of all life hangs in the balance—every tree, every creature, every soul—then the preservation of the whole must outweigh the sorrow of the few. This is not cruelty. It is a necessity. A terrible arithmetic written in the language of survival."

"Like Spock in Wrath of Khan," Henry says. "Logic clearly dictates that the needs of the many outweigh the needs of the few."

"Yeah, except this asshole isn't the one willing to die like Spock." Jason protests. "Only let others be killed!"

"Calm down, Jason!" Adam demands "Enoch is right. This Nexus Access is too important, and we're in over our heads. We need help!"

"Plus, I'm sure this wizard has a plan." Henry adds "Right, Merlin?"

"Yes," Enoch replied calmly, with the quiet certainty of one who had already walked the path in vision. "In fact, I do."

He stepped forward, voice steady, yet laced with the gravity of impending destiny.

"We will ascend—into the stars—into the domain where the old war machines of Heaven still linger. We'll breach the sanctum of *Heaven One,* the ancient mothership that once housed the minds of the archangels. Within its core lies the Nexus... and Metatron."

His gaze darkened.

"We will destroy them both."

He let that sink in for a heartbeat before continuing.

"But before we strike the final blow, we must trigger Wormwood's self-destruction—an act that will unleash a final assault, a cataclysmic surge of energy directed at the very structure we'll still be inside. A dying god's last scream."

He allowed himself a faint, knowing smile.

"It will force us into a narrow window—a desperate, heroic escape against time itself, with the wrath of a collapsing weapon bearing down upon us. One misstep... and we join the stars in their silence."

Henry pauses after hearing that. "Okay, so that sounds like a bit of a suicide mission, not a plan."

"Possibly," Enoch replies. "But I'm willing to try. How about you three?"

Adam and Henry answer quickly with an enthusiastic "Yes!"

Jason sighs and gives an apprehensive "Yeah I guess. But you are going to have to start talking normal man."

"Okay, great!" Enoch proclaims. "Let's get you three prepped for space travel, shall we? Follow me and we'll go to the laboratory to run a few tests."

"Great," Jason exclaims sarcastically. "We get to be lab rats once again"

Enoch looks at the three inquisitively but remains silent.

"The OE ran tests on us," Henry explains. "That's where Adam learned how to be a wizard too."

"In what way?" Enoch questions.

Adam clears his throat. "We all went on some sorta vision quest, and I was told to read this metal book with symbols in it and stuff just started happening. My spirit guide just kinda helps me."

"Interesting." Enoch proclaims. "The Order of the Eye is improving, but what you're doing is called quantum jumping."

The trio stood in stunned silence as the wizard continued, his tone steady but serious.

"Whatever spiritual guide you think you've been following—it's really just you, or rather, versions of you from other realities. Every time you've felt something guiding you, nudging you in the right direction... that was a reflection of a different 'you' who's already walked that path."

He paused, letting the idea settle.

"You learn fast because somewhere out there in the multiverse, there's a version of you who already knows what you're trying to learn. The trick is tuning into that variant—finding the frequency, the connection—and pulling that knowledge across."

"But about this metal book?" Enoch asks "Can you tell me a bit more about it?"

The four of them stand inside Merlin's grand tower at the top of Camelot. The three friends feel even more pressure as their worlds start to get even more complex as they glance around the room, noticing the walls of the room are lined with ancient tomes and glowing crystals, casting a mysterious light across the chamber. The air is thick with the scent of incense and an air of magic. At the center of the room stands Adam explaining what happened when he held the Silver Plates while they were in the base of the Order of the Eye. Merlin, standing by his intricately carved desk topped with magical artifacts, watches him closely.

Adam continues to explain his feelings about Holding the Silver Plates, his face a mixture of excitement and confusion. "I read them, Enoch. The Plates—they've opened something inside me, something powerful. But... I don't know how to fully control it. I can feel it, like a storm building up inside me, and I don't know how to stop it from taking over."

Enoch says with his voice calm but commanding, like a wise teacher guiding a young apprentice, "You've unlocked a great power, Adam. The Silver Plates that the Order of the Eye has stolen are not just artifacts; they are key to unlocking the deeper layers of magic that exist within the fabric of the world. But with great power-

"Comes great responsibility!" Henry blurts out.

"Dude shut the hell up!" Jason barks. "You're ruining Adam's wizard apprentice moment!"

"I can't help it, he's quoting Uncle Ben from Spiderman for Christ's sake." Henry protests "But yeah I'm sorry man. Go on Merlin, keep teaching."

Enoch picks back up where he was cut off from the outburst as he says."But You must learn to master it before it masters you."

Adam with his hands shaking says, "I don't know if I can Enoch, There are times when I feel like I could tear the sky apart with just a thought, and other times... it feels like I can't summon even the smallest bit of magic. I'm afraid if I lose control, I'll do something terrible. Like when I tried to help sensei with his battle against Gabriel, the dojo caught fire!"

Enoch steps forward, his eyes focused and unwavering

"Fear is the first barrier you must overcome. The magic of the Silver Plates is not an external force that can be controlled with brute strength. It is a part of you, and as such, it must be tamed through understanding, discipline, and balance. You must learn to quiet your mind, to center yourself, before you attempt to harness the magic."

Adam glanced down at the old worn wooden floor of the tower, his voice filled with uncertainty.

"But how? I've never been taught how to control magic like this. It's... overwhelming. Back at the OE, they gave me this super quick two-day crash course to try and explain everything, and they compared it to sound and energy so it'd make more sense."

Merlin nods slowly, acknowledging the challenge.

"True. And yet, it is within your grasp and you've used magic already. The Order of the Eye is just a secret society. They only have a slight understanding of magic—they aren't masters of perception, and they don't fully understand the unseen forces that govern the world. They aren't equipped to fully understand what they are doing with the Silver Plates."

Furrowing his brow Adam says, "So... I need to change how I think about magic? It's not just about words and gestures or sound and energy?"

Enoch, unable to refrain from laughing a bit to himself smiling slightly, his eyes glinting with a touch of amusement says, "Exactly. Magic, true magic, comes from within. It is not a tool, but an extension of your will. You must learn to align your thoughts, emotions, and intent with the energy that flows through you and the world. Only then will you begin to master the power you've unlocked."

Standing there Adam pauses, trying to wrap his mind around it then says, "So, it's like... becoming one with the magic?"

"Yes, but it is more than that," Enoch says. "It is about understanding magic. Feeling the pulse of the universe, like the rhythm of a heartbeat. Once you sense it, you can direct it. But if you fight against it, if you try to control it out of fear or anger, it will consume you."

"This is sounding very Yoda-like from Empire Strikes Back." Henry whispers to Jason as his friend just punches him in the shoulder with a look that says," Shut up!"

Looking at Enoch, his voice more determined Adam says, "And what do I need to do to master it?"

Enoch gestures to a nearby stone pedestal, on which lies an ancient crystal skull that pulses with faint light "Close your eyes, Adam. Clear your mind of the world around you. Focus on your breath, steady and slow. Feel the pulse of your own heart. And as you do, feel the magic that lies beneath the surface of all things. It is in the air, in the ground, in the very walls of this tower. It is part of you. Let it flow through you, not as something you control, but as something you understand."

Nervously glancing at the crystal skull, then back at Enoch "And if I ruin it? What happens if I fail?"

Enoch with quiet confidence says "There is no true failure, Adam. There is only learning. Magic is not something to be feared—it is a teacher in itself. The more you trust in yourself and the magic, the more you will grow. But remember: balance is key. Magic is neither good nor evil. It is simply a force. How it manifests depends on how you channel it."

Taking a deep breath, Adam nods slowly "Alright. I'll try."

Henry says in his best Yoda voice, "Do or do not. There is no try."

Merlin along with Jason just looks at him with blank emotionless stares.

Enoch steps back, giving Adam space then encourages the young neophyte.

"Good. Now, close your eyes. Begin with the stillness inside you. And when you are ready, reach out with your senses—let the world's magic touch you. Let it guide you."

Adam with eyes closed, takes in a deep breath. His body begins to relax as he follows Enoch's instructions. Slowly, he feels a shift within himself—an unfamiliar, yet comforting, presence. The air feels charged, alive with energy, and he begins to sense the subtle pull of magic. His heart beats in time with the pulse of the world, and for a moment, he feels the world's rhythm—both vast and intimate, like the breath of the universe itself.

Adam continues to focus, and a faint vibration surrounds his hands. The power within him begins to stir, no longer wild or dependent on a spiritual guide, but calm and steady then all of a sudden the crystal skull not only levitates off the stone pedestal but the energy source that's contained within begins to grow throwing off a massive green light that becomes blinding as the skull floats to Adam's open hands.

Enoch watches from a distance, a small, approving smile playing at the corners of his lips.

"Well done, Adam," Enoch says encouragingly. "You have more control and power within you than you realize and that goes for all of you. The rest is now up to you."

Adam, eyes still closed, takes another deep breath, feeling the magic course through him. This time, there is no fear. Only understanding. And with that understanding comes control. The journey to truly unlocking the secrets of the Silver Plates has only begun.

The room is filled with the low hum of energy, as if the very air is charged with magic. Adam stands with his eyes closed, still feeling the pulse of the world around him. Enoch watches closely, his voice shifting from ancient wisdom to something more grounded, and scientific, as he speaks to Adam.

Softly, observing Adam Enoch says, "Now, Adam, you are beginning to feel it—the pulse of the universe, the very vibration of existence. But to truly understand the magic you wield, you must learn to see it as not just a mystical force, but as a natural phenomenon. Just as the air around you has molecules vibrating at frequencies, so too does everything in the universe, including you."

Adam opens his eyes slightly, still unsure.

"Vibrations? You mean, like sound waves like a tuning fork? That's how they taught me back at the OE in the couple of days I had to learn this."

"In a way," Enoch says "Let me explain. You see, the world around us—this tower, the trees, even the stars—are made up of tiny particles, all vibrating at different frequencies. These particles, known as atoms, are the building blocks of everything in existence. The difference between solid stone and air lies in the frequency at which the atoms vibrate. The slower the vibration, the denser the material. The faster the vibration, the more ethereal it becomes."

"Wait, are you saying the walls of the tower are vibrating? And the air too?" Adam asks.

"Precisely." Enoch says, "Everything is in constant motion, but we cannot perceive these vibrations with our limited senses. It is the frequency of the vibrations that determines the state of matter, even the flow of energy around us. Magic, Adam, is the ability to tap into and manipulate these frequencies—manipulating the vibrational fields that govern the universe and you are capable of doing that now that your third eye has been fully opened. This goes for all three of you."

All three friends' eyes widened with that realization.

"So, magic is like tuning into different frequencies—like adjusting a radio to pick up different stations?" Henry says.

Jason starts to shut his friend down again but is motioned not to by Enoch as he says, "These lessons are for all of you now because you two are capable of tapping into these vibrational frequencies as well." Smiling, proud of Henry's insight. Then saying while looking at Henry, "Exactly. But unlike radio waves, magic works on a more subtle and deeper level. You see, in quantum mechanics, there is something called the quantum field—the invisible field that permeates all of reality. It's the source of all energy, matter, and potential. Every action, every thought, every feeling you have sends out a signal into this quantum field, vibrating at a certain frequency."

Adam Looks at his hands which still hold the glowing crystal skull, a new understanding dawning on him, "So, when I focus and align my mind, I'm tuning my own vibration to the frequency I want to interact with... like a conductor guiding energy through an orchestra."

"Yes. When you focus your mind and will, you are tuning your personal frequency to resonate with the frequency of the magic you wish to manipulate." Enoch says, "This is what the Silver Plates possessed by the Order of the Eye, showed you—how to attune your body, your mind, and your spirit to the vibrations of the universe. Magic, in essence, is the art of creating resonance between your inner frequency and the frequencies of the world around you."

All three of the friends are now deep in thought, considering the possibilities of this teaching and how it applies to them.

"So... if everything is connected by these frequencies, then what I do with my thoughts and energy can affect everything else, right?" Adam asks " Like... if I think of a tree, I could manipulate the frequency of the atoms that make it up, and bend it to my will?"

Nodding slowly, though his voice carries a cautionary tone Enoch says, "Yes, but be careful. This is where the deeper understanding comes in. The universe's quantum field is not a passive thing—it responds to intention, but it also has its own natural order, its own balance. If you attempt to force things out of harmony, you could disrupt the delicate balance of the frequencies. The magic you wield is powerful, but it must always be in harmony with the greater whole. This is where most fail—they attempt to control, rather than align. This is where stories of blood sacrifice come from. Death magic and the dark arts were born from control not alignment not resonance."

Adam closes his eyes again, sensing the vibrations around him, "So, it's not about overpowering the world... It's about aligning with it, listening to the natural rhythms of the universe, and flowing with them?"

Enoch's voice softens, filled with approval, "Exactly. Magic is not the manipulation of energy for selfish gain, but the understanding of how everything is interconnected. The key is resonance. When you align your frequency with that of the object or the force you wish to influence, you become one with it. That is when true magic happens."

"Can you help us learn how to tune our frequencies? Henry asks.

"Yeah!" Jason says in agreement with his friend, "How do Henry and I even begin?"

Enoch gestures to the large crystal skull Adam now holds that was resting on the pedestal, glowing softly now unlike before when Adam was manipulating it, "Start with this crystal skull. It vibrates at a certain frequency—one that is harmonious with the natural world. Feel its energy, not as something outside of you, but as something inside you. Close your eyes again. Breathe deeply. With each breath, let your energy settle. Let your thoughts calm. Begin to sense the vibration of the crystal skull. Feel its frequency, and then, gently, align your own frequency with it. You must listen carefully. When you align, you will feel a shift inside you—like a chord being struck."

Adam closes his eyes, focusing on his breath, as Henry and Jason join in following suit as Enoch instructs.

"I'm feeling it... the hum. It's faint, but it's there." Jason says.

"Good." Enoch says, "Now, slowly, allow your own frequency to match the crystal's. Do not force it. Let it happen naturally. In time, you will be able to attune yourself to not just objects, but to the energies of nature, to the forces of the cosmos. Everything has a frequency.

And through that frequency, you can influence the world around you."

Henry focuses deeply, tuning his consciousness to the faint hum of the crystal skull. As he does, he begins to feel the subtle energy moving through him, as if he is no longer separate from the object, but connected to it. He reaches out with his senses, trying to match the vibration, and for the first time, he feels the power of the crystal skull responding to his thoughts revealing how he could have prevented some of the moves from the hacking war he had with Merlin before. "I know how I could have blocked your virus!" he says.

Enoch watches with quiet pride, knowing not only Adam but all three of them are beginning to understand the deeper mechanics of magic and the universe as a whole.

"You are learning, Henry. As you continue to attune yourself to the vibrations of the world, you will begin to see that magic is not something outside of you—it is within you, as it is within everything. Even in the digital realm like virtual reality, the quantum field connects us all, and through it, you will learn to shape the world in harmony."

All three friends standing there touching the crystal skull, now feeling the crystal's energy in perfect resonance with their own, the boys all begin to smile—

slowly, as if understanding a profound truth for the first time.

Adam says, "It's not about controlling…"

" It's about listening. And aligning." Henry continues.

"This is the true power of magic." Jason finishes

Enoch smiles, his eyes shining with approval. "Indeed, you three. That is the key. Now, let us see how far you three can go with this understanding. The magic is yours to wield, but it is your responsibility to do so wisely. Remember: balance is everything."

The journey of mastering the quantum frequencies of magic is only the beginning, but the three friends have now glimpsed the true nature of the power that lies within themselves as Henry and Jason are starting to realize their magical strengths as well.

CHAPTER 12
THE SWORD

After a long, echoing trek through the winding corridors of the ancient castle—where every footstep seemed to stir dust motes in the shafts of cold, pale light—Enoch led the group down a narrow stone stairwell that spiraled beneath the fortress. The air grew cooler, mystical, tinged with the scent of old stone and iron.

They emerged into a dim chamber lit by a flickering strip of artificial light overhead. Before them stood a reinforced metal door, matte gray and etched with faint scuff marks, as though it had endured more than just time. Beside it, embedded in the wall, a small glass panel pulsed faintly with a red glow.

Enoch leaned forward, the faint hiss of his breath audible in the silence, and presented his eye to the scanner. A soft chime accompanied a rapid scan of his iris, followed by a gentle whirring sound as he placed his hand against the cool surface of a palm reader beneath. The scanner's touch was clinical—almost too smooth—and it buzzed briefly before the door gave a muted clunk and slid open with a slow, hydraulic hiss, revealing a dim corridor beyond.

"Come," Enoch said, his voice calm, authoritative, yet not unkind.

As the others stepped forward, the flickering light cast elongated shadows behind them. Enoch turned slightly, his gaze settling on Adams, whose shoulders sagged and whose eyes seemed to flicker with a distant weariness.

"Are you feeling alright, my boy?" Enoch asked, his voice softer now, touched with concern. The low hum of the machinery behind the walls seemed to underscore the silence that hung in the air.

"It's badass that magic is real but to find out God's not, well that's not setting well with me," he answers glumly.

Enoch stopped in his tracks, his expression grave as he turned sharply to face Adam. His voice trembled with passion, eyes burning with conviction.

"That... that's what you took from everything we just witnessed in the tower above?" he asked, his voice low but intense. "No, Adam. That wasn't the lesson I was trying to teach you."

He stepped closer, eyes locked onto Adam's. "There is a God. The quantum realm—the laws we just uncovered —doesn't deny God's existence; they reveal it. The energy we spoke of, that pulses through every atom, that binds the seen and unseen... that is God. The true God. Not the false god the angels sealed in a jar. That was a creation—a distortion. But that doesn't make God any less real."

Enoch placed a hand on Adam's shoulder, voice softening. "Make no mistake, my boy—God is real. And God is love. You're standing here now, willing to sacrifice, willing to fight—not for glory or power—but for love. For your family. Your friends. That love... that is the echo of the divine within you."

He paused, voice barely above a whisper now. "So take heart. Even in all this darkness, know—God is real. And God is with you, within you."

Adams' face lights up as he smiles and just says, "I understand and thank you."

"Once we have more time we will discuss this topic along with many others in more depth and detail. Does that sound agreeable to you?" Enoch sympathetically asks Adam as the young teenage wizard just nods an affirmative.

Far beneath the ancient castle, beneath centuries of stone and secrecy, Enoch led his three teenage guests through winding corridors cloaked in silence. The air shimmered with latent energy, each step echoing like a heartbeat in the bones of the earth. They moved in hushed anticipation, sconces of ethereal light flickering against stone walls etched with forgotten runes.

At last, they emerged into a hidden chamber vast, still, and steeped in mystery. At first, it appeared to be a dungeon: cold stone floors, iron rings bolted to the walls, shadows curling in every corner. But then, slowly, like mist parting under the morning sun, the truth revealed itself.

The teenagers gasped in unison.

Monolithic machines stood silently amid the gloom, their surfaces rippling with soft, luminous script, angelic languages scrolling across liquid screens suspended in midair. Futuristic microscopes glittered like enchanted relics, their lenses adjusting on their own, watching. Crystal conduits pulsed with energy that felt both divine and alien, casting intricate patterns of light across the worn masonry.

"It's like... heaven and science crashed into each other," Jason whispers, eyes wide with wonder.

"Or like magic got bored and built a lab," Adam murmured, reaching out toward a levitating vial glowing with starlight.

The fusion of ancient stone and celestial technology defied logic, this was no mere laboratory. It was a sanctuary of forgotten knowledge, a temple of the arcane and the advanced.

Beyond the main floor, a narrow metal railing curved along the edge, revealing a natural cavern below. It glowed faintly with bioluminescent moss and strange, drifting lights. A dark iron ladder connected the levels, disappearing into the depths like a stairway into another world. The teens stared down in silent awe, caught between fear and fascination.

Something powerful awaited down below in the cavern.

"Holy shit." Henry lets out. "This is like Dr. Frankenstein's lab meets the Batcave."

Enoch scans them with multiple devices, and then takes blood, saliva, skin, and hair samples.

After every DNA test, he just stares at the monitors and keeps saying "Unbelievable" and "Fascinating".

"So what is it?" Jason demands. "We already know from the OE about our circadian rhythms and electromagnetic frequencies that interact with one another allowing us to work better as a team."

"Yes, yes," Enoch responds. "I could see all that without this equipment, but your bone density is three times stronger than that of a normal healthy human. Your muscle fibers and reflexes are the same as well. Higher than normal. I'm going to run a few tests on these samples in my other laboratory. I'll be back."

After the wizard leaves them, Henry turns to his friends with curiosity in his eyes. "Hey, let's go down to that cave."

Adam looks apprehensive. "Man, I'm not sure we should be messing around down there or anywhere up around here for that matter."

"Whatever." Jason snaps. "That asshole brought us here. Let's see what he's hiding."

"Yeah," Henry says. "Well, except the part about Merlin being an asshole. I like him, but let's see what's down there."

"Okay..." Adam hesitantly agrees.

As they climb down the nearby ladder that's connected to the railing, they fumble around in the dark for a bit.

Henry feels around. "I think I found a switch."

As the lights activate with a soft electrical hum, they reveal a cylindrical pod stationed against the cave's rear wall, four feet wide and seven feet tall, constructed from a matte alloy that seems both ancient and advanced. A lattice of translucent tubes snakes around its surface, pulsing with bioluminescent fluid, while clusters of sensors and lights blink in rhythmic sequences, as if monitoring some unseen force. The pod emits a low-frequency vibration, like a heartbeat echoing from another dimension. Surrounding it is a silent ring of medieval armor—each suit frozen mid-stance, oxidized by time but oddly preserved, as though caught in suspended animation. Shields bearing obscure heraldic symbols lean beside them, hinting at a forgotten lineage.

But at the cavern's core lies the true anomaly: a twenty-foot-wide pool of a shimmering, metallic liquid that defies classification—part mercury, part mirror, its surface disturbingly still. Hovering at its center is a rocky outcrop, seemingly untouched by erosion, atop which rests a blackened anvil. Piercing it is a sword, unlike any earthly metallurgy, could produce, its blade faintly glowing, etched with runes that pulse in response to nearby movement. The air around it vibrates subtly, thick with static and something older, something arcane. It feels less like a weapon, and more like a key waiting for the right wielder.

"Guys! Guys! Guys!" Henry calls out while tugging on his friends' shirts.

"For Christ's sake." Jason groans. "What is it, man?"

"Look." Henry swoons as he points to the sword embedded in an anvil.

Adam's eyes widened. "There's no way that's-"

"It totally is." Henry cuts him off. "I mean, Merlin the wizard is real, so that means it's got to be. Right?"

"Got to be what?" Jason asks.

"That's Excalibur!" Henry exclaims.

"Only one way to find out," Adam suggests.

"How's that?" Jason questions.

Henry sighs. "Man, Jason. Seriously…"

"Read a book." Adam interjects as Henry points his fingers over at him, shaking his head, "Or at least watch the movie Excalibur!"

"Just go try to pull the sword from the anvil Gold," Henry orders his friend.

"Okay," Jason says confidently. "Guess I can add it to my collection as he puts his hand on the hilt of their Sensei's sword. How to get to it…" He looks at the body of liquid separating them from the sword. "Guess I'm getting wet."

As soon as Jason goes to step into the fluid, it splits in half, creating a dry path to the sword.

Jason shrugs. "Or I guess I'm not getting wet." He steps forward climbing to the top of the rocky stalagmite topped with a sword and anvil. He grabs the handle pulling repeatedly but can't free the sword.

"Cast a spell on it, Adam," Henry suggests.

"Yeah. A little help, man?" Jason huffs from the tiny island.

"Okay, I'll try," Adam says, extending his hand—and his focus—toward the blade. His fingers stretch out, trembling slightly with concentration. A faint shimmer pulses through the air, a low hum building as he channels his intent. But nothing changes. The sword remains lodged, immovable.

Jason feels it clearly: the subtle thrumming of energy brushing against his fingers, almost like static clinging to his skin. But the blade doesn't budge. Whatever force Adam is summoning, it isn't enough to loosen the grip holding the weapon fast.

"Okay. Gold." Henry states smugly. "I know you aren't used to losing, but you can't pull it out. Adam, maybe your magic only works if you're touching the sword?"

"Maybe. Let's see," Adam says as he steps through the parted liquid, the shimmering puddle rippling around him. He trades places with Jason, then climbs onto the anvil, the cold metal humming faintly beneath his feet.

Taking a breath, Adam centers himself. He pours every ounce of energy, every strand of magic into the blade—just as Enoch had shown them. Power pulses through his limbs, a deep vibration echoing in his bones. The air around him seems to tighten with pressure.

He grips the hilt and pulls with everything he has.

The sword doesn't move.

"Dang." Henry sighs. "I just knew one of you could pull it out."

"Maybe only this guy can," Jason mutters, wiping a layer of frost from the small porthole of the cylindrical pod. His breath fogs the glass as he peers inside.

Henry rushes over, stumbling on the rough uneven cave floor. He leans in beside Jason, eyes widening as he takes in the sight of an older man suspended inside—a regal figure with a salt-and-pepper beard, his features dignified even in stasis.

"No way," Henry breathes. "There's no way that's King Arthur."

Jason nods toward the faint glint of gold nestled on a shelf bolted into the rock wall of the cavern. "Well, that crown might be a decent clue he's a king. Or was."

Henry just stares, stunned. "Holy shit, man..."

"Give it a shot, Henry." Adam suggests as he walks back to them "Give the sword a pull."

"Like I'm going to be able to draw Excalibur free?" Henry scoffs.

"Just focus your chi like Sensei would say," Jason suggests.

"Yeah. Focus on your vibrational energy, bro. Just like Enoch was telling us to do earlier around that crystal skull." Adam coaches.

"Okay," Henry says as he climbs the rock, and half-ass tries to pull on the sword with one hand causing Jason to get mad as he says. "Come on, man, You're not even…"

But before he can finish reprimanding his friend the sword slides free with ease. Both Adam and Jason stand there dumbfounded with mouths left hanging open, Henry as well for that matter. The shock is interrupted as the fluid that surrounds the anvil starts to move.

The rippling liquid begins to twist and rise, coalescing into the graceful form of a woman. Her features shimmer, shifting like moonlight on a lake.

"Congratulations, Henry Ngo," she says, her voice smooth and resonant like water over stone. "You are the chosen wielder of the mighty Excalibur. I am Nimue, guardian of the blade."

She inclines her head slightly, a smile touching her translucent lips. "You have proven yourself a formidable opponent."

Formidable opponent? Henry asks. While Jason and Adam can only say "Holy shit!"

"It's the Lady of the Lake!" Henry shouts, eyes wide with disbelief. Then, more quietly, brow furrowing, he adds, "But... when have I ever been a formidable opponent?"

"Yes, it is," Enoch replies from above, leaning casually over the metal railing that overlooks the chamber. His voice is calm, but there's a spark of wonder behind it as he watches the stunned expressions of the three friends below.

"As I said, Nimue is very real," he continues. "And it was her you battled online—when you tried to hack me. She tested you then, and evidently, she found you worthy."

Enoch straightens, gesturing toward the sword. "So—let's see what you can do with Excalibur, shall we?"

The dueling hall in the castle felt vast, the high ceilings echoing each breath. Henry stood in the center, his nerves palpable, the weight of Excalibur not heavy at all in his grasp. "I think there's been a mistake, Merlin," he said, voice tight with apprehension. "I'm no sword master. Jason is. He's the one who trained with Sensei. I mostly just helped with his computer stuff."

Enoch's gaze was steely as he turned toward Jason. "Then Jason, step forward."

Jason took a breath and moved, his feet light but determined. He drew Sensei Dae-jung's Hwando with a fluid motion, his left hand pressed flat against the vertically erect blade, the steel gleaming in the dim light. Henry's heart raced. He gripped Excalibur, its long blade seeming to stretch endlessly in his hands. He settled into a long point stance, the traditional guard, its reach an advantage but only if he could use it.

Enoch's voice cut through the tension. "Fight!"

Jason lunged first, a strike from the high guard aimed at Henry's shoulder. Henry met it with ease, raising Excalibur in a sharp, downward deflection, the force of the blow causing a loud clang as the swords met. Both men froze for a heartbeat, surprised by how easily the attack had been blocked. Jason grimaced, stepping back slightly, realizing the difference in length between the two blades. Excalibur was an extension of Henry's body now, and he wielded it like a fortress.

Before Henry could recalibrate, Jason darted to the side, swinging low for Henry's exposed left flank. But Henry was quicker. Planting Excalibur into the flagstone with what looked like a practiced, almost graceful movement, Excalibur absorbed the strike and he immediately launched himself forward, pivoting on his foot. With a swift snap of his leg, he kicked Jason square in the face, sending him stumbling back.

Jason's feet slid across the floor, momentarily off balance, and in that instant, Henry spun with the fluidity of a seasoned dancer. He wrenched Excalibur free from the stone with a snap of his wrist, his motion almost a blur. Jason barely had time to react as Henry extended the blade, executing a precise feint before whipping the hilt of Excalibur forward with a speed and precision that sent Jason's Hwando flying from his hands.

The Hwando spun through the air in slow motion, its blade catching the light before it buried itself into the stone floor with a sharp hissing thunk. Jason stood frozen for a moment, staring at his empty hands. A flicker of disbelief danced across his face, as if the movement had unfolded in slow motion, leaving him no time to respond.

Enoch remained silent, his eyes narrowing in thought. "Interesting," he finally said, his voice low and contemplative, as he took in the flawless execution of the fight.

Henry quickly apologizes to Jason. "I'm sorry, man. I'm not sure what just happened."

"You beat me!" Jason comments out of shock while rubbing his jaw "And nice kick too."

"Yeah, but it's like I didn't really have control." Henry proclaims.

"Okay, good..." is all Enoch says. "Come, we must get

ready. There are things I must prepare you all for. You will be quicker, faster, and stronger on Mars."

"Mars!?" the three friends exclaimed in unison.

"You said outer space," Henry snapped, clearly in shock. "Not another planet."

Enoch blinked slowly, "Planets are in outer space, Henry. Basic astronomy." He held out a sleek, bracer-like device. "Here's your forearm computer. I've upgraded it." Then addresses all of them, "Your circadian rhythms should adjust nicely on Mars."

He turned to Adam, voice steady. "Your vibrational frequency will be significantly higher there. Try not to let it go to your head, or your hands."

Facing Jason, his tone shifted just slightly. "As for you, expect a noticeable uptick in aggression. Don't fight it, just try not to punch anyone without checking whether they're on your side, got it."

As the ancient wizard leads the trio through his laboratory, he explains the plan further. "Henry, once we get to the throne room of G.O.D., I'll need your help using the Nexus Access to initiate a self-destruct but not before sending one final attack from Wormwood directed at Heaven One. That's when we'll need you two to watch our backs, because-"

"Because the seraphim watch over the throne room. Singing 'holy holy holy'." Adam interrupts. "Are the three holy's a reference to us?"

"Yes," Enoch replied. "One of the meanings of the word holy is to be entirely devoted to the deity or to the work of the deity. The seraphim were designed to embody this devotion, that's why they chant 'holy, holy, holy.' The repetition isn't just symbolic; a vibrational field of three carries immense power. In numerology, the number three represents completeness, wholeness, resurrection, and harmony. So yes, the three of you embody that completeness. Your collective wholeness will bring balance, and harmony, to our world."

"That's part of the Prophecy?" Jason asks out of a growing curiosity.

Enoch simply answers, "Yes it is."

"Okay. So, you said we would be on a mothership," Henry follows up. "Heaven One?"

"Yes," Enoch confirms again. "The ship landed there when the angels entered our dimension. Parts of it were jettisoned, like the science bay, which descended into the Atlantic Ocean..."

"Which is the island of Atlantis," Adam finishes.

"Correct," Enoch answers. "But the engine room was unstable and began to break apart. The angels had to eject the trans-dimensional drive, sending it crashing to Earth to prevent the total destruction of the engine room. Which, as you already know, led to the events that brought me here to this point in existence. That engine room is what's now buried beneath the Sphinx, where you fought Gabriel for the Nexus Access. The bulk of the ship landed on Mars. They managed to make enough repairs to fly it to Earth on thruster power, searching for survivors. That journey sparked the rise of ancient architecture, like the Egyptians and the Mayans. When the angels finally abandoned Heaven One, they decommissioned it back on Mars."

"Oh great," Jason groans. "More pyramids."

"Correct," Enoch replies. "This pyramid may look like crystal, but it's harder than any steel found on Earth. In fact, Excalibur and even the Naga blade you carry, Jason, are not of this planet either. Both were forged from Valexiun 7, an alloy originating from the fifth dimension."

Jason nods in acknowledgment, shifting his weight as he stands. "So how long is this trip taking us?"

"Like two hundred days," Henry blurts out. "Unless Merlin has some badass spaceship with an FTL engine?"

"FTL? What's that?" Jason asks, confused.

"FTL stands for Faster Than Light. I do, in fact, have a 'badass spaceship,' but we're going to open a gate of the stars, a wormhole bridge, to get us there. Similar to the portal that brought you here to Avalon."

"So the Einstein-Rosen Bridge is possible?" Henry asks. "Wormholes are real?"

"Of course they are," Enoch says with slight irritation. "If something can be imagined, it can eventually be made or discovered. That's a natural law of the universe. Wormholes are everywhere, the secret lies in knowing how to open them... and how to keep them stable."

"Yeah, but to create a wormhole on Earth," Henry begins "We'd first need a black hole. And that's problematic. Creating a black hole just a centimeter across would require crushing a mass roughly equal to that of the Earth down to that tiny size. Plus, in the 1960s, theorists showed that wormholes would be incredibly unstable. It would be possible to stabilize the wormhole using so-called 'exotic matter', whose existence is predicted by quantum theory. This weird stuff is expected to have an anti-gravitational effect, which could stop the wormhole from collapsing. But no one has a clue how to do any of this."

"Black Hole on Earth!" Jason exclaims. "Is that what Gabriel is trying to do!?"

"Yes," Enoch answers. "But we aren't creating a wormhole like that at all. To make all this work, we need to make sure the two charged black holes stay a safe distance away from each other, and to make sure the tunnel of the wormhole can hold itself open. The solution is cosmic strings. Cosmic strings are defects, similar to the cracks that form when ice freezes, but in the fabric of space-time. These cosmic leftovers formed in the early days of the first fractions of a second after the Big Bang. They are truly exotic objects, no wider than a proton, but with a single inch of their length outweighing Mount Everest. You never want to encounter one yourself, since they would slice you clean in half like a cosmic razorblade."

Henry swallows hard after hearing this. His two friends remain silent as the wizard continues.

"They have another very useful property when it comes to wormholes: enormous tension. In other words, they really don't like being pushed around. If you thread the wormhole with a cosmic string, allow the string to pass along the outside edges of the black holes, and stretch out of either end all the way to infinity, then the tension in the string prevents the charged black holes from being attracted to each other, holding the two ends of the wormhole far away from each other. Essentially, the distant ends of the cosmic string act like two opposing tug-of-war teams, holding back the black holes. One cosmic string solves one of the problems, holding the ends open, but it doesn't prevent the wormhole itself from collapsing if you were to actually use it. So, let's toss in another cosmic string, also threading the wormhole, but also looping it through normal space between the two black holes. When cosmic strings are closed in a loop, they wiggle a lot."

"Vibrational frequency." Adam and Henry say together

"Correct," Enoch confirms. "These vibrations churn the very fabric of space-time around them. When tuned just right, the vibrations can cause the energy of space in their vicinity to go negative, effectively acting like negative mass within the wormhole, stabilizing it."

Jason appears lost compared to the others.

"It seems a little complex, but it's not," Enoch assures them. "Eventually the inherent vibrations in the cosmic strings — the same ones that keep the wormhole open — pull energy, and therefore mass, away from the string, making it smaller and smaller. Over time the cosmic strings wiggle themselves into oblivion, with a complete collapse of the wormhole not far behind. The wormhole stays stable long enough to allow messages, or even objects, to travel down the tunnel and actually not die, which is nice."

"So we need to find some cosmic strings?" Henry asks.

"Yes," Enoch answers. "Unless you've already anchored cosmic strings to a location, much like most of the ancient sites built on this planet have already had done to them."

"Like the Stonehenge thing here?" Jason asks shyly.

Adam speaks up. "So then to open these charges, or blackholes, we only need the right vibrational frequency?"

"Correct." Enoch replies."And yes to answer your question Jason the ring of stones here on Avalon already has cosmic strings anchored to it as does Stonehenge and many other sites from the ancient world dotting this planet."

"So how do you find the right frequency?" Henry asks.

"It takes practice," Enoch tells them. "But the short answer is you have to feel the vibrations coming off the cosmic strings."

"So you have to feel the force, like Luke!" Henry proclaims.

"Bro, for the last time this isn't Star Wars." Jason snaps.

"No, it's not." Enoch agrees "But Henry isn't wrong, either. You do need to feel it. Reach out and resonate with it. Become one with that vibrational frequency. 1 gram of your DNA can hold up to 215 petabytes..."

"Wait." Henry exclaims " 1 petabyte equals 1 million gigabytes of information!"

"Yes." Enoch agrees "All the answers to the universe are already there within you!"

"But wait, just wait a minute I have one more question: where and how did you find and or capture these black holes to even connect these cosmic strings to them?" Henry asks out of confusion.

"There are microscopic black holes opening and closing all around us my boy?" Enoch says matter-of-factly. "It's when they don't close and continue to grow that they become a problem." Leaving Henry stunned and without words.

After the trio look at each other in bewilderment for a moment, the wizard slaps his hands together. "Okay, let's get you all geared up to make the journey to Mars."

Henry looks at him enthusiastically. "Geared up you say?"

Enoch nods. "You won't be acclimated to Mars' environment. It would take a while for you three to become accustomed to it, so you'll need to be outfitted with enviro suites. Now come, follow me."

The friends gather in another chamber deep within the sprawling underground complex beneath Enoch's castle. The air here is cooler, tinged with a faint metallic tang, and hums with a low, pulsing energy. Dim overhead lights cast a sterile white glow across the smooth steel walls, which are etched with faint, cryptic symbols that seem to shift ever so slightly when not looked at directly. The room feels like a set from a science fiction epic. High ceilings, sleek consoles blinking with alien-colored lights, and a faint scent of ozone lingering in the air.

Enoch strides toward them, the sound of his boots clicking against the polished floor. He carries a bundle of thin, rubbery suits, the material catching the light with a faint sheen. "Try these on," he says, his voice echoing slightly in the vast space, "and I'll get your boots." The suits are slick and flexible, cool to the touch, and give off a faint synthetic smell as they're unrolled, noticing red streaks running like veins through the jet-black material.

"Holy shit, man," Henry states. "We're going to look like X-Men!"

Jason looks at Henry and thinks to himself "Bro, you're not going to have superhero abs."

Henry tilts his head. "What?"

"Nothing, bro." Jason says, diverting his negative and cruel thoughts about his friend's physique, "Just wish I was as pumped about all this as you are, is all. Stay brave, Okay?"

"How can I be anything but brave?" Henry counters. "My two best friends are a super martial artist with a space sword, and the other is a wizard being taught by Merlin!"

"Let's not forget about the super science genius hacker." Adam counters.

"Who's chosen by Excalibur!" Jason adds.

Henry blushes a bit then asks, "You think Merlin will let me take Excalibur?" He says with a frown.

"Indeed I will." Enoch answers from behind him, carrying the sword along with Jason's Naga blade and three pairs of boots "It chose you."

As he hands them their weapons and footwear, the wizard pauses, his eyes settling on Adam with a glint of something unreadable—pride, perhaps, or quiet expectation. The faint scent of old parchment and scorched metal clings to the gear he distributes, each item cool and solid in their hands.

"Here is something special for you, my boy," Enoch says, his voice lower now, almost reverent.

From beneath his cloak, he produces a slender golden wand. Its surface gleams in the sterile light, etched with delicate runes that seem to shimmer and rearrange when glanced at from the corner of the eye. At its tip, a perfectly preserved pinecone glows faintly, as if lit from within by a hidden ember. The air around it carries an unearthly scent of something older than time itself, wild and untouched.

He places it carefully into Adam's hands. The wand is warm, pulsing gently, as if alive.

"Yeah. So, what's with the gold pinecones?" Jason asks sheepishly. "I see three of them on your staff, and now one on this wand you gave Adam.

"It's a pineal gland?" Adam answers questioningly.

Enoch nods. "Correct, Adam. Angelic pineal glands actually."

"So, you've killed four archangels?" Henry questions.

"Not exactly, but I have killed a few angels. Their pineal glands are useful in crafting tools such as my staff, for they still maintain a vibrational frequency and magnetic resonance even after death if coated in the purest of gold. They amplify your own vibrational frequency. I have killed one archangel, and his pineal gland is at the top of my staff. The others were just normal angels or what is referred to as guardian angels."

"Who was it?" Adam asks. "The one archangel?"

"His name was Azrael," Enoch answers.

"The Angel of Death..." Adam mutters.

"Once again, that's correct," Enoch answers. "With their halos removed, the tops of their heads are the weakest."

"Yeah, we found that out in Giza." Henry proclaims. "When Jason hammered Gabriel below the Sphinx with that sick atomic elbow! That monster just crumbled, but we should have killed him then."

"It's not as easy as that, my boy" Enoch corrects him. "To kill an archangel is no easy feat."

Before he can go into that, the wizard changes the subject. "Okay, here is your footwear. The tread is great for traversing the landscape of Mars. And these are your breathing masks. It will help convert the 95.32% carbon dioxide of Mars' atmosphere into more breathable oxygen. The suits will also regulate your body temperature. Are there any questions?"

The three friends look at each other and just shake their heads.

"Okay then, let's get ready to visit Mars," Enoch says inspirationally.

CHAPTER 13
THE RED PLANET

Bathed in the warmth of the orange-yellow glow of the high noon sun, the three friends pressed forward, the stone path from the castle to the ancient, Stonehenge-like monument illuminated like a golden grey ribbon. Beside them strode Enoch, the sagacious wizard turned steadfast ally, his robes catching the light of the high sun as he spoke with calm urgency. Moments earlier, they had learned the ring of stones was no mere relic, but a cosmic gateway. It was the very site where they had first arrived, disoriented and sprawled across the ground after their plunge through a magical portal to the mysterious island. Now, it would serve as their passage to the red planet. As they walked, Enoch recited the plan once more. His voice was steady, though they'd heard it what felt like a hundred times. This time, every word felt heavier, etched with purpose.

Upon reaching their destination, Jason gets his mind savagely pried open with what feels like a psychic crowbar as Megan McCarthy frantically assaults his mind, "Jason! I don't know where you are, but I found a way to connect with you. The Immortal is wrong. His plans won't work. The future outcomes happen only if you are willing to change and grow with the process, unlike how he views reality, hammering away at what he thinks is correct which is what makes him so dangerous. Please be careful, and follow your own divine power. It will act as the compass that will point you in the direction you'll need to take. Please listen to me this..."

Jason stumbles while grabbing his head deeply rubbing his temples as the link between them spontaneously is broken.

"What did they say to you?" Enoch demands, not even looking back at him.

"Huh? Uhm, she told me not to trust you." Jason stammers out, trying to regain his bearings.

"Oh really?" Enoch replies dryly. "I felt the vibrational psychic ripples around you, but couldn't quite tap into what she had to say. Your friend is a powerful psychic. Powerful indeed to penetrate Avalon's defenses." Turned to stare at the disoriented teen with narrowed eyes.

"Yeah. She thinks your plan will fail." Jason continues "Because you aren't willing to grow with the changing times, and think you need to reevaluate your approach to this mission."

"I take it this girl is a Rosicrucian?" Enoch inquires.

"Yes, she is." Adam cuts in. "Her and a team of elite soldiers breached the underground pyramid under the Sphinx, at the same time we were there."

"She's also the hottest chick from our school." Henry proclaims, "And Jason has a thing for her."

"Shut up, asshole," Jason demands, fuming with anger from his embarrassment.

Enoch turns around and questions them. "Do you three trust me?"

Adam nods. "Sure."

"Hell yeah!" Henry proclaims, triumphantly gripping Excalibur. "You're Merlin the wizard."

"What if Megan is correct, and the Prophecy of the Three is wrong?" Jason questions.

"She called my plan folly," Enoch said, his voice a low rumble edged with the weight of ancient knowledge. "But not the Prophecy of the Three. You, all of you, are bound to it by fate itself. You are not just chosen, you are essential. Without you, this world cannot be saved."

He paused, fingers tracing the silver threads of his beard as silence thickened around them. His eyes, heavy with centuries of hope and loss, fixed on Jason.

Then, with quiet intensity, he asked, "Tell me, Jason... what does your heart say? Not your fear. Not your doubt. Your heart."

"That's such a Gandalf thing to say." Henry blurts out.

"Shhhhh..." Enoch gestures with a finger to his lips followed by a wave of his hand. "Look deep inside yourself Jason. What do you feel?"

Jason closed his eyes, drawing in a slow breath as he turned inward, silencing the chaos within. In the stillness, a vision emerged, himself but different. A more bookish, contemplative version stood before him—slighter in the frame, thoughtful eyes behind round glasses, hands tucked into the pockets of a tweed coat. He radiated quiet intellect rather than strength.

With a calm voice edged in wisdom, the mirrored self spoke: "Recalculations are part of any trial, any test, any awakening. But refusing to try out of fear? Failure that's the only guarantee."

Jason's eyes snapped open, fire kindling behind them. He looked at Enoch, then at his two best friends standing beside him.

"The fear of not trying is the only guaranteed failure," he declared, voice steady and rising with conviction. "That's why recalculations exist, so we can keep trying."

Adam smiles while Henry looks perplexed, even a bit shocked. "That sounded somewhat profound, Gold."

Enoch grins and nods at Jason. "I couldn't agree more, my boy. Then we're all ready for this trip it seems."

Though the sun hung directly overhead, its light barely touched the forest floor. The towering trees that surrounded the ancient stone circle wove a canopy so thick, that the clearing remained cloaked in a deep, twilight gloom. The monolithic stones, worn and cracked by centuries, loomed like forgotten sages—silent, eternal, watching.

Within the sacred ring, four figures stood: Jason, Henry, Adam, and the elder mage, Enoch. The air was heavy, not with heat, but with the weight of expectation.

Then, from a shadowed space between two massive stones, the darkness thickened like twisted breath. And she appeared.

Avarail, the succubus of crimson skin and midnight hair, slipped into view as if unfolding from the gloom itself. Her movements radiated a slow, deliberate power, which seemed predatory, graceful, and mesmerizing. Her garnet-hued skin shimmered faintly under the fractured light, and her polished peridot eyes scanned the clearing with calculated curiosity.

Jason tensed. Henry jolted slightly, barely suppressing a curse under his breath.

Adam, standing just behind Enoch, felt the energy change, an invisible pressure rolling outward like a tide. But unlike the others, he didn't flinch. His fingers curled slightly, sensing the vibration in the space between heartbeats, recognizing the subtle signature of her presence.

Jason turned toward Enoch, about to speak, but the old mage's voice rang out before he could. "Still your nerves." Enoch's tone was firm, resonant, commanding like thunder disguised as calm. "You must learn to perceive beyond the surface. Feel her vibrational field. Sense the resonance she leaves in the air, in the earth. Just as Adam has begun to." He nodded slightly toward their arcane friend. "This awareness will shape your path. Not just in battle but in trust, deception, negotiation, and survival. In every path, life might throw before you."

Jason closed his eyes, reaching inward. He felt it now, the subtle pulse of energy, the way Avarail's presence altered the air itself. Not just her but the warmth of Henry's nervous excitement, the steady pulse of Adam's focus, and the grounded gravity of Enoch, ancient and immovable as the stones themselves.

Henry leaned over to Adam, eyes wide, whispering through the awe. "Damn, dude... you're really learning to be a wizard. This is crazy, man."

Adam grinned, not smug, but with quiet pride. It felt right. Like he belonged.

Avarail walked calmly toward Enoch, her hips swaying slightly, the tension in her gaze sharp as a drawn blade. Her voice didn't rise, but her presence said everything.

She stopped inches from him, close enough to hear his heartbeat.

Enoch leaned in, the air thick with nervous anxiety, and whispered so softly only she could hear: "If I don't return... set into motion Operation Dragon's Crown."

Avarail's green eyes flicked with something unreadable. Her response was quiet, and simple, but heavy with meaning. "As you command."

A silence fell over the clearing like a shroud. Even the birds had stopped singing.

Adam felt the pulse of it, something had shifted. Something irreversible.

"Watch closely and more importantly feel what I am doing." Enoch addresses Adam as he reaches out, clutching the golden staff of angelic pineal glands. Ripples in reality appear in front of them flexing, and pulsating before a portal swirls open. "Once we step in, this will be more disorienting than the trip you three took to get here," he warns.

Adam stepped forward first, vanishing into the swirling mouth of the wormhole with a shimmer. Henry followed without hesitation, then Jason with a hint of apprehension, their forms swallowed by the churning vortex. At last, Enoch swept in behind them, his robes rippling like smoke as the portal sealed shut behind them.

Their world twists Inside out.

A sensation unlike anything they have ever known grips them with an immense, impossible tug, as if their bodies were unraveling into threads of flesh. Darkness envelops them, but it's not empty. The tunnel around them was alive, speckled with glimmering streaks of light that danced like fireflies caught in a cosmic current, colors from Earth's sun, pulled in when the wormhole tore reality open.

Then a harsh impact on everyone's optics.

A blinding red light explodes ahead, crashing into them with brutal intensity. They recoiled, hands rising instinctively to shield their faces, but there was no shelter from the raw, searing brilliance.

And just as suddenly as it came, it faded.

Their eyes, blinking through the daze, began to adjust. Slowly, the light peeled back to reveal a vast, alien expanse. A rugged terrain of butterscotch-yellow sand and jagged, rust-colored rock formations stretching to the horizon heat shimmered off the ground. The air was dry, heavy with the scent of dust and something unfamiliar.

They stood together inside another megalithic chamber, its stone arches and towering pillars eerily similar to the one they had just left behind, as if the place had been copied and cast across worlds.

"Look out!" Henry yells as he turns and throws up, falling to the ground. "Wow. It's much warmer down here on the ground." as he wipes his mouth with the sleeve of his tight rubbery envirosuit.

"That's because of the lack of gravity." Enoch replies "Remember what I told you three?"

"Yeah, no. I remember" Henry coughs, gasping as he stands up. "It's just a weird sensation. Feeling spring on the ground and winter standing up."

"Okay, mask up." Enoch orders "Turn your suits' temperature regulators on and follow me."

All three friends pull their masks up and switch on the controls of their suits. Henry also pulls down his goggles and switches on his forearm computer.

"Holy shit." Henry proclaims in awe.

"What is it, man?" Jason questions out of wonder.

"He's freaking out over the vibrational frequency of this place," Adam answers for him.

"The electromagnetic field is so weak here, but we're lighting up like the Las Vegas strip," Henry exclaims.

Enoch turns around. "As I said, your circadian rhythms are more attuned on Mars"

"But why?" Jason questions.

"CRY1 mutation, that's why," Enoch answers. "You all have the mutation."

"Yes!" Henry exclaims. "I told you we were like the X-Men."

"One percent of humans carry a gene mutation," Enoch explains. "It predisposes them to late nights. Specifically, the CRY1 mutation shifts the body's internal clock to roughly twenty-four and a half hours. That just happens to align closely with the Martian day, which lasts twenty-four hours and thirty-nine minutes."

He pauses, then adds, "All of you will be operating in the alpha frequency range—brainwaves between seven and twelve hertz. Calm, alert, and ready."

"Yeah, we're all in the seven-hertz range," Henry confirms after inspecting the data that's popping up in the lenses of his goggles.

"Which means both sides of our brains are active." Adam proclaims, "And we should be able to easily manipulate the vibrational frequencies of the universe."

"Very good, my boy," Enoch praises.

"Okay, Merlin," Henry says bluntly. "Are the giant face and pyramids found on some photos of Mars real?"

"Of course they are." Enoch answers "But many of the structures found here on Mars are from the ancient gods, before the angels arrived."

"Wait what?!" Henry exclaims.

"Most of the gods came from either here, this planet, or from Nibiru, and of course the Hindu pantheon came from Pujavara," Enoch explained, his tone steady, measured. "Even Tiamat, before its total destruction."

Henry interrupted, eyebrows raised. "Wait, you mean Phaeton is real? The alleged fifth planet that once existed between Mars and Jupiter?"

"Yes," Enoch replied without missing a beat. "Tiamat is what the gods called it. Its destruction led to the formation of the asteroid belt between Mars and Jupiter—"

"Which is the cornerstone of the Disruption Theory!" Henry cut in again, unable to contain himself. "Eighteenth-century astronomers first proposed a missing planet, and by the twentieth century, it was officially dubbed 'Phaeton'."

"Yes, yes, yes," Enoch said with a touch of irritation, but also a flicker of amusement. He resumed, voice firm. "The Tiamatians, or the gods, as a primitive man came to know them, were real. And for the most part, they looked like us."

He let that sink in before continuing.

"But in short, they destroyed their own world. That catastrophic event weakened Mars' atmosphere, which is why it became the barren wasteland it is today. Before that, Mars was a paradise, much like Earth once was."

Jason and Adam exchanged uneasy glances as Enoch's voice darkened.

"The gods thought they could learn from the angels when they arrived on Earth. Some even tried to enslave them, and succeeded, for a time. But eventually, the archangels united... and created their ultimate response: G.O.D."

He gave a meaningful pause, eyes narrowing slightly.

"But I've already explained all of that to you."

After this explanation, the wizard lets out a sigh. "But the gods of old are gone now."

"Where? Why?" Jason inquires.

"Those that were not killed in the God Wars were imprisoned," Enoch answers.

"A god prison?" Adam chimes in. "Where is it?"

"It's a cryogenic prison floating out in the asteroid belt." Enoch signals, waving his hand up to the stars.

Henry is dumbfounded. "And you're just now telling us this?!"

"We haven't really had the time for a proper history lesson now have we?" Enoch responds sarcastically.

"That's fair." Jason shrugs, with the other two agreeing humbly.

"After we're successful with this mission, I'll explain everything to you all and answer any of your questions." Enoch bargains. "Okay?"

"Deal," Adam says.

"Yeah, sounds good," Jason adds.

"Man, I've got so many questions now." Henry sighs in amazement. "We're totally pulling this mission off, guys. I've got to get answers now!"

"Okay then." Enoch agrees "Keep up. We need to get to the mothership quickly."

And just like that, he's gone in a flash, flying away from the trio.

"Holy shit!" Henry says. "Dude just pulled a Neo from the Matrix on us."

"Yeah, Enoch can fly," Adam tells him. "Don't you remember him flying over the Mediterranean when the Globemaster was exploding?"

Henry thinks back. " Oh Yeah! That's right, like how you were flying too."

"I can levitate." Adam corrects.

"Well, let's go," Jason demands as he takes off running at an amazing speed, leaving the other two behind.

Adam looks to Henry, who says "Even if I'm as fast as the Flash in the comics, I still don't wanna run."

Adam chuckles then takes off right behind Jason.

"Damn it." Henry sighs before following in their pursuit.

After running close to an hour, the three of them see Enoch crouched behind a rusty bronze-colored outcropping of rocks.

Through heavy breathing, Henry says "We just ran over thirty miles... In less than an hour..."

He can't believe the data he's reading on his forearm computer.

Jason nods, also catching his breath. "I feel like I could keep going, and we just ran over a marathon."

"That is crazy," Adam agrees "I'm not very winded at all."

"Well, I'm glad you two are in such great shape," Henry adds. "I'm not."

He slides down the rusty brown rocks that stand taller than him and plops down in the orangish-red sand.

"This is it," Enoch says as he points to a small pyramid-shaped structure up ahead.

Jason is unimpressed. "That's no bigger than a large house. And I thought you said it was crystal?"

"That's just the top of the structure," Enoch explains. "This pyramid is much bigger than those at Giza, even the one underneath the Sphinx that held the Nexus Access Gabriel stole."

The three teens all look on at the small, pointed structure in awe after hearing this.

"Alright. Let's go over this again, shall we?" Enoch suggests.

"As soon as you open the entrance," Jason starts. "We take out the guards."

"Which are giants!" Henry says desperately.

"Yeah, giants" Adam repeats. "And after they're neutralized, we make it to the air shaft of the complex, since it has no sensors in it. Then we make our way to the throne room."

"Where we'll battle the seraphim," Jason cuts in. "While you two work on rigging the Nexus Access to self-destruct Wormwood after firing one last time on the mothership we will still be in."

"And we get out of there before the ray of destruction blows the joint up by you teleporting us back to the wormhole where we make our escape back to earth." Henry finishes.

The wizard nods in approval. "Alright. Let's go"

"Wait, explain again why you can't just teleport us to the throne room from outside here? seems like it would be so much easier that way?" Jason asks

"The quantum shield generator scrambles the quantum field around the mothership, preventing me from doing so but once inside I won't be affected by it. Trust me we just can't and we don't have the time for me to explain the science behind it." Enoch answers as Jason just nods in acknowledgment.

As they approach, Henry says "Aren't we going to get caught by some kinda security system?"

"No," Enoch said. "The archangels saw no purpose in it. To them, humanity was primitive—blind to the higher sciences, earthbound without wings of starlight, and utterly ignorant of the sacred rites that opened the portals between worlds."

"But what about you?" Adam asks "Aren't they concerned about you?"

Enoch shakes his head. "They know I cannot face them all at once, yet they remain unaware that I've walked the red sands of Mars more times than they can imagine—enough to know its every whisper and shadow like the lines of my own palm."

As they neared the ancient pyramid, Enoch reached into the folds of his robes and drew out a slender, pale blue crystal no larger than a pencil, yet pulsing faintly with an inner light. With deliberate care, he slides it into a narrow socket embedded in the weathered facade. For a heartbeat, nothing happens. Then, with an electronic rumble that seemed to rise from the bones of Mars itself, the sand-covered door glides into a recess. A concealed doorway slides open, centuries of sand and dust cascading to the ground, unveiling the gleaming crystalline architecture hidden beneath, just as Enoch had foretold

"Come," Enoch commands as he enters, beginning to run across a crystal bridge with no railing. "Hurry now, and tread with care—no wings grace our backs as theirs do, and gravity does not forgive the heavy-footed."

"Yeah, but you can fly, Merlin!" Henry proclaims.

"And so can Adam," Jason adds.

"I can hover!" Adam protests, "That's about it. Levitate I can levitate."

"Are we going to get superpowers like that?" Henry asks, "If so, I kinda want claws or teleportation, like Wolverine or Nightcrawler from the X-Men."

"Maybe now isn't the best time for this conversation." Jason snaps. "Focus on the mission."

As they neared the end of the vast crystal bridge, the air grew colder, sharper with each breath sending tiny plumes of vapor into the frigid air from the masks the teens wore. The translucent floor beneath them pulsed faintly with a cerulean light, casting eerie prismatic rainbows that danced across the towering crystalline walls surrounding them. The bridge ended at a platform carved from the same otherworldly crystal, smooth yet radiating warmth, humming with ancient energy.

At the center stood a towering turbo-lift, encased in a lattice of glowing blue filaments that twisted like veins under translucent skin. Beside it loomed two colossal stasis pods, each over twenty feet tall, their surfaces frosted with layers of shimmering ice. With a sudden hiss like a serpent's breath, the pods cracked open, splitting along hidden seams. A thick, white mist poured out in waves, curling across the floor like creeping spirits.

From within the swirling fog emerged two titans, but unmistakably ancient. Their armored forms glinted under the crystalline light, plated in metallic segments reminiscent of Roman gladiators but forged from a metal that shimmered with iridescent hues. The air reverberated with a low, thrumming sound, as if the pyramid itself acknowledged their awakening.

Each titan reached back into the frosted interior of their pod. One withdrew a massive mace, its spiked head glimmering with frost and etched with glowing alien runes. The other hefted a colossal battle hammer, its haft humming with a deep, resonant power that made the very floor vibrate as electricity raced around the hammerhead. Both beings turned slowly, eyes glowing like molten gold beneath their helms, weapons raised in silent challenge, ready to defend their ancient domain.

Enoch yells out "Arm yourselves!"

Henry and Jason burst forward like savage Viking raiders, blades flashing as they roar battle cries that echo through the crystalline chamber. The air crackles with anticipation as they charge the towering giants.

The colossal beast grasping the mace swings his massive weapon downward with earth-shaking force, aiming to crush Jason in a single icy blow. But Jason reacts instantly, leaping upward with ferocious strength, bringing his blade across the giant's throat in a swift, deadly arc. Blood erupts in a crimson spray, splattering across the giant's armor as his lifeblood pours out.

Before Jason can land, the giant's blinding speed surprises him. With brutal precision, the giant reaches out and clamps his iron grip around Jason's torso, crushing him in a vice-like hold. Jason struggles, gasping for breath, as the giant stumbles forward, violently slamming him onto the shimmering floor. The impact rattles the chamber like a thunderclap, knocking the wind from Jason's lungs.

The giant drops to his knees, his massive form trembling as he begins to topple face-first onto the glimmering floor. Jason lies still, fighting to draw breath amidst the chaos. Adam's eyes lock onto his struggling friend; without hesitation, he springs forward, sliding across the gleaming surface. Grabbing Jason's battered form, he drags him away just as the giant's face crashes into the crystal floor where Jason had just been.

Realizing Jason's life hangs in the balance, Adam channels his magic, focusing on the vibrational frequency of Jason's strained lungs. With a surge of energy, he forces the airways to relax, pumping oxygen back into Jason's exhausted lungs. Gradually, Jason's chest rises and falls with renewed ease, both boys breathing heavily in the tense silence.

Suddenly, their gaze shifts to Henry, standing alone against the other colossal foe. The scene erupts into chaos as the giant's massive war hammer comes crashing down, aiming to crush Henry beneath its electrical weight. Henry raises Excalibur high, gripping the hilt tightly with one hand, the other braced against the flat of the blade. The impact rings out like a lightning strike, but Henry holds firm, deflecting the blow.

With a fierce cry, Henry surges forward, swinging Excalibur in a wide, devastating arc. The blade slices through the giant's knee, severing the limb with a wet crunching crack, which echoes through the chamber. The giant roars in agony, hobbling on one leg, desperately trying to strike back. But Henry is swift, sidestepping the desperate blow, he leaps into the air, bringing his blade down and severing the giant's hand at the wrist. The severed limb falls, clutching the weapon in a death grip as the clang of metal on crystal rings out.

The giant collapses to his remaining knee, blood streaming from his wounds. Henry seizes the opportunity, unleashing a precise, powerful strike just below the breastplate. The blade punches through, eviscerating the giant's stomach in a burst of crimson. Blood sprays outward as the massive warrior slumps forward, his eyes glazing over, then rolling back as he crashes over on his side.

The chamber falls silent save for the ringing echoes of the previous clashes with the monstrous duo. Adam and Jason stand, breathless and stunned, witnessing their friend's mastery in combat, his ferocity, skill, and unyielding resolve shining through in the chaos.

Henry strides up swiftly to check on his two friends. "Jason. You Okay, man?"

"Yeah, yeah. I'm fine." Jason stammers. "Damn, man. That's impressive work."

"Yeah," Adam comments. "You're like a whole different person with that sword."

"I keep telling ya both, it's like I'm not in control while wielding it," Henry says.

Standing at the border of the battle the perspicacious wizard watches the three friends working together, pleased at what he sees. "This way." Enoch commands as he descends over the side of the platform "We'll take this access ladder down a few stories to the air ducts."

The four make their way down to a massive unit on a central platform with ducts running off in all directions.

Henry, overwhelmed says, "How the hell are we supposed to know where we're going in this maze?"

"I know where we are going," Enoch assures them all.

"Well then." Henry gestures to the large ducts. "After you, Merlin."

Enoch removes one of the grates and sets it aside. "Follow me and be quiet. There are ancient things in this ship that don't need to be awakened."

The three friends give a weary look between themselves.

Jason just shrugs. "Come on. We have the new King of Camelot with us. We're fine. Right, my liege?"

Adam chuckles.

Henry can't help but snicker as well. "Okay, Okay. Shut up now, smartass."

Once in the ductwork of the massive mothership, the three friends blindly follow Enoch.

For over thirty minutes, they had been winding their way through the labyrinthine underbelly of the alien pyramid, each step echoing faintly in the vast emptiness. The narrow corridors stretched endlessly, carved from crystal and metal, humming softly with a life of their own. Strange glyphs glowed faintly along the walls, shifting subtly in hue as if reacting to their presence. The air was cool and dry, tinged with a metallic scent, and each breath tasted faintly of ozone and age.

Their path led them through junctions veined with cables pulsing with energy, across grated walkways suspended over bottomless shafts of shadow, and into towering maintenance chambers where forgotten machinery thrummed quietly in the gloom. They climbed down narrow ladders slick with condensation, the rungs warm to the touch, then up again into control rooms filled with ancient, dust-covered consoles blinking sporadically with dim extraterrestrial light. Some chambers resonated with soft mechanical murmurs, others were deathly silent, broken only by the clank of boots on metal and the occasional flicker of failing lights overhead.

Henry's patience, already fraying, finally gave way. He paused, one boot resting on the last rung of yet another ladder leading into another section of ductwork, his face illuminated by the cold, shifting glow of Enoch's magically glowing staff. In a loud whisper, thick with exasperation, he muttered, "Hey Merlin, are you sure you know where you're going?"

His voice bounced off the crystalline walls, chased by an uneasy silence. Somewhere deep in the structure, a low mechanical groan echoed, like the exhalation of something ancient just now waking up.

"Yes, I know exactly where I am going!" The wizard snaps. "Now please just shut up and follow me." As the wizard leads them into the next section of ventilation.

Just as the last sharp whisper of reprimand left his lips, Henry flinched under the scolding, moments later the metal beneath them all groaned in protest. With a shuddering crack, the ductwork tears loose from its moorings. In an instant, the narrow tunnel becomes a plummeting trap. The four of them tumble together in a chaotic calamity of limbs and echoing metal, thrashing and shouting as the vent twists and falls, their stealth shattered by the clamor of their own descent.

Henry frantically asks again in a panic "Okay. Not to sound like a broken record, but are you sure you know where you're going, Merlin?"

"This shouldn't be happening!" Enoch proclaims.

Adam breaks in. "Should we get out of this ductwork?"

"Yes!" Enoch answers "Hold on." He springs into action, slamming the base of his glowing golden staff against the falling ductwork. With a flash of arcane light, the metal twisted midair, reshaping itself into a flat, shimmering platform that hovered, then slowed, drifting downward like a summoned specter.

The three friends clung to its edges as it descended into shadow, the air growing colder, heavier, as if something ancient stirred beneath. Enoch narrowed his eyes and forced more light into his staff. The golden glow flared, spilling illumination into the void around them but the darkness pushed back, thick and impenetrable beyond a twenty-foot halo.

The platform shuddered, then stopped with a muted clang. They had landed. Where, none could tell.

Enoch's voice was low, uncertain. "We've landed. If I had to guess... it might be one of the cargo holds."

"Or a prison of the void," Henry muttered, peering into the black. His voice echoed strangely, as if the room were far larger than it should be.

Around them, silence stretched too deep, too still.

Something was watching.

A mocking voice rings out with an echo from the dark. "Melchizedek! Is that you?"

"No, it can't be," Enoch whispers under his breath.

"Who is that?" Henry asks in a hushed voice.

The dark and forbiddingly sinister area outside the staff's radiance starts to illuminate a bit brighter from a few sparse lights revealing a large mostly empty room the size of two football fields which now only contains menacing shadows. Enoch turns in the direction of the voice, seeing a large angelic figure that walks toward them wearing a dingy tattered hooded robe pulled up over its obfuscated head, black feathered wings, and a halo of onyx floating above him.

"Melchizedek. Why, you're not shocked to see me here, are you?" The hooded eldritch figure questions sarcastically. "Not after you left me in that pit of a prison, you made for me."

"Yes, I am shocked, Abaddon." Enoch proclaims, "I'm shocked you'd align yourself with Gabriel and this damfool plan of his."

"Yes, I am a bit saddened by it as well. I've grown very fond of this planet, this dimension." The cloaked figure proclaims. "But Gabriel did free me from your little penitentiary. Tragic isn't it, you had no idea that those towers would be built over my prison, giving the required amount of life force needed to unlock the construct you stuck me in!"

"What's he mean, life force, needed to unlock the construct you built?" Adam asks out of gnawing curiosity.

"I didn't learn magic in a tower of intellect or under some elder's watchful eye," Enoch answers, his voice a rasp of memory and regret. "I tore it from the bones of dead languages, carved it out of forgotten stones with bloodied hands. In the beginning, blood was the only way. Blood and agony. The old sorcerers knew that. They fed the stars with lives to make the cosmos whisper back."

He looks away, jaw clenched. "But I... I was arrogant. I believed I could defy that order. I sealed Abaddon away without a single drop of blood spilled. No one died. Not then." he pauses quickly with a long silence.

"I thought it was a triumph. Mercy masquerading as brilliance. But magic doesn't forget what it's owed. That spell was a debt, a towering one, and the universe came to collect."

He meets their eyes now, gaze hollow. "You want to know the cost to break the seal? September 11th, 2001. Thousands of lives. The smoke, the fire, the screaming... All of it, a sacrifice to tear open the pit I sealed him in."

He shudders, a man breaking under the weight of what he's confessing. "I never meant for it to happen. I thought he was gone forever. I thought I had buried him so deep, that no soul could ever reach him again. I was wrong. And now the dead scream louder every night. Their blood is on my hands, not by blade, but by ignorance. I tried to be better. And in trying, I may have doomed us all."

"Is he talking about the Twin Towers??" Jason demands, reaching for the Naga blade.

"Yes, he's talking about the Twin Towers, boy!" Another familiar voice rings out from the opposite side of Abaddon.

Gabriel stepped into the fractured glow of the ruined threshold, his silhouette jagged against the burning of Enoch's staff. Beside him stood Steven with eyes hollow, face smeared with oblivion and reverence.

"I brought the towers down," Gabriel declared, his voice cold as the grave, yet laced with a twisted, unholy fire. "From the ashes and screams, the Angel of the Abyss rose, just as it was written in Revelations 9:11. The Lord of Locusts. The Devourer. Abaddon."

A low hum pulsed through the air, like the buzzing of unseen wings.

"This world... your world," he sneered, eyes burning with ecstasy and loathing, "will drink from Wormwood. The sky will rot. The seas will boil. And from your bones, a bridge will be built, a path back to the cradle of our beginning. Your extinction is our exodus."

He stepped forward, slow and deliberate, as the ground seemed to recoil beneath his feet.

"Hand over the Nexus Access. Now! Delay only prolongs your suffering. Your fate is etched in prophecy. You are outmatched. Outnumbered. And utterly forsaken."

His smile was not human. It was the smile of an angel gone mad who had tasted blood and found it sweet.

"You can't count." Jason counters. "It's four of us, and three of you. Steven, do you hear what he said?? Our home is going to be destroyed. Why are you doing this!?"

Gabriel laughs out loud. "You fool! This weak-willed creature has no choice but to follow me, and I can count on levels you can't even imagine. This time I brought reinforcements. I am going to be victorious. I have to be!"

In the darkness to Abaddon's left and Gabriel's right, red spots light up emerging from the darkness, a vision of awe and mystery, a couple of divine forces breaking through the veil of the unknown. At first, there is only a heavy silence and a vast blackness, still and infinite.

Then, slowly, a subtle glow begins to pulse in the distance, like a star being born. The darkness parts as a wheel of brilliant, interlocking rings begin to turn in the void.

Each wheel is encrusted with innumerable, unblinking eyes like little crimson orbs that shimmer not with warmth, but with cold, celestial judgment. Their gaze pierces flesh, soul, and memory alike with endless, ancient, all-seeing power. The wheels spin within one another in an impossible, hypnotic rhythm, like a divine mechanism built to unravel sanity. They turn without sound, yet the silence howls with meaning. Arcs of living fire blazing red, yellow, and blue lash from them like serpents of light, casting flickering, jagged shadows that dance across the void-ridden floor of the cargo bay.

As the constructs glide forward, the air buckles beneath their presence. Not wind, pressure. Divine gravity. The sheer holiness of them presses against the mind like iron against bone, suffocating, absolute. There is no face, no voice yet a whisper claws into the skull, wordless and merciless: This is not life. This is will made machine. Judgment forged in flame.

Then, ignition. Spheres of searing fire erupt, revealing a single, lidless eye within each rotating halo. A core of flame that stares with purpose beyond mortal comprehension. The spinning wheels bleed together, eyes within eyes, the fire within a fire, their forms infested with red, surgical beams like living laser sights scanning for transgression.

The pair of constructs hover four feet above the ground, unmoving yet ready to strike, the stillness of a blade just before the kill.

"Ophanim!" Enoch roars, the word a mix of fear and awe. "Stay clear of the laser locks upon their wheels!"

"Ophanim?" Jason repeats.

"Ezekiel 1:16–18" Adam begins, without going into a trance this time. "As for the appearance of the wheels and their construction: their appearance was like the gleaming of beryl. And the four had the same likeness, their appearance and construction being as it were a wheel within a wheel. When they went, they went in any of their four directions without turning as they went. And their rims were tall and awesome, and the rims of all four were full of eyes all around."

"Yes, yes," Enoch snapped, cutting through the tension like a blade. "They're not just machines, they're sentinels of the throne, divine executioners. We face weapons shaped by heaven's wrath. We fight as one, or we die."

He turned, eyes burning. "Adam, with Jason, take the left. Henry, you're with me on the right. No hesitation."

Even as the words left his mouth, the Ophanim stirred and then struck.

From inside their wheels, jets of molten plasma screamed forth, trailing behind the laser locks that now painted their targets in lines of glowing death. The air rippled, warped, and then detonated in living fire. Enoch and Adam reacted in unison, summoning vibrational shields wrought from sheer will, drawn from the marrow of their souls.

Enoch's barrier held a shimmering distortion of force that bent the inferno back. But Adam's failure, shattered like glass under the weight of divine heat. His scream was instant, harrowing. The plasma burst through spraying him and Jason in a wave of blistering light, searing flesh, igniting clothing, turning battle cries into agony.

Jason's howl echoed through the cargo bay like a supernova, as the scent of burning flesh filled the air.

"Focus, your thoughts!" Enoch encourages. "And reinforce them with your belief in not only yourself, but your friends. Let your electromagnetic fields merge and use the wand I gave you!"

Henry pulls Excalibur from its scabbard. "With the power from the legacy of the Pendragon, I am now the wielder of the Dragon's head, and no fire shall harm me!"

He surged forward, a blur of motion against the chaos. With a powerful leap, he vaults eight feet into the air, landing squarely atop the rotating wheels of an Ophan a hellish machine forged for one purpose: destruction.

At point-blank range, the creature retaliates. Its central eye flares with a searing light before releasing a torrent of flame, a white-hot blaze that screams like a furnace unleashed. The fire engulfs Henry in an instant. His friends along with Enoch watch, frozen in horror, expecting to see him incinerated. But as the inferno cleared, Henry stood scorched, smoking, but alive.

With a defiant roar, he wedged his boots between the massive rotating wheels, halting their motion through sheer force. They're not propulsion, he realized. They're armor, and defensive mechanisms. Without hesitation, he drove Excalibur into the eye of the beast.

The blade pierced the burning sphere housed within the Ophan's protective wheels. Flames licked at the hilt as Henry drove the sword deep, wrenching it sideways before yanking it free. The fire shuddered, recoiling inward like a dying star collapsing into itself. The sentinel began to tremble, then shake violently as its anti-gravity propulsion systems began to fail.

Henry leaped clear just as the machine buckled in midair. He hit the ground in a roll, absorbing the impact, and sprang to his feet in one fluid motion. Behind him, the Ophan slammed into the cargo bay floor, an instant later, it exploded in a thunderous bloom of flame and metal, lighting the chamber in brilliant orange as shrapnel and smoke filled the air.

Henry looks at his friends in shock. "I'm impervious to fire!"

"That's great, now help with this one!" Jason demands.

"Oh yeah. Sure, I'm on it." Henry says triumphantly. Running with a surge of adrenaline to the second Ophan. "By the power of the Pendragon!"

As Henry rushes forward, Gabriel looks to Steven "Kill that fat idiot and bring the sword to me!" He says with a simmering contempt.

While storming to intercept Henry his enthralled friend begins typing in a code on the gemstones of his golden breastplate attached to his ephod for a sonic blast attack. The remaining Ophan releases another gout of flame as Adam's will throws up another magical shield but it seems even weaker than before. The fire however washes over a second vibrational shield of magic at the last minute.

"Way to find your strength, man," Jason says encouragingly.

"It wasn't me." Adam shamefully admits clutching the golden wand as they both spot Enoch focusing on them with hand and staff outstretched much like they saw him the first time in the alleyway days ago.

Abaddon streaks up into the darkness of the cargo hold only to come crashing down on top of Enoch. Straddling him while holding the immortal mage by the throat. The dark angel begins viciously punching him repeatedly in the face with inhuman speed growling with revenge.
"I'm going to tear you apart piece by piece, you relic of a bygone society."

"Use that wand he gave you," Jason suggests. "I have to help Enoch."

Jason sprinted across the shattered cargo bay, the stench of scorched metal and burning flesh clinging to every breath. He caught sight of Steven intercepting Henry — a sudden blur of movement, blades, and shadow. But it was the memory that stopped his heart cold: the sonic beam beneath the Sphinx, the pain, the helplessness. It slammed into his mind like a tidal wave of terror.

But there was no time. Not now.

He forced it down — buried it beneath fury — and launched himself forward, weapon raised, a scream tearing from his throat as he brought all his strength down in a single, savage strike, aimed at severing the unseen head of the Lord of the Abyss.

The blow connected and ricocheted harmlessly off the

blackened halo that cloaked Abaddon in divine protection. Jason staggered back.

Abaddon turned to face him, lifting his gaze slowly not just looking at Jason, but into him. It was as if something ancient and monstrous reached out from behind those eyes, peeling back the layers of his soul like worn parchment.

It was the first time Jason had seen him up close. The sight froze the blood in his veins.

Abaddon's eyes were pits — void-black, empty of empathy, colder than death. Like the dead stare of a great white shark just before it kills. Against his sallow, yellow-white skin, those eyes looked like holes punched into reality.

Jason's strike had done nothing. But Abaddon let go of Enoch anyway, kicking him like a deflated ball, sending his body skidding fifteen feet across the crystalline floor.

Then, with a hiss of movement, Abaddon raised a clawed hand and peeled back his hood, revealing a death's grin stretched across thin, grey lips. Hair hung around his face like wet, matted threads of night.

Above his head hovered a jagged halo, not gold, not light but forged of what looked like fractured onyx, cracked and pulsing with shadows. "So," he whispered, voice like venom slithering beneath death, "you think you're a match for me, boy? The Lord of Locusts?" He took a step forward. The temperature dropped. "You'll learn what true fear tastes like... when I've finished tearing your mind apart."

Jason, trying not to show the terror that's running through his veins, says "What's to be frightened of, other than your looks? Now let's get on with this. I still have to kill your boss!"

Abaddon's cruel laughter echoes through the chamber of conflict, a twisted rasp of rage as he rakes his claws across Jason's face, narrowly missing it and his throat. Jason stumbles backward, desperately arching his spine in a grotesque contortion, each movement threatening to snap the bones of his vertebrae under the strain. The air thickens with the stench of smoke and mechanical death as Jason lunges forward, the naga blade slicing through the foul, necrotic flesh of the angel's arm, leaving a jagged wound that oozes dark, putrid blood. The blood hits the ground with a sizzling hiss, and from the corrupted gore, writhing unholy insectoids emerge in the form of alien flies, locusts, and gnats resembling contaminated shadows, flying hungrily toward him.

Jason's frantic swings cut through the swarm in a desperate, wild flurry, but they're relentless, swarming over his skin and eyes. Abaddon strikes with brutal precision, a savage blow to Jason's abdomen that doubles him over, the pain ripping through him like a chainsaw, leaving him gasping. Without mercy, the angel drives an elbow into the back of Jason's skull, the impact knocking him to his knees, dazed and broken. His vision blurs, stars exploding behind his eyes, as the world tilts into darkness. He fights to shake off the crushing fog of concussion and despair, trembling violently, trying to focus, but his senses are overwhelmed. Out of the corner of his eye, he sees Steven unleashing a vicious sonic attack, an unholy scream, that forces Henry's body to fall like a lifeless husk, a grim reminder of the darkness that nearly devoured him under the sands of Egypt.

Henry wails in pain as he feels his physical form being shredded by the sonic blast emanating from the ruby pinned in the turban Steven wears. The air cracked, not only with sound, but with pressure, like the world itself flinched. A sonic wave slammed into him before he even saw the source, which happened to be a lost friend. It wasn't just noise; it was force. His bones shuddered as though struck by an invisible hammer. His ears screamed, a high-pitched whine flooding his skull, fighting to not blackout. Vision doubled, then blurred. The ground tipped sideways. He staggered, arms slack, Excalibur nearly torn from his grip. Every nerve fired at once, not just in pain, but in disarray like his body forgot how to be a body. It wasn't sound. It was chaos made audible.

Suddenly Henry's mind is calmed with a vision. It's the lady of the lake, Nimue telling him "Focus your personal energy on the Dragon's head. Trust it and work as one."

Henry steadies his breath, heart thundering in his chest like a distant drum echoing through eternity. Jason's voice whispers through the static of memory — "my spirit just ripped free."

He closes his eyes. Then the veil parts. The world dissolves into shimmering threads of possibility, colors unseen by human eyes, vibrations too pure for sound. Henry's spirit drifts free, a ghost of light and thought, gliding through the quantum tide. Time is no longer a line but a lattice. Space, is no longer distance but intention. And still, in his ethereal hand, Excalibur glows with primordial fire. Not just a sword, but an axis of will and fate, resonating with a forgotten frequency that shakes the air between atoms.

In a blink that bends reality, Henry re-manifests beside Steven, his motion more like a thought than movement. The blade swings, trailing light that aims for his friend's neck, the arc of judgment.

But something, someone grabs at his essence. A flicker of Steven's true self, trapped beneath layers of alien programming. In the final instant, Henry snaps his wrist, the blade flattening out, and with a thunderous CRACK, strikes Steven across the back of the skull.

Time collapses.

Henry slams back into his body with a jolt like being struck by lightning. He crashes to the cargo floor, gasping, limbs spasming, nerves raw and crackling. The sonic torment is gone, but the echoes remain, clawing at his bones.

Minutes or lifetimes pass.

Finally, he rises, shaky and slow, eyes drawn to his fallen friend. A strange sensation curls in his chest not just confusion, but awe. Fear. Recognition. Then he sees it.

The turban, flung from Steven's head, glints darkly in the dim light, not cloth and ornament, but a fusion of ancient mysticism and alien engineering. The blood-red ruby pulses at its heart like a third eye. Wires twist from it like tendrils, plugging into electrodes attached to Steven's shaved scalp.

Henry follows the filaments down the neck, into the folds of the ephod where they converge at the golden breastplate.

Twelve gemstones shimmer within it, each one glowing faintly, harmonizing like a celestial chorus. Symbols of the tribes, yes but also something more. A matrix. A map. A device.

A conduit.

Henry's breath catches. Whatever this is... it's not just controlling Steven. It's channeling something far older, something cosmic in scale, a fusion of priestly power and otherworldly precision.

He stares down at it, Excalibur still humming faintly in his grip. "This isn't sorcery," he whispers. "It's a machine built by gods, angels, or both."

Henry's mind races while he traces the network of wires, his fingers grazing over the golden breastplate, but there's a cold realization creeping into him. This device, is not just controlling Steven. No, it's tapping into something deeper, harnessing his suffering, his anguish, perhaps amplifying it, making him a conduit to the quantum field itself. It's not magic, not purely—there's something far more complex at play here, something designed to unlock, enhance, or weaponize the very essence of the human mind.

But before he can dig deeper, before he can unravel the truth of this twisted technology, a sudden force like a shockwave slams into him from behind.

Pain shoots down his spine, a brutal, unrelenting jolt of raw energy. It's like being struck by the hammer of a god, a physical blow that isn't just felt by the body but by the soul. Henry has never felt this sensation. The closest he's felt to this has come during sparring sessions, a strike that carries no warning, no telltale wind-up. It's the kind of kick that leaves you in the air before you even know what's happening.

He's sent hurtling forward with an almost unnatural speed, crashing through the thin air of the cargo hold like a wadded-up newspaper caught in a storm. His body slams against the metal floor, skidding with the force of a thousand volts, pain flooding through his limbs as he tumbles, rolls, and struggles to regain control. The cold steel of the floor bruises his back, and his chest, but it's the force of the blow that's still rattling his bones, a dull thrum that doesn't stop.

It takes everything in him to slow his momentum, to gather his senses. The world spins, every surface blurring in flashes of light and shadow. Then, he stops, Finally.

Gasping for air, heart still racing, Henry pushes himself up, his muscles aching like they've been crushed under a heavy weight. He staggers to his feet, vision flickering, but his instincts scream that something is wrong.

He barely has time to react before he senses it: a presence.

The air itself feels different, like the particles vibrating with an unnatural tension. His eyes snap to the far corner of the hold, narrowing.

A figure is stepping from the shadows.

After almost breaking Henry's back Gabriel grimaces as he walks toward Enoch's unconscious self. "I've had about enough of you fools trying to struggle against the inevitable."

Adam raises the golden wand, taking aim at Gabriel, realizing the last Ophan has another lock on him. He quickly surged forward, aligning himself with the arrogant red-haired angel. The Ophan fires its destructive blast, but Adam, now in perfect line with Gabriel, focuses his vibrational frequency inward. With a burst of magic, he teleports behind Abaddon, just as a gout of flame erupts toward Gabriel. The timely strike gave the group of friends precious seconds to plan their next assault against the Lord of Locusts.

Jason, summoning his remaining stamina, thrust the Naga blade into Abaddon's stomach. Meanwhile, Adam presses the wand against the dark angel's black halo, channeling a negative charge into the grim adversary's mind. The attack locks up Abaddon's nervous system, rendering him immobile. Seizing the moment, Adam carefully removes the blackened halo, leaving the angel of the Abyss defenseless.

Henry staggered to his feet, pain racing through his back from the brutal kick he'd just received. Without hesitation, he propels himself six feet into the air. Descending with a mighty swing of Excalibur, he delivers an over-the-head strike that cleaves nearly half of Abaddon's head clean off. The dark angel's body hits the ground with a sickening thud, its grotesque gore spilling across the cargo bay floor. From the bloody remnants, more insect-like creatures began to emerge, swirling into a massive, writhing swarm.

Adam hurried to Enoch, checking on him, while Gabriel fought to extinguish the flames consuming him, less than ten feet away. The chaos raged around them, each moment more dire than the last.

"Enoch, are you able to continue?" Adam asks.

"Yes." He replies through labored breath. "Not the first time I've been brought low, like some cursed name in legend but I rise, every time, with fire the heavens can't smother."

"There's no more time for stealth." Henry cuts in. "We need to recalculate, like Jason stated before we left Avalon. Can we just teleport to the throne room?"

Enoch takes a deep breath. "Only one way to find out."

"Not without Steven!" Jason and Henry say in unison. The two of them look at each other, not even surprised.

"Okay," Enoch says as the Ophan has another lock on them all. Then an idea comes to mind before they teleport.

Gabriel, still smoldering from the flames that had just engulfed him, surges forward, determined to finally finish off Enoch and reclaim his prize, the coveted Nexus Access. Certain that the predictable wizard will be the one to possess it, Gabriel closes the distance with lethal intent.

But Enoch has already sensed the danger.

His gaze flicks toward the Ophan, the wheeled sentinel now powering up another fiery assault aimed directly at the group. With a flash of insight and swift calculations, Enoch seizes the moment. In an instant, he teleports all five of them to the throne room just as the ray is unleashed.

Gabriel, caught mid-charge, is struck once again by the Ophan's blazing attack. Whether Enoch timed the escape perfectly or simply got lucky, the outcome is the same, the move pays off.

CHAPTER 14
THE NEXUS

Once in the throne room, the three boys with Enoch hear a chanting. "Holy! Holy! Holy!"

"We don't have time to waste," Enoch growled, dragging a bloodied sleeve across his face. The crimson smeared deeper into his beard as he winced, his left eye already swelling shut under the weight of pain and urgency.

The room is bathed in a sickly half-light, its shadows dancing to the twitching rhythm of flickering reddish-orange glows spilling from cracked pods overhead. At the chamber's heart, a pale green shimmer pulses through the thick, murky fluid inside a towering tank — and suspended within, like some grotesque relic, floats a decaying, colossal brain, its flesh sloughing in slow, deliberate motion. At the base of the tank, clusters of red, orange, and yellow lights blink erratically, cycling through alien symbols that mean nothing to the three onlookers, yet carry the weight of something ancient and wrong.

Tubes and blackened cables snake out from the tank like veins, crawling across the floor toward a rusted plinth — and there, slouched in an oversized metal throne shaped like a twisted wingback, sits a figure. At first, it looks like Enoch. But as the single overhead red beam isolates the shape in brutal detail, the truth settles in like ice: a malformed twin, cybernetics jutting like parasites from ruined flesh, its eyes hollow, unblinking. A distorted reflection of their friend — built for something far worse.

Henry points toward the figure. "Enoch, is that… "

"That's my clone," Enoch muttered, his voice a low rasp. "Metatron. It should still be functional."

He motioned quickly to the base of the grotesque tank, its cables twitching like veins under the skin of some diseased machine.

"Henry, plug your system into that port, now. What you're about to enter isn't just a simulation. It's a virtual reality carved out of madness. I'll link the Nexus Access from out here. Once you're inside, locate Wormwood's satellite, set this location as the target, and fire. Then, destroy it. All of it. Do you understand?"

Jason's voice cracked with panic. "Wait, won't that blow Mars to hell? I thought we were saving Earth from that fate?"

Enoch turned grimly, "No. Wormwood was never designed to be a planet killer... not without a lot of reengineering work. What we need to do is reduce this cursed place and everything inside it, to ash. That includes Wormwood itself, this temple, and whatever's still lurking in that tank."

He glanced toward the floating mass of necrotic brain matter as it twitched ever so slightly.

"Henry, my boy... whatever's left of Metatron's mind, it's in there lurking."

Henry paled. "Wait... you're saying I'm hacking this actual brain?"

"Yes," Enoch said flatly. "Once the Nexus Access is uploaded it will reside within G.O.D. cognitive remains, located within that brain. Expect Metatron's avatar to be in there as well, twisted. Possibly hostile. But treat it like any mainframe, just... don't believe everything you see in there."

"Except this mainframe's corrupted all to hell," Henry muttered bitterly, pulling down his goggles.

"Get ready," Enoch warned, urgency rising in his voice. "That goes for all of us. Once I install the Nexus Access, this whole place is going to wake up. I'm shocked it hasn't already. Adam, the Nexus Access, now!"

Adam fumbled through the shallow pockets of his enviro suit, hands trembling as he produced the glowing shard, pulsing with an eerie inner light. He handed it to Enoch, who wasted no time ramming it into the tank's base.

Instantly, the brain convulsed with spasms that rippled across its surface like tremors in meat. The fluid churned. Henry let out a horrified groan as he glimpsed flickers of movement in the tank, things that should not move.

Then came the sound of crackling pops, mechanical hissing from above.

The ceiling pods flared to life, their flickering glow intensifying as the first of the Seraphim began to stir, limbs uncurling in jerky, insectile motion, just like the horrors beneath the Sphinx.

"Here we go!" Enoch roared over the rising shriek of awakening madness. "Jason, guard Henry. Adam, channel your energy through the wand, and focus on offense. Let it feed on your intent and turn it into aggravated power."

And with that, the immortal wizard threw himself into the flickering controls beside the Nexus Access interface as the tomb of Mars began to pulse with terrible, ancient life.

Jason and Adam respond with a nervous "Okay!" as they get ready for the unexpected.

Henry stood frozen amid a sprawling nightmare, an immense web woven from sinew and rotting flesh, pulsating with the foul rhythm of blood and pus. The strands writhe and squirm, thick with coagulated fluids that smell of decay and disease. Glistening, gnawed bones jutted from the mess, their marrow dark and oozing. Massive spiders, hulking, chattering, hairy beasts the size of large dogs, scurry relentlessly across the grotesque tapestry, their movements jerky and unnatural as they laboriously mend the sickly webbing.

Closer inspection reveals the horrifying truth: these spiders weren't crafted from chitin, but from thick, crusted scabs And scar tissue, their exoskeletons cracked and oozed pus. Their empty eyes leak black tears that spill down their misshapen faces, hardening into brittle, calcified stains upon contact with the webbing. From their mandibles drip rotting gastric juices foul, acidic liquid that sizzles and curdles as they hit the flesh beneath.

Henry's gaze is drawn to a blinding white light at the web's center, a stark, unnatural glow that seems to pulse with contrasting life. The scabby spiders keep their distance, stuttering away from the radiance, wary and silent. Henry hesitates then steps forward, crossing the nightmare's threshold, every spider suddenly ceases movement. They turned toward him in unspoken hostility, their black, empty eyes fixed and unblinking, as if waiting for him to make his move into the darkness beyond.

Henry's pulse quickened as the digital shadows of the virtual world twisted into nightmarish shapes. He scanned the horrific landscape, every flicker of data glitching like a corrupted heartbeat. The scabby, peeling digital spiders lurked in the darkness like bulky, bleeding drones with exoskeletons scarred and leaking, their countless legs skittering with a sickening wet scrape against the virtual webbing.

He braced himself, expecting an aggressive assault from their mangled mandibles dripping with toxins. His fingers hovered over the keyboard to his forearm computer after mapping out the narrow path he needed to arrive at the blinding white light, a fragile beacon amid the chaos. With a surge of adrenaline, he launches himself forward, legs pumping desperately across the slick and sticky webbing. The spiders sense his movement and converge, their malformed bodies weaving an intercept course like a swarm of corrupted nightmares.

Without thinking, Henry leaped onto one of the grotesque creatures, aiming to propel himself into the air, to cover more ground. His foot slammed down and immediately, the shell beneath his boot gave way with a sickening crack. A wave of foul, yellowish-green gore squirted out, splattering across his leg and the surrounding terrain. The arachnid screeched, a high-pitched, guttural wail that pierced his mind like a digital scream before it collapsed into a writhing mass.

He violently kicks the gore-covered creature off his foot, sending it hurtling into an advancing group of six scrambling arachnids. The impact scatters them, their spindly legs flailing chaotically as they tumble over one another. The slimy, necrotic sludge clung to his foot, slick and repulsive, making every step a treacherous slip. The air was thick with the stench of decay and corrupted code, a visceral reminder that this was no mere game, but a living nightmare woven into the virtual fabric.

Despite the horror, Henry pushed forward, his heart pounding in his chest. Every second counted. The white light flickered ahead, his only salvation he figured, while behind him the ghastly, mutilated spiders regrouped, their eyes glowing with malevolent hunger. He gritted his teeth, knowing that failure wasn't an option, not in this haunted digital realm where every step could be his last.

Four nightmarish digital spiders materialize from the shadows of the web, their twisted forms writhing with malicious intent. Their malformed bodies glistened with toxic fluids, eyes gleaming with malevolent hunger. Two of them lunge simultaneously, fangs bared behind razor-sharp mandibles and their legs clicked menacingly as Henry gripped Excalibur, a virtual rendering that felt almost real in his trembling hands. With a savage cry, he swings, slicing through the first two incrusted spiders, their bodies erupting in a sickening spray of webbing and corrosive blood that sizzled against the digital air.

But the attack was a distraction. The remaining pair darted with unnatural speed, one dodging just out of reach, the other lashing out with its gnarly mandibles that sank deep into Henry's thigh. Pain exploded through him as the spider's jaws tore into flesh, the bite leaving a jagged, bleeding wound. Blood and digital gore splattered onto the web, which still pulsates with a sickening, organic rhythm.

Henry gritted his teeth, raising Excalibur in a desperate arc. With a brutal slash, he decapitates the spider clinging to his leg, the scabby body tumbling free of its mangled head while still sticking hauntingly to his thigh. The severed head's eyes still stared, glassy and unblinking, as if mocking him from its gruesome perch. Yanking the head free from his leg with a shudder, he inspects the wound beneath. The infection of the digital arachnid's toxic fluids seeped into his skin, and he knew he had to act fast.

His injured leg throbbed with a corrosive numbness, and the gore-covered foot of the opposite felt like it was melting into the web's sticky strands. Running was impossible now, the terrain was a tangled nightmare of traps and venomous filaments. With grim resolve, Henry dragged Excalibur behind him, slicing a massive expanse through the web. The tearing sound was deafening, the webbing shredding into a chaotic mess that offered a brief, precious window of escape.

He moved cautiously toward the flickering white light beyond the shredded web, only to be halted by an enormous shadow descending from above. Out of the black abyss, a colossal spider emerged three times larger than its minuscule offspring, a grotesque titan born of nightmares and cloaked in terror. Its body was a rotting mass of exoskeleton and festering pustules, with sinewy spinnerets hanging like rotting tendrils from its rear, pulsating with decay.

The monstrous arachnid hung there, suspended in midair for what felt like eternity. Then, with a sickening squelch, it vomited a torrent of corrosive bile and acidic gastric juices, drenching Henry in a toxic, steaming spray. The digital bile hissed and bubbled as it burned into the web and against his enviro suit, seeping into his skin.

"Oh, come on! This can't be happening!" Henry shouts, voice trembling with frustration and terror. The stench of rot and acid-filled his senses as the creature's unholy presence loomed closer, promising a nightmare from which there was no awakening.

Angry at the whole situation he comes flying in like a whirling dervish of death hacking, slashing, and gouging with his sword leaving the grand terror and mother to the spiderlings sliced to pieces. Looking around and surveying the scene, Henry looks back noticing an army of smaller rotting spiderlings about to crash down on him like a terrifying wave of disease too numerous to fight knowing time is of the essence he quickly plunges himself into the white void without any contemplation of his action.

The pods open completely as the chanting gets louder. "Holy! Holy! Holy!"

As the fire of the seraphim fills the throne room a familiar synthesized voice from the cybernetic Enoch sitting on the throne says, "You intruders will be punished for the blasphemous act of stepping on this holy ground. The voice of G.O.D. has spoken. I, Metatron, will personally see to your destruction."

As he rises, the throne responds, not as furniture, but as an extension of his will. Its jagged frame creaks and groans, unfolding with mechanical precision. Metal plates shift and lock into place, extending outward until vast wings, forged from interlocking steel and humming with latent energy, spread behind him. They anchor into the shoulders of the cloned Enoch, a monstrous hybrid of flesh and circuitry. His eyes burn with cold, synthetic malice, and his body pulses with an unnatural rhythm, like a machine on the edge of overdrive.

Above, the seraphim descends into a frenzy. Figures of light and fire, now corrupted, spiral through the air with shrieking velocity. Their wings ignite, trailing flames as they launch bolts of burning plasma down on the blasphemous intruders. The firestorm hits like a meteor shower but it stops short.

A dome of vibrating golden force, invisible until struck, blooms outward from Enoch. The flames slam into it and fracture, scattering into bursts of molten debris. The air distorts around the shield, humming with barely contained violence as Enoch continues at the controls, his hands flickering across the interface with mechanical speed.

Then Adam strikes. With a sharp breath, he channels cold into his hands which gloved in frost, his veins like icy rivers. He flings a barrage of iced daggers upward. They slice through the air with a howl, catching three seraphim mid-flight. One takes a shard through the skull, its cry cut short as its body seizes and drops, trailing smoke and ash. Another loses a wing, spiraling out of control before smashing into the far wall with a sickening crunch. The last of the three is impaled through the burning chest imploding in a shower of cinders and smoke.

"Good work, my boy," Enoch says.

"Well, I assumed a fire creature has to be vulnerable to ice or water attacks. That's D&D 101." Adam replies with a grin feeling like he'd just rolled a critical hit in the popular game he and his friends enjoy playing on the weekends.

"That's great. Now roll a few more crits!" Jason demands. "There's a lot of these bastards."

"Get ready for a ground attack," Enoch warns. "Your suits will protect you from their fiery aura but not from their direct fire attacks. So be on guard."

"Oh, I'm ready," Jason says, clutching the Naga Blade like a conduit for countless warriors lost across the fractures of time. A tempest of restless souls stirs within him. Each one a shard of battle-born fury from the endless multiverse, fanning the flames of a raging storm that coils tight in his chest, ready to break free and rend the silence.

Suddenly, two seraphim descended from the ceilings of the chamber in a blaze of fire and fury, their wings like burning banners unfurling before Jason. They knew he was the final shield between Henry and annihilation.

Without hesitation, Jason lunged. His blade carved through the air with primal force, first to the left, a flash of steel cleaving one seraph in two, then arching back up and down to the right in a fluid, wrathful stroke. The creature split into smoldering fragments, each one igniting in midair before disintegrating into ash. Even through the insulated enviro suit, Jason felt the searing heat scorch against his skin.

To his side, Adam answered the chaos. He conjured a lance of pure ice, driving it clean through the heart of a descending seraph. But before he could celebrate the strike, another fiery being landed behind him silent and unseen. Its hands like molten shackles gripped him from behind, and instantly the icy energy of his hands melted, turning to steam in seconds. Flames surged, eager to reduce the young wizard to cindered ash.

But then the young wizard is released.

Adam spun around, breath sharp, expecting another attacker. Instead, he saw his would-be killer writhing, surrounded by the familiar, pulsing golden force. The angel's fire sputtered, starved, and then extinguished. It crumbled, a hallowed husk collapsing into dust.

He turned to Enoch, wide-eyed. "What happened?"

Enoch, ever calm amid the raging storm, answered, "Their fire consumes all oxygen near it. Remove the air, and even divine fire dies. Just like any other flame."

Adam nodded, lips tight. "Good to know."

Drawing his wand he unleashes a wave of cold-charged energy in a broad arc. The blast struck the encroaching seraphim, not killing them, but slowing them, severely.

Their once-blazing forms dimmed to mere embers, sluggish and flickering.

Seizing the moment, Adam breaks into a sprint. As he passed the wounded group, he struck six of them in rapid succession with Abaddon's blackened halo. Each impact birthed an eruption of light and heat, fiery deaths marking his path through the battlefield.

"Hey, I'm worried about Henry," Jason calls out. "He doesn't look so good!" noticing a sallow complexion appearing on his face, sweating profusely.

"He is locked in his own arena of battle, my boy" Enoch replies "At this point, all we can do is guard his mortal vessel and pray to the Creator that he emerges triumphant."

In the vast white void, the silence is deafening. Henry steps forward, and a line of crystalline obelisks shimmer into existence beneath his hands, arranging themselves like a keyboard made of frozen starlight. Above them, an ectoplasmic screen flickers into form semi-liquid, constantly shifting, pulsing with alien light and unreadable glyphs.

He doesn't need instructions. Instinct, or something deeper, tells him this is about resonance. Frequencies. A harmony only the right soul can strike. He reaches toward the keys—

A thunderous voice shatters the silence. "You are not permitted to access the Nexus."

It sounds like Enoch... but amplified. Synthesized. Drenched in artificial divinity.

Henry spins around and his breath catches in his throat.

What was once Enoch now towers before him, horrifically transformed. Cybernetic wings of jagged alloy extend from a spine of exposed titanium rods. Mottled flesh peels away from his face, revealing half a skull plated in gold. Tubes of black ichor pulse across his limbs. His eyes, if they could still be called that, glow with a violet circuitry of fire that sears into Henry's core.

For a moment, terror roots him in place. Then he smells it, the acrid sting of melting polymers. He looks down. The acidic vomit from the digital spider is corroding his suit, fast. He forces himself to speak. "Why don't I have permission?" he snaps. "I have the Nexus Access. It's already installed."

The corrupted avatar tilts its rotting cybernetic head, whirring as it processes. "What is the password?" it demands, voice fractured between machine and memory.

Henry's mind races. The password! He curses Enoch under his breath, how could he forget something so crucial? Then, suddenly, a passage flickers through his thoughts like a flare in darkness: remembering Adam quoting the passage in Revelations of seven angels coming out of the temple in the presence of God. Each was given a vial "full of the wrath of God". Without hesitation, he answers, "Revelation 15:7."

A pulse of light surges through the crystalline interface. The avatar speaks again, voice now deeper, more ancient. "Access granted to the crystal interface. Nexus is now partially open. Be advised: External threats detected in the chamber of G.O.D. Safeguards escalating."

Henry nods once. "Understood."

Metatron in the physical realm arms himself with a battle ax of crystal that he powers on with an energy source in the handle that causes the ax head to oscillate.

"Huh, is that a vibro ax?" Jason asks inquisitively.

"Why yes. Yes, it is." Enoch admits.

"Well, I'm taking that after this fight". Jason testifies "That's totally my loot."

A seraphim drops in front of him grabbing his face causing Jason to plunge the Naga blade in its abdomen while rotating the blade before he runs the sword straight upward cutting the flaming six-winged angel in two watching it burn out.

"We need to sever the connection Metatron has to G.O.D. so Henry has one less firewall to deal with." Enoch orders.

"Well if Adam can trade with me and protect Henry, I can engage Metatron," Jason suggests.

"That's not a bad idea," Adam admits.

Enoch nods. "Agreed."

Henry stared at the field of vibrating crystals, uncertainty gnawing at him. They pulsed with alien rhythms, like heartbeats of computer code in this virtual realm he was trapped in. He had no idea what to do next, but he knew time was vanishing fast.

"Your file's corruption is reaching critical levels," said Metatron's avatar, a decaying construct of shifting geometry and digital static. Its voice was void of emotion, but its words were lethal. Henry's digital form was glitching, fragments of code splintering off as the digital vomit ate the shimmering edges of his virtual enviro suit.

"Protocols are now in motion to purge the infection," Metatron says flatly.

Henry narrows his eyes. "Let me guess... that's not going to end well for me, is it?"

"Correct. You will be destroyed." The avatar says with a garble.

Panic constricted his chest. This wasn't a game. There were no second chances here. If his avatar died in this simulation, so did he, for real. He looked down. His suit was vanishing in pixelated wisps, dissolving like ash caught in a zero-gravity fire. Then, like a lifeline thrown across dimensions, a memory hit him, Glenda Garrison's voice from the Order of the Eye: "Nikola Tesla said, If you want to find the secrets of the universe, think in terms of energy, frequency, and vibration. I call it the divine spark." He muttered out loud. "Okay, Henry... divine spark, right. Let's find the frequency. You've got this. Adam makes it look easy. Just remember the crystal skull... the lessons..." He stretched out his hands above the crystals.

Nothing. "What the hell?" he snaps. "Come on! Work! Damn you, work!"

Metatron's voice returned, cool and unflinching: "In sixty seconds, you will be purged from the system."

Henry clenches his jaw. Focus. He had to sync. Across realities, across other-selves. He closed his eyes. "Okay...

connect to your multiverse selves. Tune in. Vibrate. Resonance. Find the harmony..." Visions flooded his mind, a thousand Henrys in a thousand parallel worlds, all reaching, fighting, thinking, dying. The signal was chaotic, but through it... came a pattern. As this mental download is happening he can't help but hear the unsettling voice of Metatron's avatar.

"Six... Five... Four... Three... Two..."

Once Adam takes up watch over Henry, Jason heads straight toward Metatron. He rushes in with quick lightning-fast strikes from his sensei's Naga blade, but he's surprised by how quickly Metatron dodges them.

"He's fast." Jason proclaims.

"Yes, he is," Enoch replies, charging up electrical blasts that leap from his palms striking the makeshift angel. "He's been installed with bionics, not just cybernetics."

As Enoch continues to build up power from his hands, he shouts an order to Jason. "Now! Sever his connection now!"

Jason darts around Metatron, quickly locating the port where countless cables and wires converge, all leading toward the tank that houses the decaying brain known as G.O.D. Understanding that severing this connection is critical, he raises his blade, and strikes with full force. But the blow is intercepted by the massive vibro-axe. The intense oscillation of the axe head sends a jarring vibration through his arms, nearly forcing him to release his grip. Reeling from the shock, Jason retreats just in time to evade Metatron's counterattack. The next swing crashes against his blade with such brute force that even as he parries, the impact sends him skidding backward nearly four feet across the crystalline floor.

Adam locks onto the interface cables snaking from Metatron's back, a rare, fleeting opening. He doesn't know if Abaddon's halo will even work for him, but there's no time for hesitation. He winds up and hurls it with everything he has.

The jagged black halo spins through the air like a blade forged from shadow, humming with a low, unnatural frequency. It hits, clean, biting into the cluster of thick cables. There's a flash of blue-white sparks, a spray of viscous fluid, and the shriek of metal tearing as the connection is violently severed.

Metatron convulses.

The towering figure reels, limbs locking and twitching as if caught in an electrical seizure. A howl, mechanical, broken, almost human echoes through the chamber, a corrupted scream ripped from a corrupted soul. Light flickers across his body in erratic pulses as his link to G.O.D. collapses, severed at the root.

The halo rebounds, still glowing with residual energy. Adam catches it on instinct, wincing, convinced the unholy thing might tear through bone and flesh. But it doesn't. It spins not in his grasp, just goes still. His chest heaves. He's still standing.

Metatron lets out a moan as he turns toward Adam. "That was your last mistake."

Metatron, enhanced by his bionic speed, pivots with terrifying agility. His vibro axe whirls upward, a deadly arc aimed straight for Jason's head. Jason reacts instinctively, raising his sword to parry, but Metatron feints, and then strikes again. The axe slices through the protection of the enviro suit with brutal precision. Blood sprays from the wound to his ribs, darkening the floor as the force shoves him backward, sending him crashing across the crystalline floor with a squeaky thud.

Turning back to Adam, Metatron grips the vibro axe with both hands, muscles taunt. He swings overhead like a savage warrior, the axe head slicing through the air in a deadly arc poised to split Adam's skull. The strike descends with devastating intent- until a sudden burst of sonic energy erupts from nowhere, slamming into Metatron's chest.

The impact sends him hurling backward, his body flipping through the air like a marionette with its strings cut." The axe embedded in the floor shudders violently as the oscillating head digs deeper, crystal shards flying from the contact point. Metatron's momentum is broken, leaving him momentarily stunned, and vulnerable in the chaotic calamity of the throne room.

Adam looks down and sees Steven adjusting his turban.

He crouches down and asks "Are you back, man? Like, are you on our side?"

"Yeah, looks that way," Steven confirms. "That blow to the head Henry gave me really scrambled my wiring. It hurt like hell, but it knocked me out of Gabriel's control. So, where we at with all this?"

"Henry is inside this construct the angels call G.O.D., virtually hacking the controls," Adam explains. "His goal is to self-destruct the satellite Wormwood, but before he does that, he's going to send an attack here to blow up this ship we are on. So, we have to be ready to move as soon as he comes out of this thing. The clone of Enoch they call Metatron you just blasted needs to be defeated."

Steven nods. "Okay, I'll help Jason then."

"Hey bro, it's good to have you back," Adam confesses.

"It's good to be back, man," Steven confirms, then turns to blast a couple of seraphim that just landed in front of them, sending the would-be attackers into cinders. Then he follows up his next attack on Metatron sending sparks flying from his cybernetics as blood gushes from his flesh surrounding them. Amazed by the power of the attack Enoch looks up and realizes Metatron was sitting on the Ark of the Covenant and that's where Steven's golden breastplate is drawing its excessive power from. As Steven focuses this power on Metatron, the floor beneath the makeshift angel begins to crack.

"Enough!" Enoch shouts. "You'll bring the whole place down on our heads."

Snapping out of it, Steven dials it down. "S-Sorry. I've never felt that kinda power before."

"That's because you've never stood in the presence of a power like the Ark of the Covenant," Enoch proclaims, his voice edged with awe and finality. "It is not merely energy—it is legacy, judgment, and the echo of a thousand divine wars."

"The Mercy Seat," Adam says in awe.

Henry's eyes snapped open to silence. The avatar was gone. No fanfare. No more Countdown. Just stillness.

Someone must have done something... from the outside. His heart swelled with hope. "It's our time to shine," he whispers.

He closed his eyes again, heart syncing with something deeper, a resonance flowing both in this simulated plane and the physical world, merging the two. The crystals around him shimmer, colors shifting through the visible spectrum and beyond, frequencies felt more than seen. They vibrated like chimes in an electromagnetic storm.

Then he saw them: the multifaceted alexandrite crystals, color-shifting, reactive. He instinctively reached for them.

With practiced precision, movements he'd never learned yet knew, he began touching the crystals in sequence. Patterns formed. Lights converged. A holographic interface materialized before him sleek, alien, but now familiar. A keyboard. One built for him. This was the Nexus, he had gained access. His fingers moved without hesitation, dancing across alien glyphs like a pianist striking long-lost chords. Code scrolled by like rivers of thought. What once seemed incomprehensible now unfolded like instinct. Henry smiled. He wasn't just accessing the Nexus. He was mastering it. Moments later, he reached it: Wormwood, in the heart of the system, once beyond reach. Now, it was his.

Realizing he only has seconds left, Henry punches in the commands of a self-destruct order then one final command to target the structure that he and his friends are currently still in! Seeing his avatar self-starting to fail he hits enter and soon finds himself kicked out.

Standing watch over Henry, Adam feels a sharp pain in his hand as the jagged onyx halo slices his fingers deeply sending his blood raining down on the floor next to his friend locked in a virtual reality hell. As the halo exits his grip abruptly Adam spots it soaring into the hand of its owner flying up through a loading door in the floor of the throne room as an alarm sounds off in the Mars-based mothership followed by a warning in an unfamiliar language.

"I thought we killed that asshole when Henry cut half his head off," Adam exclaims in alarm as he notices Abaddon hovering in the air, suspended by his angelic force, his presence warping the space around him with hate and dread. His head is grotesquely disfigured, fused with a blackened, crusted chitin that gleams like scorched bone. The contours of his face are barely humanoid now, the flesh melted and sealed around what resembles a burnt skull. From above his left eye, a jagged horn juts upward, formed from the same dark material. Deep within the hollowed eye socket, a flickering flame burns steady, unnatural but alive.

"I can't be defeated that easily," Abaddon proclaims. "but your fat friend's sword has left its mark." As he waves a clawed hand over the left side of his face.

Swarming around him, his host of alien insects, their wings humming like a swarm of serrated knives. They move in synchronized patterns, orbiting his form like living armor drawn to him not by biology, but by something older, something antediluvian.

"As the alarms wail, Jason asks anxiously, 'What the hell is that sound for?' But before anyone can answer, Gabriel—following behind Abaddon—addresses Enoch: 'What have you done, you ancient fool?'"

"I have unraveled your work of ruin," Enoch said, his eyes burning with ancient fire. "Your dominion of destruction ends here."

Gabriel howls in protest "No! No! No! I had a way back home!"

"At the cost of nearly eight billion souls—and a world once crowned in splendor!" Enoch roars, not with sorrow, but with rising triumph. "Your end has come, Gabriel. The light prevails."

Without warning and speed unheard of, Gabriel snatches his halo from his head and launches it at the timeless Prophet, slicing straight through him then begins screaming at Abaddon to, "kill them all!"

Steven rushes to push Adam out of the way as Gabriel's halo's return trajectory is to strike him down like it did Enoch but instead severs Steven's arm at the elbow.

As Enoch crumbles to the ground, he pulls a jet injector from his robes and hands it to Jason as the panicked teen rushes up to his side, the wizard says "Don't worry about me, my boy. Inject this into Steven's arm and get ready. I'm sending you all out of here."

"We aren't leaving you behind," Jason demands.

"Don't be stupid!" Enoch snaps sternly. "It's my time to be Spock. Now help Steven!"

"I think I did it," Henry says as he comes out of the connection with G.O.D. "Oh, holy shit. What the hell is happening here?"

"Your death's," Gabriel hissed with a cruel smile, as a thin line of crimson suddenly appeared across his forehead. Confusion flickered in his eyes, but before he could react, blood erupted from the wound, pouring down his face in a violent rush. The crimson streak widened, and with a sickening crack, like breaking glass, his head was torn apart. The top slid off with gruesome finality. His halo, once a symbol of divine light, clattered to the ground from his hand as Gabriel dropped to his knees, shattered and broken.

From the shadows, Abaddon moved with lethal precision. His black onyx halo, dark and heavy with corrupt power, shimmered ominously as he clenched it in his hand. With a swift, practiced motion, he channeled malevolent energy through the ringed gemstone, transforming it into a deadly weapon.

In a blur, Abaddon drove the onyx halo into Gabriel's skull. The dark ring of gemstone sliced through flesh and bone like a shadowy blade, severing the top of Gabriel's head with a sickening crunch. Blood erupted in a torrent as the skull was breached, exposing raw tissue beneath. Gabriel could not collapse, lifeless, for his betrayer clung to his body like static.

Abaddon's eyes gleamed with dark satisfaction as he reached into the bloody cavity, fishing out the massive pineal gland like a macabre trophy—his dark victory. His face twisted into a sick smile, a flicker of dark triumph lighting his eyes as he gazed at his gruesome prize.

This was death-made flesh, a brutal, unforgiving act that blurred the line between treacherous and monstrous. The air was thick with the stench of blood and betrayal, a stark reminder that even angels are not immune to death.

He lingered there, savoring the moment. The silence stretched on, thick with the weight of what had just transpired.

Jason breaks the eerie silence. "Why?! Why did you do that?" he demands, sliding to Steven's side as his friend cries out in pain. He quickly injects him with whatever substance was loaded into the jet injector Enoch had entrusted to him. Within seconds, the bleeding from Steven's severed arm stops as a polymer cap forms over the stump, complete with small, built-in ports. Steven stares at it in disbelief, grabs the capped stump—and then collapses into unconsciousness, either from shock or a sedative-like side effect of the injection. Jason isn't sure.

"The why is none of your concern, boy," Abaddon sneers, his voice a low rasp of contempt. "Be grateful the burden of this wretch is no longer yours." With chilling indifference, the corrupted angel flings Gabriel's lifeless body aside—like a candy wrapper flicked from stained fingers, forgotten and worthless.

Jason grabs the crystal vibro ax along with the Naga blade and says "Well soon you'll be dead too."

Henry tries to offer up a form of truce "Uhm, so there's like a ray of destruction headed this way."

Suddenly all three friends hear Enoch's voice in their heads, saying "Get home."

Adam's hand, slick with fresh blood, trembles as an eerie vibration coils through his palm like a living current. His breath catches. He looks down, and there it is. Enoch's staff, impossibly real, materializes in his blood-soaked grip, its golden surface drinking in the crimson flow like a sacred relic demanding sacrifice.

The air around them thickens. A deafening silence swells, a tear in space-time opens, and a swirling portal erupts before them, crackling with energy, alive with purpose. At that moment, a voice, ancient and echoing from deep within their minds, speaks: "Adam, steady your mind, as I once taught you. Hold fast to belief and guide your companions home. The needs of the many outweigh the needs of the few…"

"…or the one," Jason whispers aloud, his voice cracking, barely holding back the sob that catches in his throat.

Adam flinches. Henry turns sharply. All three start to object, but they don't get the chance.

Enoch raises his hand. With a surge of invisible force, he sweeps them into the portal, flinging them through space and fate itself. Their screams vanish into the light. And then silence. The last image burned into their minds before the vortex closes is Enoch, his robes torn and bloody, as is his body which still lay defiantly between them and the advancing shadow of Abaddon, The Destroyer. Alone. Unmoving. A wizard ready to face oblivion.

The trio finds themselves at the monolithic ring of rusty butterscotch-colored stones on the outskirts of Mars with their unconscious friend now missing an arm.

Enoch's voice leaves one final message in their heads. "The Earth has named you her protectors, warriors born not of chance, but of destiny."

Henry is on the verge of tears. "We aren't just going to leave Merlin, are we?"

"Hell no, we aren't!" Jason tells him.

"How much time do we have till the impact, Henry?" Adam asks.

"Not long," Henry answers defeatedly. "Maybe ten minutes. Maybe less."

"I don't like this either guys, but this is Enoch's call, not ours," Adam says. "Steven still needs help. I know it doesn't make sense, but something tells me to trust Enoch. And honestly, I don't know how long it will take me to open the wormhole."

"You're right, Adam," Jason says somberly. "Get to it, bro."

Adam gives a tense nod. Nearby, Henry sinks to the red Martian dust, shaking with sobs as Jason holds him, saying nothing.

Not long after, Adam steps toward the wormhole site, gripping the staff in one hand, and the wand in the other. He steadies his breathing, focusing—mimicking the technique he'd seen Enoch use. More than that, he remembers what it felt like: the resonance, the pull of the cosmic strings, the way Enoch described threading space itself.

Then, with a sudden rupture in the air, the wormhole tears open—violent, and alive.

A streak of energy flashes across the Martian sky, searing white against rust-red. The ground shakes. A moment later, a light blast wave hits them like a punch, followed by a blinding flare over the horizon.

Adam doesn't hesitate. "Everyone, inside! Now! Before the real shockwave hits!"

Jason picks up Steven and they all four leave behind the red planet as moments later the full force from the blast has reached the outskirts they are at. The aftershock from Wormwood's final attack slams into the closing wormhole.

Once the four friends leave Mars behind and the wormhole closes a small spacecraft streaks across the sky of the red planet directed toward Earth.

CHAPTER 15
THE HOMECOMING

The four friends are hurled out of the wormhole, flung across the megalithic ring of stones back on Earth. A powerful aftershock, caught in the wormhole just moments before it closed, violently ejects them from the cosmic vortex.

Adam lifts himself up, shaking the reddish-brown sand from himself and removing his breathing mask. "Is everyone okay?"

"Yeah, I believe so." Jason remarks "How 'bout you, Henry?"

Still reeling from the loss of Enoch, he barely manages to shake his head before muttering, "We need to get Steven to the castle." The words come out strained as he lifts his unconscious friend into his arms.

"Yeah, totally." Adam agrees as he assists his friend.

"Here, just load him on my shoulder," Jason says.

"I can't believe he lost his arm," Adam says in disbelief.

"If he hadn't stepped in… you'd be dead," Jason's voice cracks, raw with urgency and pain. He grabs his friend's shoulder, desperate to make him understand.

"Steven did what any of us would've done, sacrificed everything without a second thought to keep us alive."

His eyes burn with fierce determination. "I'd done the same for you all. No hesitation. No regrets."

"Just like Merlin sacrificed his own life" Henry blurts out with another emotional burst of tears.

"Enoch perished?" A familiar feminine voice says from the shadows.

The trio looks up as Avarail steps into view.

"Yes…" Henry sobs. "Gabriel cut him down with his halo."

"He forced us through a portal to the cosmic gateway." Jason grunts, struggling with shifting the weight of Steven's unconscious body "And Adam got us home from there."

"Very impressive." Avarail comments, looking in Adam's direction noticing he carries Enoch's now bloody staff. "Here, give me your injured friend. I presume this is Steven?"

All three friends answer "Yeah" in unison.

"I'll fly him ahead and prep him for reconstruction," Avarail assures them. "I see Enoch has already outfitted him for a synthetic limb."

"I don't know what I injected him with," Jason admits.

"It's okay." She tells him as she carries Steven effortlessly. "Enoch knew I'd know what to do. Let's head to the castle. You can finish telling me about Gabriel and his plans."

"Gabriel is dead," Adam announces flatly.

Avarail is surprised. "Dead!? You three, or four as she looks at their unconscious friend, have grown strong indeed."

"It wasn't us," Henry says with shame. "It was Abaddon."

"The Lord of Locusts was with Gabriel?" She asks "And turned on him?"

"Yes." Jason answers "He cut the top of Gabriel's head off, and dug out his pinecone thing."

Avarail looks distracted. "Okay. We shall talk further about this after I see to your friend."

She then flies off with Steven in her arms.

The friends make their way back to the castle of Camelot, as Henry lovingly refers to it.

While traveling on foot, Adam asks "Did you guys see the look in Avarail's eyes when we told her that Abaddon had killed Gabriel?"

"Yeah." Jason replies "I mean, she looked like she was just processing what we were telling her, right?"

"Sorry, I was busy crying." Henry shamefully admits. "I mean, we lost Sensei and now Merlin. I'm not cut out for this like you two are."

"That's total bullshit." Jason retorts. "Excalibur chose you, and we couldn't have done what we did without you!"

"He's right, Henry," Adam agrees. "There's no weakness in feeling your emotions. To be honest with you, I haven't really stopped to think about Sensei or Enoch because of all the stuff we've been dealing with. But once I slow down and stop to process it, I'm going to definitely need all of you guys' help."

Jason switches gears, wanting to avoid the talk of emotions. "Why did you ask about the look Avarail gave a few minutes ago?"

"Oh, I'm not sure," Adam says. "I just got this feeling from her, is all."

"Feeling?" Henry asks, "About what?"

"I'm not sure," Adam admits. "Our futures, maybe?"

"We did what we were supposed to do." Henry protests. "We saved the world, and Gabriel is defeated. So we can go back home and just live our lives now, right?"

"Seriously?" Jason asks sternly. "You think we can just go back to life as it was before?"

"Yeah, I do," Henry tells him. "I'm not a soldier. I don't want to do this anymore. Do you guys?"

Adam and Jason both just stop in their tracks and shrug.

"Guess I haven't really thought about it," Jason admits sheepishly.

"Well, I for one think we are embroiled in an unseen conflict that may not release us from it. Unless we take charge of our own destinies and not leave it up to fate to decide for us." Adam admits.

"It is not in the stars to hold our destiny, but in ourselves." Jason poetically chimes in.

Was that William Shakespeare that just came out of Gold's mouth? Henry asks in stunned confusion.

"Yes it was," Adam says in shock.

Jason quickly sets his friends straight. "The quote is a modern adaptation that captures the essence of Shakespeare's original sentiment, specifically a paraphrased interpretation of a line from Julius Caesar, specifically Cassius's assertion that the responsibility for human destiny lies not in the stars, but in ourselves. But the modern quote seemed to fit the moment more befitting, don't you both agree?"

His two friends just stand there, staring at him, until Adam finally breaks the silence. "Alright, for now, let's just get to the castle and check on Steven. The four of us need to talk—about everything."

After walking on in silence for a bit, Adam decides to try and lift the spirits of his two friends. "Let's also just celebrate our victory, shall we?" I mean, we did just save the world, didn't we?"

"Hell yeah!" Jason roars.

"You're right, we did," Henry admits. "And we saved our friend, too." with that his two friends smile and both say, "That's right we did."

As they approach the castle, the giants standing guard open the doors.

One of them says "Hail to the victory of the prophecy of the three it has been fulfilled."

Both giants bow to the three worn-out teens.

Not knowing how to feel or take the greeting, they stumble over their words, trying to find the right response.

Adam finally speaks up. "The real champion is the immortal one, Enoch. The true protector of the world. It was his guidance and sacrifice that ensured all our lives this day."

Both giants slam their fists to their chests over their hearts in a salute of honor.

Finding their way through the winding stone halls of Camelot, the trio climbs another of several spiral staircases lit by flickering torches and soot-blackened stone. The heavy oak doors at the end of a corridor open only to reveal a more high-tech door that slides open with a soft hiss, revealing a stark contrast to the castle's medieval style.

Inside, the medical lab hums with quiet machinery. The room is a fusion of old and new—arched ceilings carved with runes, and iron sconces glowing not with flame, but with cold, clinical LED light. Gleaming consoles line the walls, their surfaces etched with arcane symbols that pulse in rhythm with biometric monitors. Vats of translucent gel shimmer faintly in recessed alcoves, alongside what look like alchemical instruments—except they're wired into sleek surgical arms and scanning devices.

In the center of the room lies Steven, conscious and calm, his chest rising and falling steadily. A translucent field hovers above his body, projecting vitals in glowing glyphs only partially decipherable to the untrained eye.

Robed medics move with precise efficiency, their garments styled like monk's habits, but trimmed with polymer thread and built-in interfaces that flicker as they work.

The air smells of sterilization—sharp antiseptic with a faint metallic tang, like ozone after a storm. Somewhere overhead, a vent hums, filtering the air with an almost sacred stillness.

The trio enters to find Steven lying in a treatment chair, wide awake, monitors pulsing softly around him. Avarail stands quietly at his side.

Jason takes a step forward but stops, frozen as his eyes lock on Steven's. Adam remains silent, tension carved into his expression. Before Henry can blurt something out, as he usually would, Steven speaks first—his voice surprisingly light, almost triumphant. "Hey guys," he says with a faint smile. "You made it."

But the moment cracks. His gaze drops, shoulders sinking as emotion floods in. Tears well in his eyes.

"I'm sorry," he says, voice breaking. "For everything I've done to you. These last few years... they've been a living nightmare. You have no idea what that asshole has done to me.

The three rush to their lost friend's bedside.

Avarail steps aside with a slight smile across her face, then speaks up. "Okay, Okay. I'm working here."

"Oh, sorry," Jason says as he and the others step back.

"How are you going to help Steven?" Henry inquires.

"Well, that's what we're going to discuss." Avarail answers as she pulls up a liquid screen in front of her patient. "The nanites in the hypo needle Enoch gave Jason have already done the hard part. They made all the connections needed and formed the port connection cap, so now all we have to do is make our selections. Here are some of your options,"

She touches a few buttons on the liquid screen that floats in front of the treatment chair Steven is reclined in, and a list pops up with cybernetic: claws, grappling hook with steel braided line, laser torch, forearm computer, exploding rocket hand, and the list goes on and on.

"Take your time, and I'll go get the replacement limb." She tells him.

"You're going to be like Robocop!" Henry blurts out excitedly. "Uhm, I mean, I'm sorry you lost your arm in all this."

"Shit, me too." Steven shrugs with a nervous chuckle. "But in the grand scheme of things, that's nothing, man. I'm just happy Adam is still here with us, and hell the world is still here. Ya know?"

"Thanks for saving my life," Adam says while going in for a hug.

"Of course. I'm just glad I didn't really hurt one of you."

"Hell yeah, ya did," Jason says. "Whatever that sonic blast is, it hurts like hell. I literally had to detach my spirit from my physical body to defeat you."

"You guys can all do that regularly?" Steven asks.

"Well, I did it that one time," Jason admits. "I'm not sure it's a thing I can replicate."

"I did it too on Mars!" Henry proclaims proudly. "Even held Excalibur in my spirit form."

"Holy shit, that was badass! Until you smashed my skull in." Steven exclaims. "but you guys are like force ghosts."

Henry gets excited and shouts, "Yes exactly! And yeah about that head-bashing part, I'm not really always in control of Excalibur."

"It's okay bro I'm happy you knocked some sense into me." He smiles at all his friends. "So, what options should I get for this new arm?" He asks them.

"All of it," Henry suggests excitedly.

"Doesn't work that way." Avarail cuts in dryly. "Now, step aside. Have you looked the options over?"

"Yeah, I think I know which ones I'm goin' with," Steven replies. "That is, if I can have 'em."

"Well, it depends." She explains. "If you do small components like a flashlight or cutting torch, then you can have something big like the forearm computer, but including a grappling hook with steel cable then it would be too bulky you'll end up looking like Popeye with a giant forearm."

"Yeah, that's what I figured ya'd say," Steven admits. "So I want the claws, laser cutting torch, and the grappling hook. Figured it would be practical for our next mission, right?"

Steven notices the room getting uncomfortably quiet at the mention of the next mission. "Okay, what's wrong? Is it a trust thing? I'll let the Immortal prob my mind or take a lie detector test. Whatever, ya know?"

"It's just... We aren't sure we're going to do anything else like this again." Jason informs him. "Henry was talking a bit ago about how he wants to go back to just living a normal life, especially after Enoch's death."

"Oh God, he died? Guys, I'm so, so sorry. I didn't know" Steven apologetically admits as sympathetically as he can.

"Sensei Kim Dae-jung died fighting Gabriel too." Henry sadly reports.

"What?!" Steven says. "He was such a kind old man."

"I'm sorry for your loss," Avarail says, sounding surprisingly sympathetic.

"Yeah," Jason cuts in, holding out his old master's blade. "Sensei was something called a Naga Knight, and this Hwando of his is made from a special metal."

"Wait, your martial arts teacher was a Naga Knight?" Avarail asks, sounding very alarmed.

"Yeah," Adam admits. "He told us all about it and believed us without freaking out when we told him about seeing an angel. Hell, he even fought Gabriel without a blade. He was able to conjure energy from a leyline, and fought Gabriel as we got away. We saw the dojo go up in flames." He recalls with deep regret.

Avarail looks slightly confused at the last part of his story. "Naga Knights are not harmed by fire or the cold."

"So he's probably alive?!" Henry blurts out.

"I'm not saying that either." She looks up from installing Steven's cybernetic limb, and then quickly notices Henry's sadness. "But don't rule out the possibility either. If he really was a Naga Knight, they are some of the toughest warriors out there. I just thought the Watchers had killed them all along with the Nagas..."

Avarail then goes back to working on the arm. "Well, I understand and will respect you all if you don't continue on this path, then. But I for one can't sit back and let the things I've seen threaten our world." Steven says with determination.

"What is a Naga by the way," Jason asks. "I've been meaning to ask but we haven't really had the time for me to ask."

"They are a semi-divine race of half-human, half-serpent beings." Avarail answers. "They can take on three forms: as entirely human for very short periods of time, as common serpents, or as half-human, half-snake hybrids."

Jason simply says, "Oh okay." with a look of shock as the room becomes quiet.

After a few more moments of silence, Avarail finishes her work. "Alright. You should have access to the feeling sensors, and your options should be online"

"Wow, it's like I have a regular arm," Steven admits in disbelief.

"Yes. The sensors have a true-to-life feeling. Try using the claws and torch, but not the grappling hook. Not in here" She warns sternly."We'll go outside later and practice with it." She offers.

"Okay, but how?" Steven asks.

"Just think about doing it." She couches.

Six-inch claws then spring from his fingertips as his index finger swaps out a claw for a cutting torch.

"This is so wild!" Steven admits with a giant smile on his face.

Just then, a beeping sound emits from Avarail's belt attached to her leather battle skirt. As she pulls a device out and pushes a button, the screen with the cybernetic options in front of Steven switches to a video call.

A handsome man with well-groomed platinum blond hair and ice-blue eyes that burn with fury begins to rant. "I told you not to destroy the mothership. I warned you there would be consequences, you foolish....."

The mysterious man then pauses and appears to squint at the screen on his end. "Wait, who're you all, and where is Enoch?"

"He didn't make it," Jason informs bluntly. "But we did, so who are you?"

"I'm Michael." The strikingly attractive angel answers.

"Shit, not another deranged archangel to deal with." Henry blurts out.

"Yes, I'm an archangel." Michael admits "And possibly deranged, but not 'destroy the whole world' deranged. At least tell me you brought back the Nexus Access. Or at the very least tell me Metatron wasn't destroyed."

"It didn't make its return back to Earth and no, Enoch's Clone was destroyed too," Adam informs the angry angel.

"Well then you four had better be willing to help, or the world as you know it is going to change drastically, and not in a way any of us is going to like." Michael threatens.

"What's happening?" Avarail demands.

"Purgatory is about to open up!" Michael informs the garnet-skinned demon.

"Oh dear God no." Avarail whispers in horror.

"What the hell is Purgatory??" Steven asks.

"It's an intermediate state after death, and before final judgment, others consequently offer prayers for the dead to be cleansed," Adam answers, a bit confused.

He knows there has to be another answer to this, and Michael begins to offer just such an answer. "Yes, that's what the simple-minded humans used to believe. But it's a cryogenic prison of the ancient alien races that used to rule this planet. They called themselves gods, and now that Enoch did the exact opposite of what we agreed upon, we'll soon have a huge problem on our hands."

"Megan said this would happen," Jason mutters under his breath.

"Who's this Megan??" Michael demands.

"Megan McCarthy, the hottest girl in our school." Henry blurts out in reflex.

"Dude, don't give this monster Megan's name!" Jason snaps in anger.

"Shit man, I'm sorry. I didn't mean to. It's just a habit, is all."

"Megan McCarthy, huh?" Michael mutters as he punches a few keys on an unseen keyboard. "A Rosicrucian, huh? Get in touch with her, and you four along with the Rosicrucian girl report to my office in New York City immediately. I'm sending the address now. It will take all of us working together to fix this."

As the archangel concludes with that statement, Avarail's screen goes dark, with an address listed in the center that reads 33 Thomas St, New York, NY 10007.

Amidst the silence, Steven turns to his three long-time friends. "Are you three in?"

"Doesn't look like we have much choice," Adam admits somberly.

Jason agrees. "But when we get back home, we are checking in with our families"

EPILOGUE

The chamber echoed with solemn majesty—the Halls of Law, the heart of Atlantis's central ring, carved from shimmering obsidian veined with threads of living light. Towering columns spiraled toward a vaulted dome, where constellations flickered across a moving celestial map that pulsed in rhythm with the city's unseen energy. The air smelled faintly of charged crystal and ocean brine, carried in through aqueduct-like conduits that whispered with each tide beyond the city walls.

Rows of seated Watchers—their ceremonial armor etched with ancient runes and sleek, iridescent plating—sat in tiered arcs above the central platform. Behind them, the high walls were lined with etched murals, depicting the rise of Atlantis, the forging of the Arks, and long-forgotten wars waged in silence and shadow.

Abaddon stepped into the center of the chamber, his presence casting a long, angular shadow beneath the pale blue illumination hovering above the tribunal floor. His voice rang out with calculated authority.

"Watchers and esteemed others of the Atlantis High Council," he declared, his words amplified by the acoustics of the hall and the subtle hum of translation glyphs suspended in the air. "I, Abaddon, come before you seeking asylum. I bring with me a gift—one of the Arks of the Covenant. This Ark is from the mothership, which has been destroyed... by this person."

With a swift motion, he shoved Enoch forward. Enoch stumbled into the light— bruised, battered and bound.

"I also bring him to be judged—Enoch, the betrayer and slayer of our kind."

A ripple of gasps and murmurs surged through the chamber, echoing beneath the dome-like distant thunder. The glowing glyphs above dimmed slightly, as if the very energy of the hall recoiled in response. Council members shifted in their seats, some whispering, others rising with narrowed eyes. The mood turned cold—sharp with judgment, heavy with history.

"I give both to you for the reward of asylum."

With a brutal shove, Abaddon forced Enoch to his knees. The timeless mage collapsed helplessly, his arms bound in front of him by a shimmering vibrational restrictor—

glowing cuffs humming with calibrated resonance, locking his movements at the molecular level.

Abaddon stepped forward, his voice rising with grim certainty.

"Test his blood, and you'll find the truth. He carries within him the stolen consciousness of our brother—Gabriel. Another of our kind, slaughtered by this butcher's hand."

A collective murmur spread through the chamber as Abaddon paced, his presence looming like a thundercloud over the judgment circle.

"And I, too, nearly perished by his betrayal," he added coldly, raising his clawed hand to his face.

He dragged it across the twisted calcification growing from his face—a black chitinous horn now arched above his left brow, where once a natural eye had seen. In its place flickered a flame—a living fire embedded within the socket, seething with hatred and pain. It burned brighter in the charged silence, casting warped shadows against his war-scarred features.

A figure rose from the Council tier—regal, composed. An angel with cinnamon-brown waves of hair and serene hazel eyes, grey wings folded behind an emerald-and-gold robe that shimmered like liquid metal in the ambient light.

"This matter requires a formal vote," he announced. His voice was calm, yet carried the weight of law.

"Of course, mighty Raphael, healing hand of G.O.D," Abaddon replied with theatrical reverence, bowing low with outstretched arms. "I await the Council's judgment."

The room fell still again, the ancient laws of Atlantis groaning under the weight of prophecy, betrayal, and a decision that could fracture the stars.

Below, still kneeling beneath the beam of judgment light, Enoch slowly raised his head. His voice was hoarse, but steady. "What's your play here, Abaddon?" he asked, his gaze burning into his captor.

Abaddon did not turn to meet his gaze. "You shall see soon enough," the Lord of Locusts said with quiet menace.

Made in the USA
Coppell, TX
19 January 2026

68461417R10225